A Forgotten Murder

By

George Donald

Chapter 1

The sun is roasting the tarmac off the crowded pavements this October Wednesday, even though it was hardly turned midday. So here I am, sitting in a coffee bar in Buchanan Street at the corner of St Vincent Street or I should say a wee cafe with a fancy name so that it can charge outrageous prices, when I see the ghost. No, I know what you're thinking. I'm not off my head, I've not been at the cheap vino and this ghost isn't wearing a white sheet and saying "Boo!" to passers-by.

So, let me explain.

When I say ghost, I'm being literal, because the guy I am looking at, almost three years previously, had been reported dead by the Spanish police. I stare through the large panoramic window that looks out onto the pedestrian precinct at a long-remembered face, a passenger in the front seat of a silver coloured BMW off-road vehicle. The beamer is stopped at a red pedestrian light and he is using a mobile phone, his left hand making a fist as he seems to emphasise a point while he stares at the pert bum of a young teenage girl crossing to my side of the street. My attention is briefly taken by the blonde, her long hair bouncing on her shoulders as she smartly strides down the street and fully aware of the admiring glances following her.

I can see his lips moving and he throws his head back as he laughs, probably at some comment about the young birds' bum, now visible to me as she passes by and encased in a pair of ski type pants that are so tight, if she passes wind, she will split them.

I snap my head back towards the passenger, the cup in my left hand almost falling from my grasp and I can feel the tightness in my chest as I hold my breath. I swallow hard and stare through the window at his face, unaware that I've slowly risen from my seat as

"So, me aside," I ask when I returned to the table. "How have you been? Hear you're a Detective Inspector now, in Govan?"

He nods, unable to speak as he wolfs down the muffin then slurps at his coffee. "Sorry," he splutters crumbs all over the table, "bloody starving. Didn't get any breakfast before I left for work and this is the first chance today I've had to eat anything."

I glance at him and think he looks tired. He has more flecks of grey hair than I remember from our last meeting. I know he is divorced and spends more hours than is healthy at his office and I also seem to remember he has only one kid, a daughter.

"Keeping you busy, then?"

"Pretty busy," he nods again. "We had a run of murders and it was the usual lack of resources," which I knew was Mike's way of explaining the police mindset of running their inquiries with the minimum of manpower. Their budget way of thinking is that if you can succeed with what you've got, why give you more resources? But again, the status of the victim sometimes determined what money is spent on serious inquiries. A newsworthy victim gets a lot more attention than some poor wee wifie beaten to death in a council housing scheme.

"But let's talk about you," he deftly dabs at his mouth with the paper napkin. "You're looking well for a guy that was up to his neck in shit, the last time we met. What, eight, nine months ago?"

"Ten months it was, in January, The Horseshoe Bar. I was pissed, I think."

"Yeah, you're right. It was Liz Jennings promotion function. I remember now."

So did I. It had been a Friday night and I had popped in for a pint or three after work and some of the guys with Mike recognised, then cold shouldered me. I had gotten a bit stroppy over their attitude and if Mike hadn't been there the situation might have gotten a bit out of hand and likely I would have offered some of them a private chat in Drury Street, outside the pub. But I had never been able to hold my liquor and the condition I was, in I'd likely have had my head kicked in for my trouble. Don't get me wrong, I'm not really the confrontational type. Not to say I've not been in a few rumbles in my time, but previously I'd usually been on duty and arresting some ne'er do well, not bar fights. To cut a long story boring, Mike had shoved me into a taxi and stuck money into the driver's fist with the instruction to get me home. He grinned again at me. "So, are you working now or what?"

"I'm an Insurance investigator for a company, working out of an office in Cadogan Street. I deal mainly with road traffic accidents, witness statement, that sort of thing."

I didn't have the bottle to explain that most of my work is phoning clients and sorting out the truth of their claims and that obtaining 'witness statements' is sending out forms by post. The title 'Insurance Investigator' is a sham. I was embarrassed to admit that in reality, I am an admin guy, that's all. How the mighty have fallen, I inwardly sighed. But it paid the rent and kept me fed, so who am I to complain? That said, Mike was never a man to judge and like my old dad always says, each job, no matter what it might be, brings its own dignity.

"You make any money at that racket?"

"I get by," then staring at his questioning glance, I shamefacedly grin and decided to confess all. "It's a shitty job, Mike. I'm nothing more than a glorified clerk. But I don't have a lot of job choice these days."

"How are things between you and Lisa? Together again or is she still with her folks?"

I sigh heavily and drained my cup, ignoring the scowls I am getting from the chubby blonde waitress behind the counter. "She's still with her parents. Lisa delivers the girls every second Saturday to my flat and I get to keep them overnight, but other than the handover as I like to term it, there's no contact. To be honest, I'm surprised at that. I thought by now Lisa would have been dragging me through the divorce court. I've no doubt her father has urged her to get rid of me. He and I never had a good relationship, though to be fair I always got on well with her mum."

"Don't suppose it could be anything to do with the fact that Lisa's old man is a private school and university educated advocate, while you're a scummy with no qualifications, born and brought up in a council housing scheme in Maryhill, a former polis who was kicked out of the Force and," he grins as he stresses the word 'and', "you were running about shagging behind his daughter's back?"

If anyone else had made that kind of comment, I might have been tempted to favour them with a Glasgow nod, that's a head butt to the uneducated, but Mike Farrell? He has been a pal for a very long time and probably knows me a whole lot better than I know myself. I grin shamefacedly and shake my head.

"Mostly correct, Detective Inspector, but honestly and I know it's maybe hard to believe, but I wasn't shagging behind Lisa's back." Not quite the truth nor a wee white lie either, but the truth was a whole lot more complicated and I still hadn't gotten my own head round it, so there seemed little point in dragging the past up over a coffee in the middle of a lot of harassed lunchtime workers and tourists. I watch as he drains his coffee and I offer to buy him another, worrying that the loose change in my pocket is getting a lot more room to be loose in.

To my relief, Mike replies "No thanks," and shrugs into his jacket. "I'm at the age now that one cup means four visits to the loo. Can't have a cuppa for an hour before I go to bed or I'm looking at a three am bladder call," he quips. We both stand and he extends his hand to shake mine then, as if suddenly remembering, withdraws his hand and reaching into an inside pocket of jacket, passes me a business card. "Bugger, nearly forgot why I'd phoned you. I was speaking to Lynn Massey, the other day. Don't know if you remember her. She was a DI with the Major Crime Investigation Unit when we were both in the surveillance team."

I nod, recalling the good looking bird who had worked on a domestic murder inquiry. Our team had been tasked with tailing the suspect who, after a few days, headed to Glasgow Airport with the intention of evading arrest by fleeing the country for Thailand. The kick-out at the arrest, I recalled, had so many airline passengers flashing cameras at us I was surprised we didn't feature on You Tube.

"Didn't she recently hit the headlines, something about a shoot-out on a rooftop?"

"Yeah, a murder suspect who took a hostage and decided she wasn't surrendering. Lynn's a DCI now, my boss actually," says Mike. "Remembers you, though why she'd recall a skinny git like you, I can't think and like me, thinks you got a bit of a raw deal. Anyway, that's her cousin's card. Martin McCormack, a lawyer. His business has taken off and he's looking for somebody to do some private detective work, statement taking from witnesses and maybe a bit of surveillance, that sort of thing and I figured maybe you could use the cash. Lynn says he likes hiring former detectives because they're already trained and know the right questions to ask."

I took the card and stare at it, my throat suddenly tight. I stick the business card for the lawyer in my inside jacket pocket. I've got a regular income where I'm working and right now, don't need the hassle of settling in somewhere else, but who knows what is in front of us, so it might prove useful at some time in the future, though I wouldn't say this to Mike. He believes he has just done me a good turn. "Thanks Mike," I finally reply, "I owe you one." "One?" he gives me a scornful look, "Dozens, you ungrateful bugger," he smiles and turns to leave.

"Eh, Mike. One thing, if you've got a minute."

"Yeah, sure, but let's talk outside. I don't know what you've done, but that wee fat lassie at the counter seems to be giving you the evil eye."

I glanced again at the girl then made my way to the door, but took time to stop at the counter.

"Hope the pregnancy goes well," I loudly said to her, then saw her jaw drop and her face turn red with rage as she tries to splutter a denial. I inwardly chalk one up to me and moved quickly away.

I follow Mike into the bright sunshine and a few steps into the pedestrian precinct, away from the crowd at the door. I took a deep breath, uncertain how I am going to open the subject, but decide to jump straight in, feet first.

"Poet Burns, he's really dead, yeah?"

Mike stares at me like I've suddenly grown two heads. "Course he is," he scoffs and shakes his head. "I've seen the report. Nothing left of the bastard and good riddance, if you ask me. It saved us the cost of an extradition and a trial. Why do you ask?"

I slowly shake my head and suddenly feel very foolish. "It's nothing, just a whim. I saw a guy sitting in a car, a fleeting glimpse really. Just that, well, he looked a bit like Burns."

With a sudden burst of compassion Mike rubbed at my left arm with his right hand. "Look, I can't even begin to think what you went through, Tom. But you need to let it go. Move on with your life. Nothing will bring Alice back, no matter how hard you wish it. The debt's settled. Burns killed her and he's paid for it and every other dirty deed that he committed, with his life. Sad thing is that the car wreck that burned the bastard to death didn't last long enough for him to suffer like he should have."

I inwardly take a deep breath, grateful that he doesn't laugh or ridicule and tell me that my imagination is running away with me and has simply sympathised. But that is Mike, an all round good guy and for that I am fortunate in having him as my friend.

"Right," he glances at his watch and anxious to be gone, "I've the underground to catch back to Govan, so give the guy McCormick a call and don't leave it too late to get back to me. Next time we'll do dinner and a couple of pints, okay? And you're paying," and with that, gives me a cheery backward wave as he walks off, presumably happy that he has settled my suspicions.

But he hasn't, for the lingering doubt persists. Something continues to niggle at me. You know that feeling you get when a tune, a smell or a face on the television haunts you because you can't quite place your finger on where you've smelled, heard or seen it before? When you go through the alphabet, hoping to strike a name or try to describe it, but can't quite get the words out.

I start walking, hands in pockets and remembering as my feet slap the wet pavement beneath me. As a member of a surveillance team I had followed Burns for nigh on six weeks, seen him sober driving a vehicle, drunk driving a vehicle, staggering in the early hours of the morning from some club or pub and usually with a floozy on his arm. I'd watched him going fresh into the gym and limping out knackered. Observed him wearing all kind of different clothing in a host of scenarios and the more thought I gave it, the more I was convinced that the guy in the BMW was Burns.

But how do I go about proving it?

I hadn't realised that I had begun walking home, my thoughts overtaking my road sense as a lorry driver honks at me for stepping out into the road and causing him to swerve round me. I startle in fright and take a deep breath, but this time conscious I am now on West George Street towards the east end of Glasgow. You might be wondering by now why I should even bother, particularly as the police had got rid of me under circumstances that still rankled, even after almost three years. Truth be told, I wasn't that sure myself for after all, it was no longer my concern. But let's just say that it was unfinished business and the cause of my unhappiness for almost three years now. Unfinished business that has haunted me daily since …. Well, since that night.

I had taken a flexi afternoon off work and hadn't known why Mike Farrell wanted to meet with me and believed it would take longer than a coffee and muffin. I suppose with wishful thinking I had half hoped that Mike was going to produce some evidence that would exonerate me from the allegation that had led to my enforced resignation, some proof that I wasn't responsible for Alice Foley's death. Self-consciously, I shake my head at my naivety. The unwritten rule in the police is that the Chief Constable doesn't make mistakes, so no matter what if anything turned up in the way of new information, I am out and will remain so.

I start to walk towards my home in the east end of Glasgow, my coat buttons and tie loosened, but conscious of a rivulet of sweat running down my spine. October so far has been wet and miserable and today is the first that the good citizens had the opportunity to walk without raincoats and brollies, with some of the younger women even sporting sunglasses.

I rent a flat in Craigpark Drive in Dennistoun, a two bedroom affair in an old, red sandstone tenement building and I'm walking because frankly, I can't afford a car and almost convince myself that I don't really need one, that the buses are quite regular and I've only the city centre to travel to. Anyway, these days, I'm Tommy nae pals and work and home is about my limit of travel with work being my only real social outing. So here I am, walking through George Square and curiously, though I can hardly recall what I did yesterday, the events of three years ago are crystal clear in my head.

Alice Foley. Detective Constable Foley. Alice. Twenty-eight, a slim five foot six inches tall, short dark hair cut in a page boy style and stunningly beautiful. Or she had been, I mean, before she was murdered by Poet Burns. The very thought of her causes me to take a deep breath and I hardly notice the crowds gathering at the Cenotaph, another public protest against the latest round of council cuts to public services. I push my way through them as I head towards George Street, ignoring the women handing out leaflets and demanding a signature for their cause, my mind racing with thoughts of that night.

Poet Burns, self styled hard man and gangster. Like me, a product of the Glasgow council housing developments that commenced in the late fifties with the demolition of the old, rundown tenements in the city and continued with the construction of new, ultra modern housing developments in the suburbs.

And of course, all had inside bathrooms. A luxury to people brought up sharing a WC between three families on the tenement half landing. But what the developments didn't have was the employment and infrastructure needed to maintain and improve the life of the youth who moved with their parents to the new utopia's. No cinemas, youth clubs, dance halls, football parks or any kind of recreation facilities. In fairness to the City father's, their priority was to get the Glasgow populace out into the fresh air of what had once been arable farmland and in that they succeeded and by the thousands. However, what these new areas did have was a large number of hormone charged teenagers with time on their hands and nothing to discharge their teenage energy. And so began the rise of the new parochial gangs, successors to the inner city gangs the council fervently hoped had been dispersed to the new housing schemes. To compensate for the lack of facilities for the young, these new gangs offered a sense of comradeship, a feeling of belonging and even a pride in proprietary. 'This is my area. If you're not from here, you're getting done.' It quickly became apparent to teenagers that it was suicidal to wander where you weren't known. It wasn't long before the gang names were spray painted on the new brickwork and the territorial boundaries set. I was no stranger to the gangs myself, having in my teenage run with the Young Maryhill Tong, or the YMT as we liked to describe ourselves with spray cans. As I trudge along, I smile at the memory. I'd boasted about myself to my pals as being the bee's knees, as they say in Glasgow. Top of the tree, afraid of nobody, a James Cagney wannabe. At least, that's what I had thought, until one dark, winter night, after a rammy with an opposing gang from the Possilpark area, the cops had turned up and the rest of the gang had taken off like shit off a hot shovel. Only being me and thinking I was as wide as the Clyde, I waited that little bit longer, fuelled with cheap wine and determined to show off to my pals how tough

I was. With one hand waving an old, World War II bayonet about my head and calling out the infamous Glasgow battle cry of "C'mon, ya bastards", I almost shit myself when I realised the cops were a damn sight closer than I thought. In sheer panic, I had run like a bat out of hell with one cop on my tail, grabbing at me. The guy was a lot older than my nineteen years and I thought I'd outrun the bastard, but then twenty feet between us soon became fifteen feet. In my panic, I ducked into a newly constructed tenement, one of the few still unoccupied even though the redevelopment had long since run out of funding. Thinking that I knew the place like the back of my hand, I was shocked to find I'd stumbled into a dead end. Breathless and shaking with fear, I'd turned towards the cop, his cap held in one hand and the other holding one of the wee, wooden batons the polis were issued with back in those days. I shudder now when I think back, remembering that cornered and in the dark, I hadn't realised I was still holding the bayonet.

The cop, Gordon Roberts was his name, breathlessly told me in no uncertain terms that if I didn't drop the bayonet, he was going to shove his baton so far up my arse I'd end up with splinters on my tongue. Well, I didn't need much more persuasion after that and the bayonet slipped from my numb fingers with a clatter, to the ground. A sudden vision of jail and family disgrace passed before my eyes and the hard man I thought I was faded faster than my Auntie Jean's knickers dropping at the offer of a second gin. I almost laugh out loud when I remember that in an act of surrender, I'd put my hands out to be cuffed, but Roberts just shook his head, stuck his baton in his trouser pocket and plonked his cap onto the back of his head. Then to my utter astonishment, he really surprised me when he produced a packet of fags and shook two out that he lit before offering me one.

"McEwan's your name, isn't it?" he had asked.

Nervously, I'd taken the fag and with shaking fingers, stuck it in my mouth, wandering if this was some sort of prelude to him battering me. "Aye, sir," I agreed, now much subdued and deciding that a little humility was called for. After all he had, as they say, got me by the short and curlies. "Thomas McEwan. 65 Brassey Street," I volunteered.

"Live with your folks, don't you? Your da's a welder in the yards?"

I had nodded, too dumbstruck with shame that Roberts knew my folks. My church-going, never been in trouble with the police parents that I was now shaming. My shoulders had drooped. Life as I knew it was over.

"I know your da," he had continued. "He's an elder in my church, a Baptist, like me. And I know as sure as anything that me arresting you, that will just kill him." I stood silent, knowing that my arrest would not only destroy the faith my father had in me, but my apprenticeship as an electrician in the yards would also surely be over. I can even remember that hard man that I was supposed to be, the mention of my parents had brought on such shame that tears were tickling the back of my eyes and threatening to erupt from me.

"Ever been in bother us, Thomas? Charged by the polis, I mean?" I shook my head, which was a half truth. No, I'd never been charged by the cops, but I'd been involved in a few scrapes where the polis had attended. I'd just never been caught. Petty stuff, I now realise, being that bit older and wiser, but as I said, back then? Life revolved round work and the area where I felt safe. Oh, and Partick Thistle. And before you start scoffing, I've heard all the jokes, okay? Like it or lump it, I'm a Jags man through and through.

By this time I'm crossing from George Street across the High Street and, now mindful of the traffic, striding into Duke Street, but still the memory of that night stuck with me.

Of course, what I didn't know then was that Gordon Roberts was one of life's good guys and I've mentally thanked him every day of my life since then. What he'd seen in a gawky, tall youth at nearly six foot with a mop of what my mother calls strawberry blonde hair still puzzles me, but he'd decided to give me a break, rather than a criminal record for stupidity. Don't be fooled though. He was and is a good man, but he's also a bit devious when he needs to be, so let me explain. Gordon had reached a decision because he knew my father, a more honest, upright man you will never meet. So in that dirty and dark place, he struck a deal, offering me the opportunity to get myself out of the hole I had so stupidly jumped into, head first. The deal was that the very next morning, I was to present myself, shaved and showered and wearing a collar and tie and my one good suit, to the recruiting Sergeant at Oxford Street

Training Centre and request an application form for the police. We didn't shake on it, no. It was more of a threatening deal. Let me explain. Gordon told me that he'd be phoning the recruiting Sergeant at 10am and if I hadn't appeared, he'd hunt me down and father or not, keep good his promise with the wooden baton and that was before he'd arrest me for gangland violence. Of course, in my naivety, it never occurred to me he was bluffing. I was just so grateful for the chance to get out of the predicament that I was in and would have slobbered all over his boots with my furry tongue, if it would keep me out of jail. So, bright and early the next morning and to my parent's surprise, I announced my intention to join the polis.

Pity I hadn't seen the outcome, but there you are. Fate smiles and gives with one hand and sticks a finger in your eye with the other. However, no matter what thoughts I have as I walk along Duke Street, the nagging feeling persists.

Was it Poet Burns I had seen in the beamer?

Chapter 2

The autumn sun has brought out the areas residents, so Duke Street is busy with shoppers and warily, I dodge the young mothers and their prams, grannies with their snotty nosed grandkids slurping at ice-creams to keep them quiet and grim faced, mostly east European males, one hand offering a Big Issue and the other aggressively flicking the fingers for payment.

It's a bit of a take-on, this part of the east end. Duke Street itself could probably do with a facelift, but take a stroll from the main, arterial route that's lined with gaudily painted pubs, take-away food shops and cheap, bargain stores to the residential area behind the dirt grimed tenements towards Alexandria Parade and it's as if you've stepped from noise and chaos to a quiet, suburban housing estate. The area is a mixture of clean, sandblasted tenements, detached Victorian villas and 1950's mid terraced houses, the predominant number of which is privately owned. The side streets act as a conduit through to Alexandra Parade and to cut down on heavy traffic, the council installed traffic calming buttresses that in the dark can burst tyres and tear the underside from a vehicle, but really the only drawback to living here is the parking. To say it's chaotic is an understatement so I don't really miss having my own transport. I make my way to the tenement in Craigpark Drive, my thoughts again of Alice. I involuntarily smile, recalling her wicked grin and quick witted sense of humour. The way she would brush a loose strand of hair from over her eyes, her ready smile or how her eyes narrowed and her mouth puckered and creased to the left side when her thoughts were occupied by some problem. Did I love her, you'll be asking yourself. If I'm very honest, I'm not really certain. What I did know was I had strong feelings for her, but love?

I turn into the short path to the close mouth and insert my common Yale key into the front door of the building and slowly make my way up the stairs, savouring the aromatic smells wafting from the Ahmed's ground floor flat. Opening my front door, I hang the keys on the hook on the wall beside the door and then shake my head, remembering that once more I've forgotten to buy milk. Damn, black coffee again.

The flat is small, but neat and tidy. After the luxury of the detached three bed roomed house I'd shared with Lisa and the twins, it has taken a bit of getting used to, but if anything the size make it that much easier to keep clean and tidy. I'm not the type of guy that goes off the rails when his marriage fails. No, Lisa used to boast she'd married a domesticated man, so the general housewifery duties come easily to me and besides, I don't like clutter. Everything in its place and a place for everything, as my old mum likes to say.

Taking my coffee through to the compact lounge that faces onto the street below, I sit down on the old, but comfy leather sofa, courtesy of the Salvation Army shop on Dumbarton Road, and stretch my legs onto the solid, if slightly scarred wooden coffee table. The persistent thought that I'd seen a very much alive Poet jumps back into my head. I just can't shake the belief that it was him, but again asked myself. How would I go about proving it?

A thought strikes me. Against all police standing orders, I'd managed to keep all my old notebooks from just after I joined to my final, sixteenth year; some vain idea I'd had years ago as a rookie cop that one day I'd sit and write down my experiences for my kids. The books were all neatly stored in a cardboard box in the spacious hall cupboard. I set my mug down and fetch the box, plonking it down onto the table and begin to rifle through the books until I find the date I am looking for, the date we'd commenced Operation Timorous Beastie, the surveillance operation to snare Robbie 'Poet' Burns, armed robber and all round bad guy.

I flick through the book till I find the details and using Google on my trusty old laptop, obtain the phone number I need for the Glasgow Registry Offices in Martha Street, then reach for my land line phone and dial. A female operator puts me through to Births, Death and Marriages.

"Glasgow Registry Office, Michael speaking. How can I help you?" answers the youthful voice.

"Oh, hi," I reply. "My name's Tom McEwan, Claims Investigator with YCS Insurance Services in Bothwell Street. Michael is it?" I ask, hoping to create a mutual bond from the outset.

"That's right," he agrees.

"Hi Michael, I'm making inquiry into a claim, one of these ongoing things, you know how it is," fervently hoping he doesn't, but would not want to admit otherwise.

"Yeah? So, how can I help?"

"It's relative to a road traffic accident that occurred abroad, Spain actually. The deceased's estate is currently being fought over by several family members and my company is trying to sort things out. I'm aware that as a British subject having died abroad, his death would still need to be registered in the UK. Think you'd be in a position to assist me?"

I've dangled the carrot and fingers crossed, hope his curiosity will take over. After a slight pause, he asks, "What do you need, Tom?" I try not to sigh with relief and tell him, "I have full details of the deceased and approximate date of the accident, but as it was almost three years previously," I tail off, my heart racing in my chest, half expecting the apologetic refusal.

"Well," Michael almost gushes, "three years in the scheme of things isn't too long because these days, even in the Council, we've computerised everything, so I can maybe do a speculative check on the details you do have, Tom."

I guess I've fired up the young guys imagination, that he now believes himself to be part of an insurance inquiry and from my notebook, gave him Poet's full name, date of birth and last known address at the massive detached house he rented in Killermount Grove in the Castle Policies estate in Bothwell, as well as the approximate date of his fiery demise.

"Get many of these inquiries, from abroad I mean?" he asks.

"Oh, the odd one or two," I glibly lie, guessing he is merely making conversation while he works at his computer.

"Does that mean you get foreign travel then?"

"No such luck," then think to keep him on-side I'll try a bit of bonding. "That's for the senior investigators, Michael. Guys like you and me are stuck in the office, doing the real work, not swanning about on company expenses."

"Yeah, know what you mean," he replies. His voice sounded slightly detached and I assume he is concentrating on the screen in front of him, looking for the report.

"Here we go," he says at last, "tenth of November. That'll be three years ago this forthcoming November. Same details you gave me. Robbie Burns. He'd be, let me see, forty-six when he died? That sound about right."

"That'll be him," I try to control the excitement in my voice. "Does it say who filed the report?"

"The entry was made by a Sergeant Meikle of Stewart Street police office Inquiry Department. That's quite common with this sort of situation. When the death occurs abroad, the Scottish police get the report from the local police where the death happened and as a matter of course, the Scottish police then in turn register the death with us, so it's not uncommon to read it's a local police officer reporting the death."

"Anything to indicate who initially dealt with Mister Burns' death? Perhaps maybe even a contact telephone number or something?"

I knew I was chancing my arm with that one, but let's face it. You don't get if you don't try.

"There's an e-mail printout attachment to the report, give me a minute and I'll try to open it," he replies.

I wait impatiently, not trusting to luck but to the competence of the unknown Sergeant Meikle, my now tense fingers unconsciously crossed that he had diligently attached all necessary correspondence in the event should it later be required for retrieval.

"Got it open and surprise, surprise," says Michael, "it's in Spanish. But," I hear the pause in his voice, "there's a signature box at the bottom of the e-mail. The signature is a bit squiggly, but the officer's name is typed underneath. I don't need to read Spanish to guess from the letters 'Sjt' beside the name that the guy was a Sergeant."

"And the name is?" I try not to sound too anxious.

"J Martinez," he replies, "of the Guardia Civil. That will be the police, right? Anyway, it's somewhere called Badajoz. There's a phone number Tom, if you've got a pen handy?" He relates the number that includes the international code and which I confirm by reading back to him.

"Michael, I owe you one. If you're looking for a good deal on Insurance give me a bell," I promise, giving him my office phone number and desk extension, thinking the young guy might be a useful contact at some future time.

"No problem," he cheerfully replies and hangs up.

I sit back and sip at my cooling coffee, unable to believe my luck or how easy it had been. If nothing else, I now have a tentative lead. I consider phoning the Spanish number right away, but of course, I don't speak Spanish. No, I decide, I'll wait till I am at work tomorrow and use the company phone. Okay, it might technically be theft of a call from my employer, but I don't expect to be hauled up by the management and besides, name me someone who doesn't use the company phones for personal business at some time or other? I sit back and shut my eyes, trying to recall the fleeting glimpse of the man in the BMW vehicle. When I had been a serving detective officer, among the many courses I'd been required to attend was one on cognitive interviewing where I had been taught to coax information from witnesses who perhaps hadn't realised what they had seen or heard, who might dismiss such information from their conscious mind as irrelevant, but what might prove to be invaluable to an investigator. Really, it was simply putting the witness at ease, normally with eyes closed and softly talking the witness through a particular part of their statement, trying to induce them to recall some details their conscious mind has ignored. I willed my body to relax, closed my eyes and began by playing back in my mind entering and sitting in the café, trying to recall the surroundings. It is just over an hour later when I startle awake. I half laugh at myself; so much for bloody cognitive recall. I've fallen asleep on the couch, stupid bugger that I am and awoke with a creak in my neck. Rubbing hard at the stiffness with one hand, I reach for the control and switch on the TV. I'm a bit of a news junkie and like to keep abreast of what's happening locally. It was the usual murder and mayhem, but then again good news isn't newsworthy, or so I've been told.

I am still bothered by the sighting of the man in the BMW and it fills my thoughts as I prepare my evening meal. I'm not cordon bleu or anything, but I can rustle up a mean curry and aside from the usual traditional dishes, I'm also a dab hand at serving all sorts of pasta dishes. During my marriage Lisa used to boast that she'd married an all round good guy. I don't suppose she thinks that now, though.

You might wonder where it all went wrong, so let me take you back to a dark night almost three years ago and I'll begin my tale in the briefing room in Meiklewood Road police station. The whole team had been summoned from our rostered two days off and while we waited for our DI we knew, as Mister Holmes used to put it, that something was afoot. You didn't need to be a detective to work that out, not when six of the team had been instructed to attend at the duty officers safe and draw Heckler & Koch MP5's as well as their personal issue Glock's and everyone else not firearms authorised told to wear vests and carry the non-standard batons known in the trade as 'snoopies'. Snoopies were an assortment of pick axe handles and baseball bats, primarily used for smashing in car windows and, while screaming abuse to intimidate a suspect, battering anyone who didn't immediately surrender. You have to remember, the type of villain we usually encountered wasn't your "come along quietly please" criminal, but predominantly the product of the Glasgow council schemes, well schooled in violence and with no respect for authority, equally capable of giving out as good as they got and many a copper has the scars to prove it. And that's just the women.

The issuing of firearms at short notice was always a sure indicator it was a time critical operation and the only target we had operationally running at that time, that habitually used guns when committing crime, was Poet Burns. There were fifteen of us in the briefing room that included me and Alice Foley. The rest of the team comprised of two Detective Sergeants and ten detective constables, the last team member being a female dog handler, with the aptly named Robber being the ugliest looking Alsatian I had ever seen. Mind you, as I recall as far as looks were concerned, it was a bit of a toss-up between the dog and the handler. Even Minnie Maxwell's parents must have been hard put to describe their daughter as anything but a nice girl. And credit where credit is due. Minnie was and probably still is a fine cop and she and her dog were very useful when it came down to pursuing a suspect. Not many argued with Robber when he had his hackles up and many a thug surrendered when Robber bared his teeth.

It was a lousy night I recall, a bleak, wet October Tuesday. We waited with some impatience for Donnie Chapman, our team Detective Inspector. The usual ribald comments were being bandied about with the butt of the jokes being directed against Sandy Oates whose on-off relationship with women and the antics he got up to trying to impress them kept us going for most of the shift. He was a good natured lad Sandy, but Walter Mitty would have had a hard job keeping pace with his story-telling. I smiled as I remembered that night, Sandy recounting his attempts to woo one of the Meiklewood Road office typists with a tale of his Porsche and his offer to run her into the country for lunch on their next day off, only for her to remind him that her hubby worked for the RAC and had told her of a job a few days previously, repairing a Skoda for one of the cops that worked at her place, a DC Fleming. I shook my head and smiled as I recalled the story, Sandy was a good guy, but where women were concerned, he couldn't catch his fingers in a door. Alice had laughingly joined in the banter with the rest, avoiding my furtive glances towards her. But it hadn't escaped my notice or that of the others that she'd applied a heavy layer of make-up to her clear skin that didn't quite manage to hide the bruise under her left eye.

All hilarity in the room ceased when Donnie Chapman, five feet eight in his socks and barrel-chested, with a shock of white hair and ruddy complexion, stomped into the office and scraping a chair back from behind the desk at the front of the room, plonked himself down and loudly called for silence. I can almost recall the tension that settled among us as we listened.

I recall that night that Donnie was the stereotype grim-faced detective as he began by telling us what we suspected, that the target for the rush operation was indeed Robbie 'Poet' Burns, that information had been received from a previously reliable source that Poet intended that evening to commit a robbery, what we called a CIT – a Cash In Transit.

"The hit, lads and lassies, will be on a MacPhee Security vehicle delivering through the wee small hours to ATM's in the Lanarkshire area. What we do know is that Poet will carry out the assault on the security personnel and as is his trademark, will be using a sawn off double barrelled shotgun to terrorise the van crew. An accomplice will grab the cash boxes and no, I don't know if the accomplice will also be armed, while a second accomplice will drive the getaway vehicle. I don't know if the driver will be armed either." A mutter went up from the team and Donnie had to firmly call for silence. "Further, what we also do not know is where the actual hit will occur, the identity of the two accomplices or what type of vehicle will be used as the getaway car."

The mood of the team became sombre as we realised the pitfalls of such an operation were already becoming apparent and Paddy O'Brien, one of the two DS's, began to complain, but was waved down by Donnie who in no uncertain terms, told us all to shut the fuck up, then shaking his head, handed out briefing packs.

"Look, I know it's not ideal, but we're surveillance, we're well trained and it's out job to follow and deal with the situation as it arises. Adapt and overcome, okay?"

We shuffled our feet in agitation and like me the rest of the team had the pre-operational nerves that usually occur when gunplay might be a likelihood. Donnie read from his own notes, telling us that the security van would depart its depot at 10.30pm that evening with a driver and front passenger who, when the vehicle stopped to make a cash delivery, would stand off from the vehicle and observe the surrounding area before giving the nod for the third crew member to alight from the enclosed rear of the vehicle with either one or two of the large cash cassettes, depending on the ATM's location, that were to be inserted into the ATM's.

"First, let me clue you in as to the standing operational procedure for the three man crew of these security vehicles in the event they become the subject of a compromise. The front passenger," Donnie told us, "will carry a hand alarm that if activated will not only sound a high pitched audible alert, but also transmit a radio signal that informs the company's base that an attack is underway. In addition, the driver, who remains within the vehicle, is instructed to activate the automatic locking of all the doors and not to leave the vehicle, no matter what occurs outside."

Sandra Donnelly, the other DS in the team, piped up, "But what if the two guys outside are getting a kicking?"

"It's their company Lisa, their rules," replied Donnie, waving his notes at her. "You might also have reasoned that if Poet can grab two cassette's full of cash that is likely preferable to grabbing one, which might, just might, be an indicator as to when the hit could occur. Not definite, but keep it in mind, okay? Now, children, here's what we're about tonight," then proceeded to allocate the teams, two firearms officers to a car driven by an unarmed officer who would remain with the car no matter what occurred at the location if in the event the hit went wrong and turned into an armed vehicular pursuit. With nine of the team now designated three surveillance vehicles and Minnie Maxwell and Robber within their own unmarked van, which left five of us and the DI in three double manned vehicles. It was by chance that Alice and I were teamed together and I recall inwardly drawing a sigh of pleasurable relief.

Donnie finished his briefing by calling for any questions and Graeme Fleming got his in first.

"What route is the van taking boss? I mean, can we pre-empt the hit by staking out the likely locations?"

Donnie audibly sighed and shook his head and like the rest of the team, I guessed what was coming next.

"Intelligence suspects that because Poet seems to be spot-on with his information, there might be a tout in the company providing him with the security vehicles routes and stops, so we're staying clear of any contact with the company. If we were to flag up an interest in a particular route or van, we might tip of that tout and you know the rest. Poet will be told and simply cancel the hit till such times he believes we've lost interest."

Something else had been nagging at me so I was next to raise my hand.

"This previously reliable source you spoke of, boss. We've been tailing Poet for almost six weeks and he's hit at least one CIT that we missed," I reminded the team, "so why has the informant now suddenly produced this wee nugget and who exactly in our outfit did the informant tell?"

Donnie had shook his head and I realised I'd raised a doubt in his own mind. "All I know," he sat with hands outstretched as he'd shaken his head and addressed us all, "is that somebody in the Covert Handling Intelligence Section contacted the DCI to pass this information on. I can't vouch for the veracity of the intelligence other than to tell you that we are instructed to treat the information as A1. The source, whoever he or she might be, has satisfied the management that Poet is going out tonight and tooled up, with the intention of collecting himself a couple of cash boxes, each apparently containing twenty-five grand in unused notes. But I will remind you," he glared at us, "don't be taking it for granted Poet will go after two boxes. He might just decide on one cassette and twenty-five grand isn't to be sneered at, so we stay alert for all the ATM visits. Got that?"

Almost as one, we all muttered to confirm we understood.

I couldn't know it then, but I wish to God now that I had made more of that question.

Since that time and believe me, I've had plenty of time to think about it, I thought it odd that as the team was going out on such a time critical and dodgy operation, none of the senior management attended the briefing to offer their support and give us the "We'll back you guys, no matter what" speech they usually hung on us. Of course, it might be because Donnie Chapman was such a gung-ho bastard and made it known he was keen to move from DI to a cushy DCI post and wanted any glory to come directly to him. But then again, as I later thought about it, it might have been because none of the management wanted to have their fingers burnt just in case the operation went apeshit, as it so spectacularly did. Either way, nobody questioned or even gave a thought to why the management weren't present. We just wanted to get out there and do our jobs and let's be honest about it here. We've all watched the Hollywood blockbusters and the prospect of gunplay in an operation excited us. As a unit, we wanted to be the ones featured in the papers next day, the cops giving it to the bad guys. Jesus. How naive we were.

The memories of that night came flooding back as I stand and stretch my aching back, collect the now cold cup of coffee and walk into the kitchen, filling then switching on the kettle. I stand with my hands on the worktop, my brow furrowing as I remember trying to ignore Alice, not daring to be anything other than a team member, collecting the car keys and bag of maps and sundry equipment that a surveillance team used during an operation. Unconsciously, I swallow hard as the memory of her courses through my thoughts.

My relationship with Alice, if you can call it that, had begun some months previously when I joined the team. Alice had preceded me by about six months. I'd previously been with the Shettleston CID and had already passed the surveillance course, but waited nearly a year for a vacancy to occur.

My first week with the team had been training exercises, designed simply to integrate me and the other new member Sandra Donnelly. I had noticed Alice as soon as I arrived. It wasn't difficult. She was by far the best looking woman I'd ever met. No, not Miss Scotland pretty, but an attractiveness that was hard to describe. I won't give you any of that old 'our eyes met' shit. It wasn't like that. Not by any means. Now, yes, I know what you might be thinking. So there I am, a married man with twin daughters', fantasising about another woman, herself married and too another cop. You'll note I didn't say I was a happily married man. I wasn't unhappy, but I think the euphoria of the first two years had passed and Lisa and I had settled into a comfortable relationship. And now here I was, lusting after another woman. Not cool, not by any means. But I just couldn't get Alice out of my mind. You might think my own marriage was going down the pan and that complacency had set in after such a short time, but the truth was I had a good-looking, head turning wife and two smashing kids, so why would I put my relationship in jeopardy? Why would I risk not only my marriage and my kids, but my career?

I sigh heavily and rub with the heel of my hand at my brow, my mind concentrating on her face, the shape of her eyes, her dimpled chin and the way she turned her head slightly left when she smiled. There was something about Alice, something I just couldn't get my head around. She was a hard working cop, of that there was no doubt, capable and competent and with her exams passed, she had the opportunity to advance her career. Her husband, I later found out was a Sergeant in the Airdrie division. No kids. Of course, cops being cops and the world's biggest gossips, it soon became apparent that the marriage wasn't happy and I learned that before I joined the unit sometimes Alice turned up for work with make-up plastered on to hide the bruises. Some of the team, the guys that curiously included Sandra Donnelly, whispered about paying Alice's husband Wallace a wee visit and I know from at least one conversation with Sandra that if Alice decided to leave her husband, she and her own husband Paul had offered Alice a room until she got herself together. I never understood why she didn't take up the offer and leave the bastard. Over the course of the next few weeks I fought the urge to offer my shoulder.

But the simple truth is, I don't really know what I felt about Alice. Call it what you want; stupidity, an adult crush, some kind of need to protect her. No matter how you try to analyse it, I fucked my life up and in the worst possible, straight to the bottom, nose-diving fashion. The worst thing is, I didn't just commit professional and personal suicide; I dragged my wife Lisa down with me.

Chapter 3

We left our base about 9.30pm on that wet, overcast evening, the driving rain battering against the car windows, the windscreen wipers working overtime and the heaters set to demist working at full pelt.

The perfect weather for surveillance because we knew for experience that any target driver would be too engrossed on looking ahead at the hazards of the road, rather than mind what was behind him.

Our first port of call was the security depot located in the old Wills Cigarette factory on Alexandria Parade and coincidentally not far from where I now live. A square, solid brick built building surrounded by a fifteen foot wall that was itself topped by razor sharp barbed wire. It didn't take a genius to work out the place looked and was likely as solid as Fort Knox. A bank in every sense of the word, but not one the public had access to. The exit from the premises was into Hanson Street, so the surveillance convoy deployed into the surrounding streets to await the departure of our target vehicle.

In my time within the unit, I'd followed a variety of vehicles and once even a suspected robber who used a pushbike, but this was a first to me, a yellow and green liveried security van and I had reckoned even in the darkest of nights like that it was, we wouldn't have any problems following the van round Lanarkshire.

Alice elected to drive our surveillance car, a charcoal coloured Ford Focus and so as her footman, I shrugged into the covert radio set in its body harness and plugged the earpiece into my left ear. Under my green waxed three quarter length coat, I also had room to carry an old hickory baseball bat, my very own persuader. I close my eyes, remembering that night. Alice had tied her jet black hair back into a tight pony-tail and was wearing a loose fitting navy blue sweater and black coloured denim jeans with the dark grey hiking boots she favoured for night operations. In the confines of the car with the heater working overtime, the light scent she wore intoxicated me and made my head spin. I wanted nothing more than to hold her close.

"Alice," I had said, turning towards her and tried not to stare at the swell of her breasts, but she held up her hand and stopped me.

"No, Tom, This isn't the time to talk about you and me, not here."

I remember feeling foolish, like some overgrown schoolboy on heat.

"Your face…" I tried again, but once more she cut me off, this time turning towards me, her eyes betraying her embarrassment.

"Is it that obvious?"

I had been angry, outraged that her bastard of a husband and himself a police Sergeant, used her like a punch bag. I wanted nothing more to get a hold of him and big as he apparently was, kick him till my feet hurt.

"It was my fault," she stared ahead through the rain swept windscreen at the darkened road. "I'd forgotten to iron him a clean polo shirt for work. He's very particular about his appearance."

"And that's an excuse to hit you?" I had replied with more sarcasm than I meant.

She slowly shook her head and continued to stare ahead at the road as she drove, her brow knitted in concentration or fretting at the memory, I wasn't certain. "I told him yesterday I'm leaving," she softly said. "I told him there was someone else. I'm sorry Tom. I used you as an excuse. I told him about you."

I remembered holding my breath, both surprised and shocked, a wave of emotions sweeping through me. Till that point, that moment in time, I had been the ideal husband. Lisa had never any cause to doubt me, never suspected that my affection now lay elsewhere and here was Alice identifying me as the other party in her failed marriage and as far as my own marriage was concerned, I was the perfect betrayer.

The phone in the front room rings, startling me from my memories. "Hello?" I answer.

"It's me," Lisa curtly replies, "about the arrangements for getting the girls on Saturday?"

"Ah, yes. Usual time, if that's okay with you."

"Fine, I'll drop them off at your flat," she tells me then abruptly hung up.

I take a deep breath and sit heavily down on the worn couch. I have no right to expect anything from Lisa, least of all courtesy. I treated her badly. No, not violence or anything like that, I could never be abusive. It just isn't in my nature. But cheating? I am a past master at that as far as Lisa was concerned. As I said, my betrayal of her trust was enough and Lisa is not a forgiving woman.

I thought back to that time when I first met Lisa at a CID colleagues promotion function in a bar in Sauchiehall Street. She was with a couple of mates and I was so pissed I started slobbering all over her pal, who clearly was on the pull that night and rightly didn't want a drunk hanging about her. Lisa was more tolerant of the drunken me, even suggesting that sober, I might be worth seeing again. So I woke up the next morning with a crumpled piece of paper that had the name Lisa Farquhar and a mobile number scrawled on it. Took me three days to work up the nerve to call her and when we did meet at Slattery's Irish themed pub in the Merchant City area of Glasgow, I worried that I might not remember what she looked like. Turned out, that wasn't a problem, because Lisa is a real eye-catching beauty. A natural blonde and just a few inches shorter than me at five foot nine, she turned more than my head when she walked into the bar. I smile with self-conscious embarrassment as I pour myself a fresh coffee, my mind recalling how I tried to give her a line about me being the big city 'Tec and talk about a whirlwind courtship? Before I knew it, three months had passed, she's pregnant and I'm whisking her off for a week in a two star hotel in Torquay and a registry office. Her father John has never forgiven me for stealing his one daughter away and losing him the opportunity to walk her down the aisle and parade in front of his affluent Law Society cronies. John Farquhar, how would I describe him? Well, let me say he wasn't slow in name-dropping his senior police officer friends he plays golf with and he has the sort of personality that sucks the atmosphere right out of any room he is in.

Her mum Joan is a different kettle of fish, though. Nice wee woman and at all not stuck-up like her snobby husband. She's more of a Glasgow wifey, if you know what I mean. When I first met Joan, on that first occasion Lisa plucked up the courage to invite me to her parent's house, she introduced herself and her hubby as the Derby Club pair. I politely laughed along with her, wanting to make a good impression on my future in-laws, but John didn't laugh; didn't even chuckle and it seemed obvious to me even then that he thinks he's married beneath himself, twat that he is. As for my folks, let's just say the parents didn't mix socially. Mum and dad still live in the semi-detached council house in Broughton Drive in sunny Maryhill, where I was brought up and where I occasionally return every couple of months to top up my tan. The only thing they have in common is the girls, the twins Sophie and Sarah, aged six now. Me being an only child, my folks dote on their grandkids as does Lisa's mum. Minutes after the girls were born, John Farquhar simply made it known and I suspect continues to do so that he'd have preferred grandsons.

But I'm getting off the track here. I was recalling how it happened that I became the villain of the story.

So we're back to that fateful night. The surveillance convoy arrived in good time to plot up round the area of the security premises, engines switched off and radio chatter at a minimum as lost in our own thoughts, the team readied themselves for the departure of the target security van. Alice and I were deployed in the nearby dark of Milnbank Street, the car pointed towards Alexandria Parade and ideally located to immediately get onto the van's tail when it left to make the rounds of the ATM's in the Lanarkshire area.

I remember sitting in uncomfortable silence, almost too afraid to breath let alone ask Alice about her revelation. Part of me was overjoyed that she had made the decision and I secretly hoped that maybe we could be together. But any joy I felt was overshadowed by the explosion I knew would come later in my own life when I told Lisa that I was leaving her. Yeah, I'd made my decision as quick as that. Leaving her and the kids I mean, because I knew that Lisa would give up her last breath before she would let me take the girls. My mind raced at the complications Alice's simple statement would make to my life. When I think of it now, I can hardly believe what a selfish bastard I was.

The more I thought about that night, the more I have come to decide that Alice was distracted by something, though what, I can't imagine. I remember her silhouette against the darkness of the rain splashed window, her eyes fixedly staring straight ahead.

"I know that I can't expect anything from you, Tom," she had told me, breaking into my thoughts. "I don't want you to give up your marriage for me, your wife and kids. This is my decision. I'll get myself a place and get my own life back on track before I commit to anything. I just can't live with Wallace any longer, not now.... God, I'm such a fucking mess," she had sobbed, the tears trickling down her cheeks.

Now, I don't know if you've ever tried to offer comfort to someone in the drivers' seat from the front passenger seat, but let me tell you from experience, it isn't easy. Try as I had to give Alice a comforting cuddle, the gear stick threatening to dislodge my bollocks from their bag didn't help so the best I could offer her was a hug as she softly cried and leaned into my jacketed shoulder. The radio harness hampered me even more and the awkwardness of the situation hit us both at the same time, causing us to giggle. I can't quite remember how it happened, but the next thing is we're kissing and I remember tasting her salty tears that made my own cheeks wet when we were both startled as the radio burst into life with a message from the team member, who was hidden in the observation van.

"Standby, standby, that's the electric gates swinging open and the target vehicle about to depart. Standby," the voice repeated.

Alice suddenly pushed away from me, rubbing with her sleeve at her eyes and shuffled back into her driving position as she hurriedly snapped on her seat belt.

"And it's an off, off, off," said the voice on the radio, "now turning right towards the Parade. Convoy?"

One by one in numerical order, the surveillance vehicles acknowledged the signal, with me using the car radio to let the other vehicles know that Alice and I would take the first eyeball on the security van.

I won't bore you with details of the follow, but almost immediately we're heading east on the M8 toward our first port of call that turned out to be the ATM that was located on the outside wall of the Bothwell service station, located on the M74. I can remember the tension of the moment as the convoy gave way to the armed cars to permit the Heckler-Koch guys to get into some sort of position while the rest of us pulled into the hard shoulder and switched off our lights.

The weather hadn't let up and I didn't envy the armed guys, quickly getting out of their cosy vehicles and finding somewhere to hide each time the security van stopped and the cash delivery was made.

Throughout the follow as the surveillance cars switched eyeball position, each car driver provided a running commentary that over the next five deliveries sounded almost word for word.

"The van now stopped near to the ATM and the passenger out, out, out and taking up the guard position; rear door now opening."

"Bag man out, out, out and carrying one cash cassette and towards the ATM," said the voice. "The bag man unlocking the safe below the ATM and removing cassette and now inserting new cassette; bag man towards rear of the van and passenger safely returned to vehicle and it's now off, off, off. Convoy?"

It was on the third delivery at the Bank of Scotland in Bellshill, when the rear bag man got out carrying two cassettes that as a team we unconsciously held our breath, thinking this was the hit. The rain continued to spatter off the car windows and the deserted streets where we parked, dimly lit by the overhead halogen lights, had an almost surreal eerie feeling to the location. Two cassettes, the informant had said. But it turned out to be two ATM's side by side and again, each of which received a new cassette. Within five minutes, the drop was complete and we were off again.

Breathing a sigh of relief, the surveillance continued to wind its way round Lanarkshire and by now, the seed of doubt had crept through the team like a furtive itch. I could hear it in the voices over the radio. At one point Donnie Chapman broke into the wavelength and ordered us to cut the cackle, that the van was still making deliveries and instructed us not to get complacent.

By now, seven drops had been successfully completed and it had just gone 3am. I remember my eyes were beginning to droop. The warmth of the car with the heater going full blast to demist the windscreen and the hypnotic motion of the wipers combined to cause me to drift off and it was only when Alice sharply dug me in the ribs with her fist that I startled awake. I rubbed at my eyes and yawned and I remember wondering if I could persuade Lisa to go into work an hour late and get the girls to nursery so that I could go to bed and crash. She worked in the Glasgow University library and I knew she hated being late, but it wasn't as if I made a habit of asking her.

"Where are we now?" I had asked Alice as I peered through the windscreen at an unfamiliar road.

"Just coming into Holytown," she had replied and then with a grimace, added, "Apache country."

"You know this place?"

"Yeah, I worked on a murder inquiry here a couple of years ago. It's a small place, a village really and a bit insular. Former mining town and everybody knows everyone else's business. The victim was a local man, as was his killer. It started out as the usual Saturday night bevy session then turned into a pub quarrel gone wrong. The history of the West of Scotland; too much drink and a failure to recognise that football difference doesn't mean religious divide. It seemed that whole community knew who did it, but nobody was talking. Didn't take us long to identify the killer, though. It was gathering sufficient evidence to charge him that presented the difficulty. The old story; knowing and proving are two different things. It was one of those inquiries whereby if anyone spoke to the cops, they were shunned by the rest of the community. Even with the loss of one of their own, we were still the bad guys, the outsiders. In any event, the murder team finally obtained enough evidence to arrest the bad guy and he went down for murder.

"Standby, standby," said the now bored crackly voice on the car radio, "Van stopping beside Cooperative shop. There's an ATM there. Passenger out, out, out and taking up an eyeball position. Rear door opening. Bag man out, out, out and carrying two cassettes and towards the ATM. Just one ATM," the voice added and I remember it had seemed to me at the time there was slightly higher pitch in his voice. Two cassettes, but just one ATM?

"Bag man unlocking the safe below the ATM and removing a cassette, now inserting one new cassette…Wait!"

That one word, "Wait" echoed from the radio like a gunshot. I recalled snapping out of my sleepy stupor, Alice tensing beside me as the seconds seemed to drag on.

"Two suspects approaching, running … Jesus, they're hooded. One's got a shooter, a shotgun I think! The radio man's run off. It's going down! Back-up?"

"Armed response! Armed response!" shouted Donnie Chapman's voice as he cut into the radio, "get in there now!"

Now, I said earlier that we, the team that is, all liked the idea of being involved in a Hollywood type gunplay situation. The reality is completely different. Right then it was sweaty hands and dry mouth time and I remember I needed to pee. I turned to stare at Alice, her mouth open, eyes wide and almost together, we cried out, "Fuck!" and jerked open our doors. I didn't at first understand why I couldn't get out of my seat, but quickly realised in my haste I'd forgotten to unlock my seat belt. Alice hadn't and by the time I exited the car, she was five yards away and running down the poorly lit side street where we'd parked towards the Main Street that led to the Cooperative, nearly two hundred metres away. "Alice!" I shouted after her, all pretence at covert surveillance now gone. She shuddered to a halt at the junction and I saw her raise a hand to stop me, her head cocked round the corner of the building to take in the scene outside the shop. In my ear, I could hear orders being barked as Donnie tried to direct the armed officers to the location. I pulled up behind Alice, gasping for air from the short burst of running from our car and knowing the adrenalin was already beginning to course through my body.

"I can see a car, a saloon car, parked across the road, lights off, but" she breathlessly whispered then added as if explaining. "Funny, it looks like …well, it's the same type of car that….but it can't be…" I was squeezing in beside her to also look round the corner when she was interrupted by the discharge of a firearm, but not knowing that at that time Poet Burns had fired his shotgun into the air to intimidate the security man carrying the cases. To me then, in the quiet of the night, it sounded like a cannon going off. Donnie Chapman shouted in my ear for an update, but all that I could hear was someone screaming on the channel, "Shots fired! Shots fired!"

"The armed guys are going in," I whispered to Alice. Now, I'd been on plenty of armed operations before and while most were concluded with the bad guys being arrested without the need for gunplay, this was the first time I'd been involved in one where a gun had been discharged. Scared? Not at the time, probably because I was too hyped up for any emotion other than shock and the realisation this wasn't Hollywood. In truth and believe me since then I've given it plenty of thought, it sounded like a real fuck-up, that nobody knew what the hell was happening. Donnie continued to ask for an update, but radio control had gone and everybody seemed to be trying to break into the channel with their tuppence worth.

"I can see somebody running," said Alice, her head still pressed against the cold brickwork of the building as she peered east along Main Street towards the Cooperative. "They're coming this way," she added, her voice strained, a hand reaching for me as if trying to keep me safe behind her. "Wait, whoever it is," she turned towards me, "they've turned off down a side street parallel to this one. Come on!"

With that, she dashed past me and run down the slightly sloping street into the darkness. I had no option, but to follow her, presuming what she had seen was one of the bad guys making off from the robbery. Now, back then I was and even today am no slouch when it comes to running, but I was hard pushed to keep up with Alice on that dark and wintery night. Legs pumping and chest heaving, I followed her shape into the darkness, past the short row of one storey tenement buildings to the end of the street, my chest heaving as I tried to keep up with her, but watching as she slowly outpaced me. The street lighting was nonexistent and the darkness seemed to envelop her. I strained my eyes and concentrated on the slowly disappearing figure, my efforts hampered by my constraining jacket and the snoopy I'd thoughtfully remembered to lift from the car. "Alice!" I wheezed at her back, now twenty metres in front of me, but whether she hadn't heard or simply ignored me, I can never be certain.

And it was about then I came a cropper. I later learned that some kids had been collecting wood for a November fifth bonfire that they had stored at the bottom of the road and dropped a plank on the roadway. Running as fast I as was, I unfortunately found the wood and connecting with my right foot, went arse over tit to land in a crumpled heap. By the time I got myself together, Alice had disappeared into the darkness.

The radio chatter had calmed down and from what I could make out, one suspect was arrested, but of Poet Burns there was no trace. A frantic voice in my ear shouted that a car had made off and was being pursued. Donnie Chapman was again patiently asking for any call sign who knew Burns whereabouts to shout in, adding that Burns had been seen running from the location westwards and cautioning all unarmed officers to return to their vehicles. The fall had left me slightly dazed and with skinned knees as well as trembling fingers, but I managed to call in and tell Donnie that Alice was pursuing a possible suspect into fields to the south of the Main Street.

"What's your location now? Is she alone?" he demanded.

"Eh, not sure," I hesitantly replied, then said, "No, wait. We're parked in Holly Grove, I think it's called."

"Armed response," Donnie interrupted and spoke over me, "get yourselves down to the fields behind Main Street. Minnie, you and your dog meet with one of the armed guys and join the search there. All unarmed officers make your way to the security van location. Armed response, the first priority, find DC Foley, over."

Dusting myself down, I decided there was no way I was going back to the vehicle with Alice out there alone, chasing what sounded to be an armed Poet Burns across a darkened field. Limping slightly, I made my way into the darkness and deciding to hell with discretion, began shouting Alice's name. I could see torches switching on to my right as the armed guys used their flashlights to scan the area in front of them. Like me, their priority now was finding Alice.

It took fifteen minutes; fifteen long, worrying, heart stopping minutes before Alice was discovered, but not by me or the armed guys. Robber, Minnie Maxwell's dog, found her lying face down in a narrow, waterlogged ditch, the back of her head matted with blood that glistened in the torchlight night. Minnie, her mouth stained with dirt, had dragged Alice onto the unforgiving ground, turned her and valiantly tried to resuscitate Alice, but she'd been dead too long.

I don't realise it, but I'm almost holding my breath as I remember standing over her with the rest of the team. Minnie, tears coursing down her cheeks, knelt in the mud and gently wiped the soft earth from Alice's face, then Donnie Chapman, the consummate professional, reminded us all this was now a murder scene and ushered us back from her body.

The rest of the night was a blur. A host of uniformed cops appeared as if from nowhere. A full blown murder incident began right there and then and also, as if by magic, the top brass appeared, everybody talking and issuing instruction at the same time, but nobody apparently in charge. If it hadn't been so serious, the circumstances might have been described as farcical.

As for myself, I was bundled into the back of a marked police van and driven to Motherwell police station where I was dumped alone into an interview room and left for over an hour. The police belief was that I was the last person to see Alice alive so that, in their mindset, initially made me the prime suspect. My first visitor was a middle aged doctor with uncombed hair, wearing an ill-fitting suit who complained incessantly of being dragged from his bed and who spent ten minutes examining my hands and knees, all the while complaining that his examination should have occurred in the medical suite and not in the dimly lit interview room. I was too numb to protest and didn't at first realise the fix I was in. The doc gave me some sticking plasters for my knees and with ill temper, banged shut his bag and slammed the door behind him when he left.

I waited another ten minutes then they came in, two suited detectives from the rubber heels or, to give them their proper title, the Police Standards Unit. No offer of a cuppa or even a glass of water, just straight into it. I can't remember exactly what I said, but as it was all tape recorded there was no need for them to take notes. I lost track of the time and after what seemed like hours, they left me again, but this time had the courtesy to offer me what they called a comfort break. It didn't escape my notice that one, the younger of the two, accompanied me to the toilet to watch me pee. But I didn't just pee. The situation took over my body and I vomited into the toilet bowl, discharging time and time again till I was left feeling weak and shaking.

I recall being driven home that morning by a dour faced and uncommunicative uniformed Inspector about midday to find a note from Lisa berating me for not calling and complaining she had to make arrangements to get the girls to nursery. Exhausted as I was, I couldn't sleep, going over and over in my mind the night, playing back all that I remembered. I'm not ashamed to say I sobbed myself into a fitful sleep.

Chapter 4

Wednesday morning dawned again bright and sunny so the walk to work was pleasant enough. I'm a bit of a people watcher and can't help noticing my fellow pedestrians as I make my way to Bothwell

Street. I see and guess at the committed walkers, intent on getting to the office first; the dawdlers, reluctant to spend their time inside on such a sunny day; the partygoers, frantically downing their takeaway coffee in the hope it'll refresh them enough to face another day; the bad timekeepers, skipping through the busy traffic as they race to get to work on time. Then there's the type like me, those who meander along in the full knowledge they've left enough time to pop in to purchase a newspaper and a latte before committing ourselves to another eight hours of their lives they will never get back.

But today for me anyway, there was another purpose in going to the office. Today I intended making an international phone call that might go some way to appeasing my fears, inwardly hoping that I am wrong, that I didn't see Poet Burns sitting in a BMW, supping from a cup and admiring a young blondes arse.

I sincerely hope I am wrong and do not at all feel uncharitable by praying that the bastard is dead.

I pushed through the large glass doors to be greeted by, "Morning Tom."

Gerry Higgins, one of the concierges at the building, nods as he hands me a Metro. Like me, Gerry is a former cop, having served his thirty years as a beat man in the Govan Division, but with a daughter still going through University, he decided retirement wasn't on the cards just yet. I know Gerry is aware of the circumstances surrounding Alice's death and both the police and media witch-hunt that ensued, with me being the publicly identified whipping boy. But to my surprise, not long after I started working there, Gerry had invited me in to the closet of a rest room used by the concierges' to confide that shortly before he had retired, he had himself been the subject of a rubber heels inquiry when a local lad in Govan, being pursued by Gerry, had inexplicably tripped and cracked his head open. The experience, he told me, opened his eyes to the narrow path cops tread when involved with violent death and suggested that if there was anytime I wanted someone to speak with, to give him a call. We've been more than work colleagues since then and have on occasion, swapped stories together over the odd pint or three.

I get off the elevator at the fifth floor and make my way to the office I share with about forty other desk bound inquiry agents. Most are kids, whiling their time away while they decide what meaningful path to take to enjoy their lives. Some, a very few, are older guys looking forward to retirement and wishing their lives away. I nod to a couple already at their desks, but apart from casual conversation there isn't anyone in the office I routinely spend time with. It isn't the worst place in the world to work and while the money isn't what I had previously been used to, it keeps a roof over my head and bread on the table. Lisa doesn't need any kind of financial support from me. Her own salary now easily dwarfs mine and the profit from the sale of the house, for which driven by guilt I rejected any claim, went some way to providing her with a reasonable standard of living, particularly as living with her parents I guess she had no household overheads.

The only problem I have working in the office is Cathy Williams, my line manager. In her mid forties and married with two teenage kids, Cathy has almost from the outset had her eye firmly on me. Expensively styled blonde hair that complimented her womanly figure and a couple of inches over five foot, she isn't a bad looking woman, keeping herself fit with regular attendance at the company gym on the second floor and frequently wears short skirts to show off her admittedly good legs. I'd made the mistake of attending the last office Christmas bash on the sixth floor, one of those functions where the management like to be seen to be bonding with the plebs and providing free wine and canapés. Some of the younger staff quickly got pissed, though I suspect that was to more to do with the illicit vodka in the girls' handbags than the cheap wine. The party atmosphere, with balloons and paper hats and false bonhomie quickly thinned out and quickly turned to snogging in the nooks and crannies. I'd shown my face at the request of Archie, one of the older guys, who was too embarrassed to go alone and needed to kill time before meeting his wife and grandkids later for a pantomime show. I had been sitting alone by a window while Archie fetched us a couple of glasses of the cheap stuff and didn't immediately realise that Cathy was sitting beside me till I felt her hand resting lightly on my thigh.

"So, Tom," she had asked, "how are you enjoying yourself?"

It seemed obvious to me that she had indulged in more than her fair share of drink and not wanting to cause a fuss, I smiled and tried to make polite conversation, but it soon became apparent it wasn't chat she wanted as her fingers run smoothly up to my groin. I made some kind of lame excuse and stood up, but that didn't deter her. Don't get me wrong, I was flattered and frankly, women hadn't figured in my life for a couple of years, so yes, I admit it. I was aroused. I won't bore you with details, but somehow or other we ended up in an unoccupied office on the floor below the party where she locked the door behind her and well, one thing led to another. I'm not proud of what happened and had carpet burns for a week after to remind me of it. Call it the wine, the atmosphere or whatever, but since that time I've deftly avoided being alone with her. I've enough problems keeping body and soul together without the shenanigans of an affair with my boss. That said, it didn't stopped her pursuing me for some weeks thereafter, but finally she got the hint and since then? Well, you know the old saying of a woman scorned. Everything I do is checked by her and she's made it no secret that I need to watch my step, that given the first opportunity she has hinted she'll make it her business to ensure that I'm out on my ear.

I shrug off my jacket and settle into the chair behind my desk, then sign onto the company network. The internal mail has already delivered some correspondence, but nothing that seemed to require my immediate attention. Feeling slightly guilty, I fetch the scrawled notes I'd made from my pocket and dial the Spanish number young Michael from the Registry Office had given me. I selected a file from my In-tray and open it on my desk to conceal my subterfuge and listen to the dialled number ringing, going over in my mind the story I'd concocted and fervently hoping to God that I am wrong, that Poet Burns is really dead.

"Ola," said the male voice, catching me unawares.

"Ah, yes. I'm calling from Scotland. Do you speak English?" I ask, wondering why it is that whenever we Brits speak to foreigners, we always seem to raise our voice a pitch and speak slower.

"Ingles? Momento, por favor."

I hold my breath and glance round at the co-workers, wondering if any of them had heard me, but nobody seems interested and I listen to the sound of the phone being put down, then someone shouting in Spanish. A couple of minutes pass and I seriously considered hanging up before any of my co-workers became suspicious, when the phone is lifted and a young sounding female said, "Hello? I am Helena. You wish to hable, I mean, speak in English, yes?"

"Ah, good morning. My name is Thomas McEwan," I began. "I'm sorry, I don't speak Spanish."

"That is okay. I speak and comprenda some English, if you speak slow, you understand, yes?"

"Yes, thank you. I am calling from an Insurance company in Glasgow, Scotland."

"Ah, si. I am visited Edinburgh, the Castle and Tennents beer, yes?"

I hear the pleasure of memory in her voice and smile, imagining the impression the young woman must have of Scotland if the first thing she recalls is Edinburgh Castle and the popular lager. I think it best if I speak slowly and as simply as possible.

"I am making inquiry about a Scottish man that died in a road accident three years ago, in Badajoz. The officer in the case was Sergeant Martinez."

"Ah, Sargento Martinez, he not work any more here. You wish to speak with him?"

I just knew it wouldn't be that easy and inwardly take a deep breath.

"Do you have Sergeant Martinez's files? Maybe his work papers? About a Scottish man being killed in a road accident?"

I figure it can't be that many foreigners killed in Badajoz within the last few years that it wouldn't jog somebody's memory.

"You stay a momento, yes?" then without waiting for my reply, Helena puts the phone down again. A couple of more minutes pass and I become anxious, particularly as I can see Cathy Williams at the other end of the office, chatting with old Archie while she furtively glances at me. If she come close that was it, I was hanging up regardless of whether I have a reply to my query or not.

"Hello," says the voice in my ear.

"Helena," I reply with some relief.

"I speak with other policia who tell me he with Sargento Martinez. Very bad choque, I mean, how you say, cash?"

"Crash," I correct her and hope she doesn't think I am being a smart arse.

"Yes, crash. Car and driver all burned. No witnesses, you understand?"

"The man was called Robbie Burns, yes?"

"Yes," I can almost imagine her nodding, "Senor Burns, it is his motor car."

My chest tightens and my mouth is suddenly and inexplicably dry. "How did the police, I mean, Sergeant Martinez. How did he identify the dead man?"

Cathy Williams has moved closer and is now chatting with a couple of the younger women, all three of them laughing at something. As I watch, Cathy's head tilts back as she laughs, tossing her lengthening blonde hair about her shoulders. Funny, even though I'm in the middle of conducting an illicit investigation on company time and expense using the company phone, it doesn't escape me that she is looking really good now she's decided to let her hair grow that bit longer. Jeez, what am I like? Talk about the old devil raising his ugly head. I have a couple of minutes no more, then she will be at my desk. Through the phone I can hear Helena speaking rapid Spanish and it sounds like she is acknowledging an explanation from a male voice.

"Senor Thomas, the officer, he say to me that the identificación, you know …."

"Identification, yes, I understand," I reply, keen now to hurry things along before I am rumbled by the increasingly nearing Missus Williams.

"Yes, it was made by the car numbers, you understand. I not know the English."

"You mean the registration plate?"

"Yes, the registration plate," she replies, stumbling over the strange word. "The car, it was owned by Senor Burns."

I have at most thirty seconds then Cathy will be at my desk. I turn away so my back is to her and quickly speak into the phone. "Can you ask the officer if DNA, dental or fingerprints were possible?" and prayed that Helena would understand. I listened to a short burst of Spanish then Helena was back on the phone. "Not sure, maybe," I imagine her shrugging her shoulders, "Maybe too burned, you understand?"

I almost froze with shock. The body in the car was identified by Martinez simply because the number plate registered the car to Senor Robbie Burns. Shit!

"Was he buried or cremated, the body burned?" I almost whisper into the handset.

"Ah, the officer he say Senor Burns is buried. Here in Badajoz."

"Good morning, Tom. Busy at work already, I see?"

I can smell the expensive scent she wears as hands flat on the desktop, she leans across towards me, the crisp white blouse open at the neck and the top two buttons undone, exposing the enticing lure of her cleavage, a thin gold chain dangling between the swell of her breasts. Her blonde hair hangs loosely and frames her face, her make-up perfect, the lipstick a deep shade of red. Cathy isn't just trying to be provocative; she is being downright sexually aggressive and to my embarrassment, it is working.

I smile and hold up one finger to pause her, then say into the phone, "Thank you very much for your cooperation. If there's anything else, I'll certainly be in touch." It is a bit of a bummer, dismissing the young Spanish girl like that and particularly as she has been so helpful, but you can see the position I'm in here. I've no choice because the situation at hand doesn't lend itself to courtesy, not if I want to keep my job I mean.

"Good morning, Cathy," I smile at her. "You're looking very…. nice," was all I can manage because right then, my throat is as tight as a Paisley housewife's purse.

"Nice?" she purses her lips at me, her eyebrows raised. "Okay, I'll settle for that, then. So, how was your day off yesterday, Tom? Get up to anything …. nice?"

"Nothing much, just met with an old friend for lunch."

"And who paid for lunch, you or her?"

"Oh, the bill was down to me."

She half smiles because I haven't risen to the bait and I can see it in her eyes, her very sexy eyes. Oh, Oh. Better watch myself here, I'm thinking. Mind you, why should I bother when the rest of the office already have their beady eyes on both of us and likely I will, at least for the day, be the subject of office gossip. She half cocks her head to one side and slowly and very deliberately runs her pink tongue round her upper lip.

"I'm considering giving you another chance," she whispers, her eyes boring their way through to the back of my skull. "If you're a good boy, a very good boy I mean, you might be looking at a small promotion."

"And what do I have to do to earn this small promotion," I whisper back at her.

"I'll think of something," she pouts, then smiles and turns to walk away towards the lifts.

I'm only human and let me tell you that apart from the fact I have to adjust my seating position slightly, I breathe with relief and watching her pert little bum wiggle away in a tight, charcoal coloured pencil skirt was probably the highlight of my day so far. Alternatively, the news delivered by Helena that the body in the car is questionably Poet Burns?

That left a cold chill in my already overworked gut.

Chapter 5

The remainder of the day become a blur as my mind pores over the increasing possibility that I am right, the face I'd seen in the BMW is that of Robbie Burns. As the rest of the day continues, the files I deal with and the phone calls I make are conducted with a perfunctory professionalism and courtesy and absolutely no interest at all. When I speak to witnesses, I idly doodle on my desk pad without realising I have drawn up a list of 'to do's' regarding the new information, a habit I'd acquired as a divisional CID officer when mapping out my working day. I glance down at what I have written, as I listen to the voice in my ear droning on and on, providing me with a minute, detailed account of the elderly female witness's recollection of having stopped at a red light only to be rammed up the arse, if you pardon the pun, by a white van man.

"Are you still there, young man?" the nasally voice screeches in my ear.

"Er, yes madam, just taking some notes as you speak."

I then surrender another five minutes of my life that I'll never get back again.

With relief, I complete the paperwork and pass the file into the Settlement Tray for someone else to endure.

The end of the day can't come quick enough and my original plan, to catch a quick pint in the Horseshoe Bar, fades as my mind goes into overdrive. I want nothing more than to get home and consider what I am going to do next. I admit it, I was hyped up. I need to sit down and relax, think things through. I squeeze into the lift with a dozen other sweaty colleagues and wave a brief cheerio to Gerry Higgins at his concierge desk before joining the throng making their weary way to the buses and trains or wherever. Somehow, though I'm at a loss to explain it, I have a lighter step about me. I don't at first understand it, but as I'm deciding to again walk home in the fading sunshine and making my way through the Buchanan Street precinct, it comes to me. I realise what the change is that has come over me. I have a purpose.

Now, don't think that's it, case solved. Common sense dictates that I only to have to inform my former colleagues of my sighting and they will do the rest. Yeah, right.

For one, who will believe me? I had tried it on Mike Farrell, literally minutes after I saw Poet and he didn't believed me, so what likelihood is there that the CID will do so? For two, let's remember that the Force and I didn't part on good terms, so it's unlikely I'll get through the front door at Pitt Street before an alarm will sound and I'll be unceremoniously chucked out on my ear. No, I need to form some sort of strategy, provide the cops with irrefutable proof that Poet is alive and back here in Glasgow. You might ask, what will they do if I am able to provide that proof? Well, take a minute or two and let me fill you in further with what occurred after the debacle that resulted in Alice's murder.

The morning that Alice died the rain stopped by the early daylight, though the winter sun belied the fact it was a bitterly cold day. I rose after just a few sleepless hours, my head aching and my tongue furry enough to line a rat's nest. I sat wearily on the edge of the bed for I don't know how long, going over in my head again and again the circumstances, trying to figure out what possessed Alice to run off like that. A lengthy shower didn't help and it was while I was drying myself the curt phone call came, summoning me to Meiklewood Road for an operational debrief. I recall leaving a note for Lisa, surprised that the radio news bulletin about the murder of a police officer hadn't provoked a call from her to ensure I had returned home safely.

I dressed casually and in those days, with the luxury of a joint income, drove a small second-hand Vauxhall Corsa that had been lovingly restored and cared for by me, while Lisa used the family car, a Volvo saloon. The rush hour traffic had subsided so it didn't take me long to travel the distance from Bearsden to Meiklewood Road office. I turned in past the security gate, waving at the commissionaire and as I slowly drove the car towards one of the free bays, saw the DI, Donnie Chapman, engaged in conversation with a large, bullet headed, stocky guy, a cop I presumed because though he wore a dark coloured anorak, I could see he was wearing the uniform issued cargo pant/trousers. I manoeuvred my car in between Sandy Oates lime green coloured Skoda and an old, but gleaming black coloured Ford Cortina mark one, unconsciously registering that the car was a collector's dream. Donnie and the big guy both turned as I got out the Corsa and walked towards them.

"Morning Tom," said Donnie, then his face paled.

"Tom? Tom?" repeated the big guy, his eyes widening then without warning, punched me on the face.

Now, I'm not John Wayne and I'd like to say I responded by putting my fists up then ducking and weaving. Unfortunately, I was so taken aback by the sudden, unprovoked attack that I staggered back then went down like a sack of coal and the next thing I know is the big guy is astride me with both hands round my throat and squeezing like he was juicing an orange. Except my neck was the orange.

"Fuck's sake, Wally!" screamed Donnie, his arms wrapped about the big guy's neck as he tried to haul him off me then loudly shouting, "Need some help here!"

I couldn't breathe and I remember trying to break the big guy's grip, but nothing I did could release the stranglehold he had on me. His face was red with rage, his teeth showing white and I recall he smelled like he hadn't washed and had bad breath as he snarled above me, saliva dripping down onto my chin. I tried to roll over to dislodge him, but he was a good three stone heavier than my thirteen and a half. Through clenched teeth, I heard him mutter,

"Dirty murdering bastard!" at me. I began to literally see stars as I was starved of oxygen, then suddenly it was over. The big guy was pulled off me and somebody had me by the shoulders and I'm heaved to my feet, my legs spindly and feeling like jelly. I staggered some feet away to a nearby bench and sat down, shaking and gasping as I drew in air. I tried to speak, but the words wouldn't come. Then I noticed about half a dozen of my team stood staring at me, with Donnie and two surveillance detectives Graeme Fleming and Paddy O'Brien holding back the struggling big guy. I finally managed to gasp, "What the fuck…." but nobody was listening. The team, almost as one, with the big guy being escorted between them, turned and walked off to the building where we were to be debriefed. It didn't escape my notice the big guy wasn't being manhandled, but curiously I saw some of my team patting him on the back then lead him over towards the Cortina and sit him in the driver's seat. Before I went through the door, my last glimpse of him is sitting with his head in his hands, with Fleming and O'Brien standing beside the open door.

'Wally', Donnie Chapman had called him. I closed my eyes in understanding, my throat still raw from the pressure of his hands. Wally, I reasoned, must be Wallace, Alice's husband. The police trousers confirmed it. It seemed that since her death, Sergeant Wallace Foley had gone from wife-beater to grieving widower. Murdering bastard, he had called me. I was confused and wondered what that was all about?

I guessed then that her husband had already disclosed Alice intended leaving him and that I was the reason. Bloody hell, I had thought, this is getting worse by the minute.

Rubbing at the tenderness of my throat, I rose to my feet, my legs still shaky and slowly made my way to the briefing room.

I got there and opened the door to see that the team were assembled and all seated. Donnie Chapman stood at the dais on the slightly raised platform. Seated beside him on two wooden chairs was the Assistant Chief Constable (Crime) John Moredun, the universally disliked and mistrusted head of CID and Detective Chief Superintendent Frankie Jackson, the Divisional head of the CID in the south of Glasgow who also had overall responsibility for the operational surveillance teams that worked out of Meiklewood Road. I didn't know Johnson, but the word at that time was he's a good guy. A third chair was occupied by a heavy-set, balding guy in his mid forties, wearing a badly fitting navy blue suit who had Professional Standards Unit written all over his smug, florid face. Nobody introduced him to the team. As I sat down in a chair at the rear of the team, the atmosphere in the room wasn't just sombre, it was positively funeral. I glanced about and saw that Wallace Foley had been admitted to the debrief and was sitting in the front row, his head bowed. I couldn't understand the logic of why, in his supposed time of grief, the bosses would bring him into the debrief to hear the circumstances of our fucked up operation that resulted in his wife's death.

"Right, now we're all here," began Donnie, "I'll dispense with formalities and briefly run through a summary of last nights events. Thereafter, I'll hand you over to Mister Moredun whom I'm certain will wish to make some comment."

In the heavy quiet of the room, Donnie commenced his debriefing by reminding us of the dispersion of the team, our vehicular call-signs, naming us all individually and in particular the armed crews, then reading from handwritten notes and occasionally referring to the logs kept by each crewed vehicle. As Donnie recounted the nights' events, he included the armed arrest of the associate Robert 'Foxy' Fulton, who was caught while Burns ran off and the getaway driver, a nineteen year old kid, an up and coming gangster called Sean Patrick O'Halloran who, in Donnie's words, bottled it and tore off at speed, only to find himself wrapped round a lamppost when a surveillance car rammed him side on and resulted in him receiving crushed right ribs and a fractured right knee.

I saw that the three men on the dais each made notes in a pad.

"..... who told us that he had fallen over a piece of wood and lost sight of DC Foley."

I startled at that, realising that I had been only half listening, my mind still reeling from Alice's death and glanced at Donnie, aware he was staring at me. '*Told us that he had fallen,*' he had said. What was that supposed to mean, '*Told us that he had fallen?*' Some of my team had also turned their heads to stare and I saw a mixture of scorn and disbelief in their faces. I wanted to scream out 'but that's what fucking happened', but I didn't, just sat there bristling, now acutely aware where this debriefing was going. It wasn't about Alice's death; it was about finding a scapegoat for what had proven to be a fucking disastrous police operation. Concluding his narrative with the finding of Alice's body, Donnie finally sat down and Moredun took his place at the dais.

"First," he began, "let me say that on behalf of the management I would like to convey my sincere condolence on the loss of your colleague."

Not *our* colleague, I noted, but *your* colleague. That apparently was Moredun's style, clearly marking out the definitive lines between management and other ranks.

"Though I did not personally know DC Foley, I have learned she was a thorough and tenacious detective and highly thought of by both her peers and supervisory officers. She will be a sad loss to the Force and I also wish to convey my condolences to her husband, eh," he glanced down at the notes in front of him, "Sergeant Wallace Foley."

So much for knowing your lines, I remembered thinking.

"However, I can assure you that the circumstances surrounding the murder of DC Foley will be fully investigated and already a team is being assembled by Mister Jackson," he turned and nodded to the Detective Chief Superintendent, "and this suspect Robbie Burns will be hunted down and made to answer for this dastardly crime. I will also assure you that any member of your team found guilty of wrongdoing or conduct unbecoming an officer of this Force will be harshly punished."

So there it was, out in the open. Because I had been Alice's neighbour and lost her in the dark it was assumed I had hung back, allowed her to go alone into the dark to face an armed nutcase. I was now clearly and unequivocally identified as the coward who had caused her death. Nothing I had said or could say would alter the decision that had already been made. As I've said, a bad operation that resulted in the death of one our own needed a scapegoat. And that scapegoat was me.

I remembered I stared at Moredun, knowing what I really wanted to do was get up on my feet and defend myself, to scream and shout at the bastard and all the other bastards in that room who would believe that of me. But even then I hadn't the guts to do that. I simply sat and let my team's contempt wash over me.

I remember the team being dismissed and told to take a few days off, then Frankie Jackson indicating for me to stay behind. I sat heavily back down and ignored the stares as they passed me by, the only contact being a brief squeeze of my shoulder by the dog handler, Minnie Maxwell, but even she couldn't look me in the eye. I sat for a few minutes, my stomach churning in the now empty room as on the raised stage, Jackson and the PSU guy had a heated, whispered conversation that ended with the even more florid faced guy stomping off without a backward glance. Jackson uttered a deep and audible sigh, then came over and dragged the chair in front of me round, then sat down.

"You're in a shitty place right now, Tom," he said. "I know we've not met before, but I have heard good things about you." He paused and rubbed at his forehead with the heel of his hand.

"We've a pal in common," he smiled, then raised his hand, palm toward me, "no names, no pack drill, you understand?"

I nodded, wondering where this was going.

"So tell me, just between us. Man to man, as it where. What the fuck went wrong out there?"

I shook my head and a sudden thought struck me. "Can you answer me one question first, boss?"

"If I can," he nodded his head.

"Where did the intelligence about the robbery come from and why was there no senior management at the briefing? You know as well as I do, there's usually some senior officer there where it is suspected gun play will occur."

"Well," he smiled, "that's actually two questions Tom. First, as far as I know and I'll need to get it confirmed, the intelligence was from a previous reliable source…."

"Shit!" I snapped out at him. "That's a cover story for beefing up some crap information."

I didn't need to explain to Jackson that one piece of information is simply that; information. It doesn't become hard intelligence until there is two or more 'information's' from separate sources corroborating each other, unless of course as Jackson suggested, that source is totally reliable and proven to be one hundred per cent correct on previous occasions.

He sighed and shook his head. "That's the best I can tell you at the moment, Tom. But as I said, I will be looking into it."
"As for no senior officer being present at your briefing," he continued. "That was a definite oversight and again, I'll be looking into that. So, in your own time," he said, then sat back and loosened his tie, "tell me what happened?"

Chapter 6

The rest of the sorry events of that night is now history. The post mortem concluded that detective Constable Alice Grace Foley had been murdered; she having suffered a heavy blow to the back of her head that undoubtedly caused immediate loss of consciousness and resulted in her falling face down into a narrow, water filled ditch. The water found in Alice's lungs indicated that unable to save herself, she drowned, sadly in less than one foot of dirty, bracken water. Forensic further concluded that a smudged imprint on the back of her jacket just below her neckline was likely that of a boot-print, suggesting that after having been struck on the back of the head and whether conscious or not, she would have been unable to raise her head from the water filled ditch. It made the circumstances of her death all the more hideous.
Of course I was subjected to a very one-sided investigation by the PSU, who made it perfectly clear they dismissed my statement as a fabrication to excuse my cowardice by failing to accompany my colleague in the pursuit of suspects. The PSU recommended that contraventions of the Police (Scotland) Act be libelled against me, but due in the main to the intervention of Frankie Jackson, a deal was cut whereby I resigned from the Force, forfeiting all pension rights and literally, getting out ahead of the posse. I can't vouch for my state of mind around that time, but needless to say, I didn't have a farewell party.

A fall-out from the investigation was the death knell of my marriage. The fat, florid faced PSU detective, who Jackson named dropped as Detective Inspector Hamish McGrath, felt obliged to interview my wife Lisa and probably took delight in telling her that the deceased Alice Foley had informed her husband she was leaving him to set up home with me. You'll of course know that was a damned lie, that nothing between Alice and I had been decided and that indeed she had determined at first to find her own place. Lisa challenged me about McGrath's story and during a confrontational and tearful argument, told me in no uncertain terms that she was leaving and taking the girls with her. I offered a half-hearted excuse for my behaviour, but nothing I could say would dissuade Lisa from believing the fat fucker, particularly as he was almost telling the truth and so, one wintery November morning she packed the Volvo with clothing for her and our daughters and took off for her parent's house. Though on paper to this time we remain married, the separation ensued from that day and commenced with the sale of the house.

As I said, the only one who didn't stick the boot in had been Frankie Jackson and while I didn't again meet with him, through time and reasoning about what happened, I now know it was his argument that persuaded Moredun not to have the PSU pursue me, that for the sake of good public relations, the police would be better keeping the facts of the case in house and any media attention would damage not just the Force, but maybe even Moredun's own career ambition. I'd previously heard whispers about Moredun's obsession with his career advancement and the issues surrounding the death of Alice simply seemed to confirm the rumours.

The only fly in the ointment was of course Wallace Foley. I didn't know much about him, just that he worked in some office job within a department at Coatbridge police office. Alice's funeral service made the local TV news and as I watched the solemn ceremony in my new flat, her husband walking stiffly behind the hearse, I blinked back tears and listened as the reporter, using the time tried phrase, hinted that a police source named the suspect that the police would like to speak with as Robbie Burns, whose whereabouts were at that time unknown. Of course they were. The whole of the Glasgow criminal fraternity knew that the slippery bastard had taken off for the Costa Del Crime. By that time an arrest warrant had been issued for his arrest for Alice's murder. Then, through the passage of time, the story simply died out. But a couple of months later, a page three item by the Glasgow News chief crime reporter, the self-obsessed Alistair 'Ally' McGregor reported the demise of a leading figure in the Glasgow underworld, one Robbie 'Poet' Burns who according to McGregor, met a fiery end on a dusty road outside the small Spanish town of Badajoz. To all intent and purpose with Burns being dead, the warrant was withdrawn and the case closed. No suspect, no trial, end of story. Only, it now seems that the report of Burns death was a little premature.

So here I am, walking along in trance, my mind whirling at the developments that occurred because of a simple phone call and wondering, who the hell can I tell? Who would listen?
I'm pleased to say that on this occasion, I remembered to get the milk and health conscious or not, decide on a Chinese takeaway from the shop on Duke Street. I've too much going through my head to think about cooking and am eager to go over my notes and get started on some kind of plan. I sit at the coffee table, the food by now half eaten and congealing on the plate and re-read my scribbled notes. The first thing, I've decided, is to track down Poet's current whereabouts. No easy task in a place the size of Glasgow that stretches not just across the city itself, but out to the suburbs and nearby towns. The close proximity of places like Paisley to the west, Airdrie and Hamilton to the east as well as the rural towns in Ayrshire and Dunbartonshire means all are on a good day, literally within twenty minutes driving time of Glasgow city centre. Easy enough for the police to check out known haunts and persons of interest to them and by that I mean those currently or past involved in major crime. But I'm on my own with not even a vehicle to use. Yes, I know I can easily hire a small runner, but going round the area without any idea of where Poet might be holed up is in itself a daunting task without the benefit of intelligence. And that is the key word, intelligence. I need to get help, speak to someone who is still in the know. Someone who might just have an inkling or contact with an ear to the ground, someone who won't sneer when I turn up to ask a favour and that someone, I inwardly grin, has to be an old friend.

That evening, I get off the Glasgow Underground at Cessnock close to Paisley Road West and jump on one of the buses that travels on the main arterial road that run from almost the city centre straight through to the centre of Paisley. As the bus rolls on, I reflect again that maybe I should have phoned ahead, warned of my visit. I know I'd be warmly greeted, even though I had failed to keep in touch for what I now am embarrassed to admit is more than two years. I get up and press the stop bell when the bus arrives at Ralston and alight into a cold, but bright evening sun. The houses in the Ralston area, predominantly post war bungalows, are in the main surrounded by dwarf walls or hedgerows and neat gardens, testament to the care and attention of the lower middle class owners. As I walk through the quiet streets, I can see a sign on nearly every lamppost that indicates I am in a Neighbourhood Watch area and evident by frequent twitching of curtains that indicate the suspicious glances from householders sitting by their windows. At last I turn into Marchbank Gardens and almost breathe a sigh of relief when I see the lights on at number 37. I open the well oiled gate and taking a deep breath, rattle the letterbox. I am dazzled by a bright porch light being switched on as the door was pulls open.

"Well, as I live and breathe, Tom McEwan. Come away in son. How are you?" says Gordon Roberts, pumping my hand up and down and patting me on the back, a huge smile on his face. If anything, the shock of white hair he'd sported the last time I had seen him is even whiter.

I grin as I shrug off my coat and hand it to him. Gordon's wife Wilma, an apron about her still slim waist, pops her head from the kitchen to see who had been at the door and waves in greeting.

"Hello, stranger, tea or coffee?" she calls out.

"Bugger that," interrupts Gordon. "He'll be having a small dram with me," then his brow furrows, "I mean, you're not driving are you?"

I smile at Wilma. "A cuppa will be fine thanks, at least for now," I continue to grin back at Gordon, a feeling of well-being washing over me.

"Right then, you men go away into the lounge and I'll bring the tea in," orders Wilma, herself a former policewoman, then her eyes narrow. "I'm guessing you'll have things to discuss," and with that disappears into the kitchen.

I had visited the house some years before, but at that time bringing my daughters to meet Gordon and Wilma and apart from fresh décor, nothing had really changed. Gordon led me into a comfortable front room, soft couches with scatter cushions and switches off the football match that blared from the television. The next ten minutes was spent in pleasantries and catch-up during which Wilma fetched a tray in to us with a pot of tea and plate of cake and biscuits, then ruffling my hair and admonishing me for not being in touch, leaves us alone.

"So how is retirement treating you these days Gordon? What's it been, two years now?"

"Just over two years and what you don't know because you don't keep in touch," he pointedly begins, "is that yes, I'm retired from the Force as a cop, but I'm back working at Headquarters as a civilian."

I startle at that. I heard Gordon retired as a Sergeant from some desk job at Pitt Street, but hadn't known he was back working there. Suddenly, my visit now seems pointless because there is no way I intend involving him in my problems. I just can't compromise him by asking Gordon to do something that might affect his employment.

"So," he sits forward to pour my tea, "down to business young Tom. Why are you here, after all these years, I mean? Are you in some sort of trouble?"

I smile, thinking back to a dark night when as a scared teenager, running from the coppers, this quiet, astute man had threatened then bluffed me into a career with the Force, a career that two-handedly, I'd thrown away. I take a deep breath and sitting back in the comfort of the settee, told Gordon about the day I had seen a ghost.

He listens without interruption for ten minutes, the cup of tea growing cold in his hand. When I have finished my tale, he stands up and opens a door in a polished wooden cabinet, then fetches an unopened bottle of Glenmorangie and two chunky glasses to the low table in front of us, pouring two, four-finger measures. No water, but that is Gordon's style. I'm just surprised he didn't crush the bottle top in his large hand and throw it into the bin in the old Glasgow CID tradition of 'once opened, nae sense in not emptying the bottle.'

"Of course, I'd heard of Poet Burns during his heyday committing robberies, but I never had any personal experience working on any of the Cash in Transit inquiries," he begun. "If you recall, most of my service was in uniform and doing the real job while you glory boys pranced about in suits and fancy cars," he grinned at me. The old jibe, the uniform and CID rivalry. "My last job, before I retired as a Sergeant," he explains, "was working in Criminal Intelligence, so yes of course. I had more than just background knowledge of Burns and his shenanigans."

"Do you miss it? The job I mean. Working at the hub of intelligence?"

Gordon's eyes twinkle and he slowly smiles. "Let's just say the police were quick to recognise the expertise I had built up during my time in the Intelligence Department and," he pauses, choosing his words carefully, "they wanted some continuity in the Department, some old guy who could point the younger people in the right direction, pass on his experience, so to speak. Remember, Tom. The cops and detectives who serve in the department are usually on a three year secondment so everything that they glean during that period goes with them when they leave and the replacements have to start again." He pauses to sip at his whisky. "Do you recall a CID boss called Frankie Jackson?"

I nod, again silently thanking Jackson for his part in easing me out of the Force without facing a witch-hunt.

"Jackson recognised there needed to be an on-going continuity of intelligence and also recognised recently retired officers still had something to offer. He instigated a civilian role, recruiting cops who had worked in Intelligence roles at a civilian pay scale of course," he smiles, "and to work in an administrative role, while tutoring recently appointed officers to the Department. It's not a bad number and the boss, a DI called Danny McBride who recently returned to the Department, is a good man to work for." He suddenly leans forward, his forearms resting on his knees. "So tell me, young Tom. What exactly is it that I can do for you?"

I truly didn't known Gordon was back working for the Force and again try to dissuade him, but that old wicked gleam is in his eyes and he cuts me short.

"Look Tom, you've told me about the possibility of Burns being alive. I'm not jumping onto the bandwagon and agreeing with you, just because you thought you saw him. No, it's not that. But I'd be failing in my duty, albeit I'm retired," he smiles, "if I didn't help you. That bastard killed one of our own, a wee lassie in the prime of her life and that's just not on. If there is a chance he is alive and back here, we need to do everything we can to hunt him down and ensure he gets what's coming to him. Besides," he grins again, "I like a mystery."

"I know that you run a number of touts when you were a cop, Gordon. Did you ever keep in touch with any of them? I mean, before the Force changed procedures and clamped down on informant handling. Any who might have their ear to the ground about whether or not Burns could be back in the city?"

He sits back and sips from his glass, licking his lips, his brow furrowing as he considers my question. "There are a couple of people I can speak to. No offence, but maybe better if you don't know who they are. I'm not promising anything and I don't know if any of them will have that sort of information about Burns being back here, but it won't hurt to make a couple of calls, perhaps even a wee visit to an old associate." He picks up the Glenmorangie and raises his eyebrows at me, but I put my hand over the top of my glass. One of Gordon's wee shorts is the equivalent of four pub halves. He pours himself a generous top-up and says, "You know that we'll have to keep this in-house for the moment, that I can't let on to anyone in the Department about your ..." he hesitated, "... your sighting."

I knew what was going through his mind. If I went public with my suspicion, it would merely be seen as some sort of pathetic attempt to redeem myself with the Force.

"I agree."

"There's another thing, Tom"

I sensed Gordon is embarrassed and take a deep breath and pose the question he was about to ask. "Did I have an affair with Alice Foley and is this some sort of soul cleansing, an obsessive need to find Robbie Burns?" I slowly shake my head. "I cared for her,

Gordon. Don't ask me to explain that, I don't even fully understand it myself. But did we have an affair? I suppose that would depend on your interpretation of an affair. No, I did not sleep with Alice," I tell him, sounding more like President Bill Clinton than I want to. "Hold her, kiss her, yes. Guilty as charged. I've racked my brain over the last three years, trying to come to terms with what the relationship was all about, but the only way I can explain it is, it was something like a schoolboy crush. Seems stupid, a man my age having such feelings for a woman. Would it have progressed to something else? Well, that I'll never know." I got to my feet, the whisky glass clenched in my fist, a sudden need to walk about the room as I explained to one of the very few friends that I have left who I can trust. "The DI from the PSU fired me into Lisa, telling her that we were having come sort of clandestine sexual relationship, but I swear to you. That's not true."

"The word was bandied about that she was leaving her husband and setting up home with you," he quietly says. "A lot of your colleagues were unhappy with that, particularly after it was gossiped that you had run away and left her and she was murdered because of your, eh, your....."

"I know, I know, my cowardice. It's okay Gordon, you can say the word, but it doesn't mean it's true and anyway, that's not the full truth of the matter," I hissed back at him, a desperate need to unburden myself. "The night … it happened, Alice told me she was leaving her husband and that she wanted to find her own place and get herself on her feet. Did you know he was hitting her?"

He slowly nods; his eyes boring through me. "The Force might be a large organisation, but you know as well as I do that gossip gets around and usually arrives at my Department in one form or another."

"I know about the gossip and regarding my feelings for Alice, well, it doesn't excuse my behaviour. But run away? No, that's just not true!" I almost spit out and sit heavily down on the armchair facing him, the whisky glass in my hand splashing some of the liquid onto my hand and cuff.

"That night of the Operation, she turned up with a black eye. Yes, of course she tried to hide it, but there it was, in plain sight and not one bugger commented. We all knew, but did nothing." I stop, a sudden realisation hitting me. I feel dizzy, but whether from the large whisky I'd almost fully consumed or a vicious slap to my memory, I'm not certain. Was that why I felt for her, as I did? Was it some sort of Galahad feeling, the need to protect her? I lean forward, my hands clenched and rest my elbows on my knees. "She told me that she didn't want to come between Lisa and me, didn't want me to risk losing my kids. Well guess what," I can almost taste the bitterness in my mouth, "it didn't make one bit of fucking difference."

The door is knocked and Wilma pops her head into the room. "You boy's okay?" she asked, concern etched on her face.

"Fine love," replies Gordon, winking at her, "just Tom here being his usual loud self."

"Sorry, Wilma," I sheepishly smile at her. "Didn't realise I was shouting."

"Right, well there's a coffee coming up, Tom. After one of his legendary wee whiskies, you'll need it," and closes the door behind her. We grin at each other and I sigh heavily. "What about Alice's husband? Is he still serving," I ask.

"Wallace Foley? Last I heard is that he's still with the Divisional Intelligence Unit in Airdrie. The bosses kept him there after his wife's murder. Probably figured too much change might be harmful to his mental well-being. But from what I hear the true story is that he's a shifty type, a real toss-pot and not fit to be on the street. There is also a whisper he's too handy with his fists and where women are concerned, there have been one or two rumours of him using, shall we say, inappropriate behaviour?"

Wilma returns with coffee and says, "You know you're welcome to stay tonight, Tom. We've the spare room now that Victoria's moved out to her own place."

I smiled and thank her and explain I've work to attend in the morning and need to get home for a change of clothing. Gordon sees me to the front door and warns me not to be such a bloody stranger to his home. He takes a note of my mobile phone number and watches as I get into the taxi, a choice I've made as being preferable to an hour on public transport with one of his generous whiskies in me.

On the trip home I sit and reflect on my meeting with Gordon, wondering what I am doing. Was I chasing a ghost as well as involving Gordon in my paranoia? What the hell am I thinking? But that's the thing about night-time. The dark seems to compound fear and worry and throws up all sort of doubt. But, as they say, the die is cast and like it or lump it, the hunt for Robbie Burns is now on.

Traffic was light and the taxi drops me at my close mouth just after 9pm. I'm not in the habit of drinking whisky and the first thing I intend doing when I get into the flat is brushing my teeth. I have just rinsed my mouth when there is a knock on the front door. Wiping my lips, I wonder who would call on me at this time of night, then think about it. Who would call at my door anytime of the day because, let's face it, I'm not the most popular guy in the world. The previous tenant had thoughtfully installed an eyehole in the door; one of those small glass things that provide the viewer a panoramic, if slightly distorted look at who is calling. I am surprised to see what looks like a bottle of wine held up to the eyepiece and completely hiding whoever is holding it. Taking a deep breath I reach up and take the spare Yale key down from the hook on the wall and unlock the door.

Cathy Williams has never looked so sexy. Holding the bottle in her left hand, her lengthy black coat lies open, revealing a short, tight, bottle green mini dress that shows her curves in the right places and barely reaches to her thighs. Matching bottle green high heel shoes and the dress is so low cut I could see most of her tanned upper breasts. Black stockings and yes, I mean stockings because the darker tops were clearly visible. Her blonde hair lies loosely about her shoulders and her right index finger was at her red lipstick painted, pouting lips.

"Thought I'd visit and we might discuss your future prospects," she purrs as she slides past me, her scent making me catch my breath as her free hand lightly strokes my thigh. I feel the thrill of anticipation sweep through me and as I close the door, I know it's going to be a long night.

Chapter 7

The following morning, I awake slightly later than usual, just after seven thirty to find Cathy has gone, though the scent of her perfume lingers on the pillow. You have to remember that right now, I have no marital commitment, so no matter what you think, whether or not I should have succumbed to her charms, I did what any man in my position would have done. Gave in to temptation and yes, thoroughly enjoyed the experience. I'm no fool and I don't for one minute believe that Cathy has eyes only for me. I recognise her for what she is, a predatory and highly sexual woman who likely has more that just Tom McEwan in her stable of men. I had heard stories when I joined the firm, the usual ones from disgruntled male colleagues who, believing they should have moved on further than they have, gossiped that Cathy had slept her way to her job. Frankly, whether they were true or not didn't interest me. She's good at her job and as far as I'm concerned, her private life is just that; private. The fact is it now might include me and provide me with the occasional .... relief, I suppose I'll call it. Well, I'm smiling as I'm saying this because after last night, right at this minute I'm not complaining. Cathy used the seven or eight years or so of experience she has on me to teach me a thing or two about what a woman really wants.

I shrug off the sheets and conscious of my nakedness, grab my robe from the chair by the bed and rubbing my weary eyes, stumble through to the kitchen. I didn't bother buying wine glasses when I moved in so the two chunky IKEA specials lay side by side, abandoned on the worktop and still half full. The remainder of the untouched wine was now spoiled in the uncorked bottle. I grin to myself, the memory of us clinking the glasses together then hardly taking a sip before we were tearing each others clothes off and fumbling our way through to the bedroom. I didn't expect to find a note and presumed the one night stand, for the time being, was over. That is, I grin again, until Cathy might again want the use of my body. I shower and dress, knowing I would be a little late for work this morning, but figure given the circumstances of the previous evening, a little leeway by my line manager might be guaranteed. Grabbing the front door keys from my anorak pocket, I slam the door behind me and you know that sudden feeling you get, the one where you think you've maybe left something in the house? However, I shake my head and because I don't want to kick the arse out being too late and as it is raining, use that as an excuse to hail a black hackney cab on Duke Street.

Twenty minutes later, Gerry Higgins waves good morning as I push through the large glass doors and hurry towards the lifts. Alone in the elevator, I press the button for the fifth floor and startle as the mobile in my trouser pocket activate with a text message. I flip open the cover and glance at the number. It isn't known to me and to be honest, I receive so few calls and messages I haven't bothered previously recorded the incoming numbers. But this phone number is one to keep. The message says: Calld an old frend 2day. Meetng her 2nite at 7 in Sari hed. Can u b there. Gord. I smile at the phone. Seems Gordon isn't wasting any time then. The Sarry Heid, to give it its Glasgow colloquialism. I know of course where it is, on London Road in the Gallowgate, but I've never had the inclination to visit. Some would call it the infamous Saracen Head pub where its reputed cheap wine is sold by the glass, an indication of the type of clientele the pub draws.

I'm not a natural when it comes to mobiles, not like some of the kids I work with who can both hold a verbal conversation and a text message conversation at the same time. They're bloody weird, if you ask me. The lift squeaked wearily and arrived at the fifth floor, by which time I had managed to type 'c u ther' and send the reply. I am putting my phone back in my pocket when I look up and the first person I see is Cathy Williams, standing in the middle of the floor, wearing a navy blue trouser suit and cream blouse, her hair tied back in a severe pony tail and staring at me as she taps the watch face on her left wrist with her right forefinger. A sudden fleeting vision crosses my mind of that same finger being tapped against her full and luscious lips. With suitable downcast face, I approach her, my hands held out in supplication and acutely aware of the interest my lateness is causing among my co-workers, their heads bent over their desks and ears pinned back for my scolding.

"Sorry, Missus Williams," I begin, just loud enough for the listeners nearby, "something kept me up all night."

Her face doesn't change. "Please try and be a little more attentive in future," she replies, her eyes betraying just a hint of a smirk, then turns sharply on her designer shoe heel and walks off. I smile at her retreating back, regretful that I didn't get the opportunity to remind her that I know she isn't a real blonde.

My desk is laden with the usual morning mail post and I settle down to get through it all, impatient to be gone and meeting Gordon and his friend that evening. My mind must have wandered because suddenly old Archie is there beside me, a grin on his face. I tolerate more than like Archie, who I privately consider to be an old sweetie-wife who loves the office gossip. I inwardly smile because I frequently catch him furtively glancing at the young girls and can only imagine what must be going through his wicked old mind.

"You'll need to be careful son or you'll be getting your jotters," he hisses through ill fitting teeth. "She's an awful stickler for the time-keeping that bugger."

I patiently smile and maybe I should also mention that not only is Archie's teeth ill-fitting, but his breath would peel the paper off the wall. He is a walking advert for halitosis.

"It's only the odd occasion, Archie. It's not as if I'm a regular latecomer."

"Aye, well just watch yourself, particularly with the phones. Young Paul there," he nods towards a nearby desk, "was telling me that Williams ordered a subscriber check on all the office phones. Apparently the telephone bill has been sky high this quarter and she's been ordered to conduct some sort of inventory or whatever they call it."

I smile tightly, confident that Archie can't have known about yesterday's Spanish call, but certain that it would show up on my desk phone and that might cause an employment issue. "So," I keep my voice neutral, "how long does it take to get these subscriber checks back from the telephone company then?"

He shrugs his shoulders. "No idea, but Paul says it could be any time within the next month or two."

I relax. A month or two at the most might find me elsewhere, so my philosophy is no need to worry about something that hasn't yet happened.

"Oh, the wicked witch returneth," squeaks Archie and casually sidles off to his own desk.

I don't speak to Cathy for the rest of my shift and to be honest, it didn't really bother me that much. I glance at the desk clock and realised I've ten minutes till knocking off time. I think about Cathy and supposed that no doubt she'll turn up at my front door at some time in the future, when it was my turn on her list to be shagged. I almost slap my forehead when the thing that has been bothering me finally comes to me. My front door, that's what was bothering me. The spare Yale key I'd opened the door with last night when Cathy arrived, it wasn't in the inside lock this morning and I'm pretty damn sure I didn't returned it to the hook either. Sly bugger, she must have swiped it before she left. I chew at my lower lip, a habit I've had since childhood when I'm fretting about something. Well, there's nothing I can do about that now, I'll just need to wait till she turns up and get it from her then, I decide. The only problem of course being that it gives her free and uninvited access to my flat and that is just not on. Angry now, I shake my head, determined to challenge her, but I know that the office just isn't the place and as for time, well it can't be now because I've a meeting to attend. Fuck the ten minutes I think and grab at my anorak, ignoring the surprised looks of the enslaved morons sitting around me.

The rain soaked pavements are mobbed with homeward bound office workers and I decide it isn't worth travelling to the flat only to come back out later for the meeting, so make the decision to hoof it to the Gallowgate, grab a paper and have some dinner in the small fish and chip café that sits under the railway bridge just off the Trongate. Twenty five meandering minutes later, I'm striding from Argyle Street into the Trongate while fervently hoping the rain stays off and breathing a sigh of relief as I push open the doors. I try to remember the last time I'd been in the place and sit down in a booth in the almost empty café with the evening edition of the Glasgow News for company. The only other occupants is a young, junkie looking couple who were sharing the one plate of chips, a glass of Coke and staring soulfully into each others eyes. Maybe I'm too indoctrinated by the police and that perhaps makes me judgemental and I'm doing the couple an injustice, but the stereotype of anyone who looks as they do, half-starved and with dark shadows round their eyes, is almost immediately classed as a junkie. I continue to snatch glances at them as I pretend to read the laminated menu and that's when I see two rucksacks' brimming with books stuffed under their table. Students, I inwardly grin to myself and feel so guilty I almost shout an apology over to them.

"Whit ya having pal?" says the disembodied voice. It was only then I realise that like some sort of stealth warrior, a wee Glasgow wifie wearing a flowery apron, her grey hair tied in a ferocious bun on top of her head and who couldn't have been a pubic hair above four feet six inches, had stole up to my elbow and is standing there, one hand on her hip and the other holding a well used notepad. In fairness, she is a cheery wee soul, I guess in her mid-sixties and her infectious smile is almost as wide as she is. I glance at the menu and smiling back, order a mince pie with gravy and chips, not a meal I'd normally partake but what the hell. It's the east end of Glasgow, so bugger the calories and worry later about arteries full of grease.

"Will you be having beans or mushy peas with that?" she asks.

"Eh, beans please."

"And tea or coffee?"

"Tea, a large mug please."

"One pie and chips with beans and a mug of tea, please Mario," she suddenly screams out, startling me and putting the shits up the young couple across the way. So much for the notepad then, I think.

The food, piping hot and dripping in delicious gravy is delivered within two or three minutes by a cheerful Mario, a crisp white apron surrounding his wide girth and bald head shiny with sweat from working over the fryer. I prop my paper up against the tomato ketchup bottle and read as I wolf down the grub, surprising myself how hungry I am and even more surprised at the quality of the food. The tea, hot and strong, is a welcome relief and as I eat, I think that the same meal in a city centre café would likely cost double, but unlikely to be as tasty.

I am now on my second cuppa and by now the clock above the counter is showing six thirty. Sod it, I'm thinking. Half an hour will pass quickly enough in the Saracen Head. I pay for my food and on impulse I leave an extra fiver and tell the cheery waitress to buy the young couple who are still staring goggle-eyed at each other, another bowl of chips and a coke. The grub is cheap at the price and the wee waitresses smile gets even bigger when I leave her a three quid tip. By now, it is pouring from the heavens and though I've only got just over a hundred yards to walk, I'm dripping wet by the time I get there. Now, you might recall I've already mentioned I'm one of a dying breed, a Jags man or more properly a Partick Thistle supporter, though admittedly not a diehard. I'd forgotten that the Gallowgate is the preserve of the Glasgow Celtic supporters who dominate most of the pubs in the surrounding area and bedeck them with their flags and paraphernalia, thus setting out the parochial boundaries between the Irish republican supporters of Celtic and any bastard who isn't. So imagine my surprise when I burst through the doors of the Saracen Head, expecting to find a lot of old winos with shaky hands clutching cheap booze and discover I've walked into a sea of green and white. Not just that, but most of these shaven head, tattooed guys standing at the bar in Celtic tops and shirts are known to each other and strangers are immediately identified as just that. Swallowing hard, I make my way to the bar, ignoring the suspicious glares and smilingly ask for a pint as I point to the Tennents, but nervously thinking that any fucking pint will do and wishing I'd waited till after seven o'clock so that at least I might recognise a friendly face when I'd come through the doors. The barman simply nods and pulling the pint remarks in a strong Irish accent, "Hell've a night out now, isn't it?"

Just glad to be in conversation, I agree and again try to ignore the mutters and glares from who are obviously the regulars. I pay for my drink and am just about to sip at my pint when I'm tapped on my shoulder. Turning and half expecting a pint tumbler to be smashed into my face I see with some relief it is a smiling woman. "Your name Tom?" she asks.

She is and I'm guessing here, mid fifties and not unattractive. I'd say about five foot five, with short dark hair, but well groomed and probably lightly touched with a dye. Her skin is as clear a woman in her twenties and devoid of make-up. She wears an expensive looking black coloured wool coat with a small emerald encrusted brooch on the lapel and carries a tan coloured handbag over her left arm. She is also holding a small glass of sherry in her right hand

and from the slight glow on her face I presume it's not the first of the night.

"Aye, I'm Tom," I nod in agreement, grateful for the distraction. "Mary, you can call me Mary," she says, but somehow I'm suspecting this isn't her real name.

"Shall we sit down?" she turns without waiting for a reply and makes her way to an empty table halfway down the back wall of the bar. I'm following her and can't help but notice for an older woman she's got a shapely set of pins on her. Oh, oh, there I go again. Mind you, staring at her legs distracts me and I resist the temptation to turn my head, but am now aware that the previous interest I provoked seems to have disappeared and causing me to think Mary must be known as a regular. I'm not a religious person and don't really believe in a deity, but you didn't need to be a genius to work out the small brooch in her lapel is some sort of Catholic religious badge so maybe I'm right, that she is a regular.

"Gordon should be along any time," she smiles at me. "You used to be a policeman then?"

I swallow hard, hoping that nobody nearby has heard her and reply with a sickly grin, conscious the hairs on the back of my neck have jumped to attention faster than a vicar in a brothel.

A couple of minutes pass in polite conversation, mostly about the shitty weather then I see her eyes light up and for a second time a hand slaps me on the shoulder. To my relief, it's Gordon.

"Sorry I'm a wee bit late," he begins, setting down a soft drink on the table, "bloody parking round here is a nightmare. Parking wardens is everywhere. How are you, doing these days, Ina?"

Ina, or Mary as she told me, has the good grace to blush and replies, "Fine," then hurriedly sips at her sherry. "So, I don't hear from you for what, two years Gordon? Then suddenly, out of the blue, a phone call. What's happened? You found yourself divorced or widowed and decided to pursue me then?"

Gordon chuckled and shook his head. "It's the young fella here Ina. He thinks he's seen a ghost."

It hasn't escaped my attention that without saying, our voices have suddenly lowered in pitch; all three of us now speaking softly and you would need to be a parrot on our shoulders to overhear us.

Gordon turns to me. "Ina is somebody I trust and if she can help, she will. Won't you Ina?" he says, turning towards her.

She nods, her eyes staring straight at Gordon then slowly turns to me. "So, Tom, who is this ghost you've seen?"

I didn't realise till then just how dry my throat is. Maybe it's the tension over the last few days, maybe it's because I've got not just my fingers crossed, but my toes too. Or maybe it's because though I've absolutely no right to do so, I'm hoping beyond reasonable hope that the bastard is alive, that I did see Robbie Burns two days ago. Unconsciously, I lick my lips and say, "Robbie Burns. Used the nickname Poet?"

She stares at me for what seemed an eternity, her face showing disbelief; no, more surprise, then slowly smiles. "You do know he was killed in a car accident, in Spain?"

I nod, all hope fast disappearing and I'm thinking, another dead end. Once more Thomas McEwan has made a complete arse of himself. Shit!

She sips delicately at her sherry than stares at the glass then, as she set it down on the table, says, "But that's what he wants people to think, isn't it?"

I daren't breathe as my whole world and not least my sanity, focuses on her face. This woman whom I met just fifteen minutes earlier is holding my balls in her hands. I can't speak. I just stare at her, willing her to continue. I'm almost considering begging, but my mouth isn't responding to my brain.

"The young guy that was injured in the car, the night Burns murdered the polis woman. Sean O'Halloran. His mother Deidre was a friend of mine, the two of us widows like and Sean was her only child. We cleaned the chapel together, you know, set the flowers on the altar, that sort of thing. Deidre O'Halloran loved that boy and did everything she could to keep him out of bother. It broke her heart when he got into trouble with the polis. I mean, he wasn't an angel, but he wasn't such a bad lad either, at least not till he got in tow with that wicked bastard Burns," she makes the sign of the cross and adds, "God forgive me for my language. That night," she half turns to Gordon and nods, "the night after the polis woman's murder, Deidre and me were at a wee dance in the church hall. Nothing fancy you understand, just a wee glass or two of wine and some line dancing, you know? She was upset because Sean hadn't come home the night before and she was upset because he would always phone her, tell her where he was staying the night so she wouldn't worry, you know? But she hadn't heard from him all that day either. Anyway after the dancing in the hall I went home with Deidre and the polis were there waiting for her. They told her Sean had been hurt in an accident, but that he had been arrested for a robbery and that there was a dead police officer too. They hadn't come earlier because he refused to give the polis his name. Well, she was in a hell of a state I can tell you." Ina stopped for a sip at her sherry and continued, "I stayed with her through the night. The polis had told us that we wouldn't get to see Sean, that he wasn't dying or anything, mores' the fucking pity," and crossed her self again. "Word soon got round the estate that you lot were after Poet Burns and that he had got away and left the other two to fend for themselves. Some pal, eh?"

I was patiently listening when what I really wanted to scream out was where the fuck is he now, Ina!

"Well, you know the rest. Sean and that other numpty Foxy Fulton got sent down for twelve years each for the robbery and were lucky not to have got done for …. what do you call it, corruption?"

"Collusion in the murder," interrupts Gordon.

"Aye, right, collusion for the wee lassies murder," she sighs.
"Anyway, Burns got himself away to Spain, helped by his pal. But he's back right enough, Tom," she leaned over the table towards me, her lips curled in a snarl and breath reeking of the cheap sherry, "and I hope you get the bastard, so I do."

I wanted to ask the obvious, but she wasn't finished.

"My poor pal Deidre; my very best pal, God rest her soul. She wasted away when her boy got the jail and she died within a year. The cancer got her, but the doctor said the stress and strain had exab… ecerber…what's the word Gordon?"

"Exacerbated is the word you're looking for, Ina."

"Aye, that's it," she sniffed, reaching reached into her hand bag for a tissue. "Anyway, poor Deidre's in God's hands now and nothing can hurt her anymore."

Gordon turned to look at me, his eyes warning me to give it a minute before I stuck my size tens into the poor woman's grief. With more patience than I felt, I waited a minute till Ina composed herself and then asked the obvious, "How do you know Burns is back here Ina?"

She stared at me with moist eyes like I was senile or something, then the bulb must have burned that wee bit brighter and she half laughed. "He doesn't know, does he Gordon?"

"It's your private business, Ina. I wouldn't betray a confidence."

Ina nodded and reached over to pat Gordon on the top of his hand. "You've always been a good man, Gordon Roberts. Thank you." Taking a deep breath, she turned towards me and smiled; her cheeks now damp as some tears escaped her. "The pal that helped Burns get over to Spain is Jo-Jo Docherty. That's who let it slip, you see, because that's who I'm sleeping with at the minute and that's how I know Burns is back here."

"Do you know how Burns got back into the country or where he is now?"

She shakes her head then stares at me. "I have no idea where he's hiding and ….. No, wait a minute. I was in Jo-Jo's car the other day and there was a sticker on the windscreen, one of they wee sticky parking ticket things. It was from Edinburgh Airport from about four of five weeks ago, but I don't know what the date was. I remember it, because when I pulled it off the window I wondered why he had been at an airport. Does that help?"

I nod, guessing that if he is officially listed as deceased, the Ports Lookout with his passport details must have been erased from the system. Still, he must have taken a hell of a chance to fly home and I wonder why he was so anxious to return.

We each get a peck on the cheek and leave Ina with another glass of sherry, then walk through the drizzling rain to where Gordon has parked his car. "No arguments, I'll give you a run home," he says and for that I'm grateful, for now that I know for definite it was Burns I saw, my legs feel a bit shaky and I still can't believe what's happening. Ina's revelation has been a shock for me. Knowing Burns is alive and back in Glasgow is one half of the puzzle, but Ina claiming she doesn't know where he is holed up and to ask questions of Docherty, she fervently assured me, would invite suspicion upon her. The one thing she could tell me with certainty was the Docherty had several cars that he owned, one of which he favours is a large silver BMW, so that suggests to me who Burns was with when I saw him and is another small point that just might prove useful.

Sitting in the warmth of the car, I feel a bit lightheaded and no wonder. My previous night's nocturnal antics with Cathy left me with little sleep. Added to that, the two pints I'd drunk conspired to knock me out before I got home. I fight the sleep and decide I'll have a little fun with Gordon.

"So you and Ina? An attractive lady and probably more so when she was a bit younger, so how did you two …"

"There is no 'me and Ina' so don't even go there," he growls at me. "You know my Wilma. Why would I even consider playing away when I've got her at home and besides, I've never learned to breathe through a pillow," and even in the dark of the car I could almost see him grinning. He takes a deep breath and exhaling softly, launches into his story. "Ina's man was a real headcase, I can tell you. A docker he was and handy with his fists. The first time I met her, I was a young cop on the beat when I got a call to attend at her house for a wife assault. One of the neighbours called it in because Ina was too proud to let anyone know her business. I was on my own and knocked on the door and the first thing I see is her with a sore face. He's at the back of her in his vest, yelling and screaming and telling me to fuck off. Well, I was a skinny twelve stone something in they days, but could handle myself when it came to the rough stuff. I meekly invited him down to the half landing in the close for a wee chat then knocked seven bells of shit out of him. Did him for breach of the peace and police assault and in those days they got a night in the cells for hitting the polis. The next week I was on nightshift again," he half turns to remind me, "We did six weeks in a row back in them days, when I heard he'd been at it again, hitting her. There wasn't a call or anything, I just went up to his door, dragged him out by the hair and ladled into him with my wee baton."

"That'll be the one you threatened me with?"

"The very same," he laughs. "After the second hiding I gave him, Ina and I had a sort of agreement. He'd come in drunk, mouth off to her and she'd threaten him with me. That soon cooled him off. To the best of my knowledge, he never laid another finger on her, though obviously I can't be certain. He drowned a couple of years later when he was drunk when he fell off the dockside into the water at the King George the Fifth Docks. God forgive me for speaking ill of the dead," said Gordon, the devout and confirmed Baptist, "but the bastard was no sad loss to society. I went to his funeral, though it was my day off, just to show support to Ina. I think she appreciated the gesture and since that time, she's always managed to pass the odd wee bit of information to me. Some of it's been local gossip, but every now and then, she's turned up a wee gem. Like tonight, Tom which makes me wonder, where do you intend to go from here?"

I sat back in silence and contemplated his question. I'd already decided that if Burns was indeed alive and back in the Glasgow area, what action I intended taking. Of course, the right thing would be to inform the police, but as far as they are concerned Burns is dead and based on that evidence, the murder warrant was more than likely withdrawn. Sure, if they have evidence he's alive, it'll be re-issued and they'll hunt him down. But to inform them would mean revealing the source of the information and who am I to risk Ina's life, because that's exactly what would happen to her if it was disclosed she was the source of my information and let me tell you, when it comes to keeping secrets, the police leak like a sieve. I daren't involve Gordon because he's already overstepped the mark by acting outwith his Departmental rules and he'd not only face dismissal, but probably a prosecution for withholding information as well. Being the police, I don't doubt that if they went after him, they'd probably have a go at his pension too. I already owe him too much to ask more of him. When we pull up outside my tenement building, I decide that the only other thing, the final thing, I would ask of Gordon is if he is willing, will he text me Docherty's home address? He stares at me for a few seconds then slowly nods his head.

"Just don't get yourself into bother, young Tom my lad. I could never forgive myself if I've led you to a point where you land in deep and serious trouble. You understand?"

I nod and squeeze his left forearm. "I need to do this, to find him, Gordon. I need to satisfy myself that he pays for what he did."
What I don't say is I know the action I intend taking - for after all, how can I be convicted for murdering a dead man?

Chapter 8

At work that Friday morning I again find it difficult to concentrate on what I'm doing. Cathy Williams passes by my desk a half dozen times, on each occasion pointedly ignoring me, but leaves behind a lingering scent of her fragrance. The last time, just before I leave for lunch, she half smiles when no one was looking and softly blows me a kiss. I smile tightly back at her and can see she is puzzled. I am still irked that she has pinched my door key, but the opportunity to speak to her about it just doesn't arise.

There's something about a Friday afternoon that animates people. Probably it's the thought of what antics they can get up to that weekend, no doubt. During the morning, I'd popped into the small kitchen we use for tea and coffee breaks and while the younger members of staff boasted about the drink they would consume and how wrecked they intended getting, the older ones discussed shopping, gardening and a hundred other plans. Nobody asks me what I plan and I suppose my intention to hire a car and hunt down a killer just wouldn't occur to them. The only fly in my ointment is on Saturday morning, Lisa intends dropping off the twins about ten o'clock. Don't get me wrong, I love spending time with Sophie and Sarah. They're the best part of me, the one thing in my life that I can be proud of and regardless of all else, I can't wait to see them.

When I finally leave work that in the afternoon I walk the short distance to Mitchell Car Hire garage in Mitchell Lane, behind Argyle Street and pay for a weeks hire of a black coloured, three-door Fiat Punto. It's a while since I've driven any kind of vehicle and while the wee car isn't a difficult drive and to the frustration of the cars behind me, I stall a couple of times before I get the hang of driving again. The Punto is a neat and tidy wee motor and to be honest, my choice was determined more by cost than fashion. All I have to do now is find a parking space near the flat. On the way back to the flat I stop in Duke Street outside a small newsagents and purchase a compact, reporter's type notebook. I made the decision that I would begin to keep notes, time and dates, that sort of thing. One thing the police taught me is that nobody can rely on an elephant memory and note taking is the surest form of reference.

It was late that night while watching some inane show on television that I hear my mobile phone activate and see the text is from Gordon. It simply reads: Strathbln rd, 150 yd pst helth clb, big hose on rite. G

I acknowledged the text with an: Ok. Ta. Then fetch my Glasgow A to Z from the cupboard, a gnawing excitement in my gut. Page 26 of the map book shows the location Gordon gave me as opposite the Craigmaddie Reservoir in the affluent Milngavie area to the north of Glasgow. If his reckoning was correct, the house sits just off the Strathblane Road between what seems to be a health club and Bankell House. Docherty's house isn't marked on the map so I figure it is likely a new build and that's why it's not included on my 2005 edition. I sit back on the couch and think of the run home last night in Gordon's car and his potted history of Joseph 'Jo-Jo' Docherty. Gordon related Docherty was a long term associate of Burn who had moved on from petty theft into the drug trade, but like most of his kind used a large gang of flunkies to carry out the actual transactions, distancing himself from the hands on side of the business. Surveillance on him was apparently a regular thing, which made me wonder. If the surveillance teams were on the ball, why hadn't anyone picked up on Docherty driving Burns about? I supposed that was the one day they might have pulled off, but there was no real way of knowing. Still, it is a thought.

Saturday morning is another cold, but bright sunny day and I've risen early, given the place a once over tidy and eagerly await the arrival of the girls. I check every few minutes at the window, watching for Lisa's car when bang on ten o'clock, she draws up and sounds the horn. Lisa never gets out of the car, but sits and watches till the girls are in the close then waving at her from my window before she drives off and today is no different. I accept that she prefers as little contact with me as possible and sometimes wonder why she is so insistent that I have time with the girls. I can only presume she doesn't want the girls to grow up without knowing their father and to be fair, neither Sophie nor Sarah has ever commented on anything their mum has said about me being a bad man or bad husband. They seem to have adapted well to the fact their mum and dad just live separate lives at different home. I greet the two of them, their blonde hair in ringlets and miniature versions of their mother, with the biggest hug I can muster without breaking their backs. That done, their coats are slung onto the couch and they're at the window, watching and waving as Lisa drives off.

"Can we have the TV on dad?" asks Sophie.

"Not yet Sarah," I reply, making them giggle. It's a game we play every week, me pretending to get their names wrong and expressing my shocked surprise that I can't tell them apart. They pull at me and while I get them juice and a chocolate biscuit, they jump onto the arms of the couch and I give in to their, "Please, please, please" and they catch up with the animated adventures of Barbie. By the time they're five minutes in the flat, I've promised to take them to McDonalds and to visit their Papa and Gran McEwan, so that's the day sorted, I'm thinking. Selfishly, I'm also thinking that if I leave them for an hour or two with my folks that will give me the opportunity to visit the abode of one, Joseph 'Jo-Jo' Docherty.

Barbie and Ken once more foil the dastardly plot, whatever the hell it was and I manage to get the girls coats back on, but again it costs me another chocolate biscuit. If that's not bad enough, if their mother knew they were being taken for a McDonalds there would be hell to pay.

Down at the car, I'm annoyed because frankly, it never occurs to me that I would need car seats for the girls. A silly wee thing, but I'm out of practise in matters of child safety and previously, we have usually just jumped on a couple of buses or my dad has collected us from the flat. "Wait here Sophie," I sit her in the car and lock it behind me, smiling encouragement as an idea hits me. I drag Sarah with me back into the close and knock on the Ahmed's ground floor flat. Mrs Ahmed, her face curious, shyly opens the door and looks from me to Sarah, then back at me.

"Hi, Mrs Ahmed, I was wondering if you had a spare child's car seat that I might borrow? It's for my wee girl?"

I know her English isn't great and I'm about to explain again and this time also using my hands when her son Iqbal, a tall, skinny lad of about fourteen, appears behind her. I like Iqbal and have often used him to run errands for me to the local shops in exchange for a couple of bob.

"Hi Mister McEwan," he greets me in good, but heavily accented English. "Is it for the girls? The car seats you're looking for?"

"That would be grand Iqbal, if you can spare it for the day."

Iqbal rattles off something in Urdu to his mother, who eagerly nods and waves him away while she remains at the door, smiling from me to a curious Sarah. He comes back with not one, but two well used and slightly stained booster seats. "Two wee lassies you've got, is it, no?"

"That's great Iqbal, exactly what I'm looking for."

"So Mister McEwan, what car you got? I like cars, all sorts of cars. But I like real fast cars. Man, they are the best and when I get my licence, I'm going to get me a Porsche Carrera 4S Cabriolet. That is a real babe magnet," he grins at me, then he looks thoughtful, "Or maybe an Audi TTS Roadster."

"Thanks son," I reply and not wanting to disappoint his illusion of me, decide not to tell him I've hired a Fiat Punto. Waving cheerio to them both, I return to the car to find Sophie, her lower lip trembling and about to cry because she thought her hard-hearted father had abandoned her. Bad guy that I am! Once I have them both securely fastened in the back, we're off and the rest of the journey through the city to the McDonalds on Maryhill Road is me explaining to the giggling pair where I got the car and no, I didn't steal it. I know I'm being pestered for their amusement, but I love every minute of it.

It is almost two hours later when I finally pull up outside my parent's house and they're both out the door before I've got the girls unstrapped from their seats. It's hug and kisses all round then in for a cuppa.

"You look tired, son," says my mum, the constant worrier, one eye on me and the other on the girls who having not only demolished a big Mac each, are now putting paid to a sausage roll and spaghetti. "Are you getting enough sleep these days?"

"Like a log mum. It's just the weather, it's getting everybody down. You know what it's like."

Dad, sitting opposite me at the small kitchen table, says, "See you've got yourself a hired car. Got some business to be doing?" He doesn't miss a trick, my old man. I grin and ask him how he knows it is a hire?

"The sticker on the back window," he grins back "You're not the only detective in the family, son." "Former detective," I remind him "and yes, I've a wee bit of business. So, is it okay if I leave the girls for an hour or so?"

"Silly question," interrupts my mother. "Leave them with us forever if you like."

I say cheerio to the girls and gave them a hug, telling them I was going to do a wee errand and drive off waving, but they hardly notice I'm away for when they're at their Papa and Granny's house, nothing distracts them from the attention they get.

The short journey from Maryhill to where I am going in Strathblane Road takes me no more than fifteen minutes. I pass the health club on my right and within about a rough hundred yards, I'm parallel to Docherty's place. As I drive past the house I see it is indeed a new build or more correctly, what I could see of the house for the place is surrounded by a high wall and I'm guessing six feet at least. The red tiled roof suggests a one storey construction and the formidable looking, black painted gates I also guess, are electric. Of course, this was all at thirty miles an hour so I drive on for a few minutes then pull over into a lay-by. I don't for one minute think that anyone in the house or the grounds will pay attention to a passing small, black coloured Fiat Punto, but Gordon had said that Docherty was frequently the subject of surveillance so there is every likelihood that whoever is in the house or grounds might routinely pay attention to vehicles passing by the gates.

I let a couple of minutes go by then drive back, passing the gates again, but on this second pass I notice what seems to be a CCTV camera located on top of one of the gateposts, pointing down to where a car or visitor would stand in front of the gates. I continue driving and this time turn into the grounds of the health club. I had seen that the club's car park is located on the north side of the building and with the level fields between the two properties it looks like it might provide an uninterrupted view of Docherty's house. I find a bay among the couple of dozen cars that are parked and nose the Punto in towards the two foot wire fence that marks the boundary of the club grounds and marvel at the quality of expensive vehicles parked about me. I haven't considered what I might gain by sitting there, because all I can see is the same as when I passed on the roadway; a high wall that seemingly went round the entire property and the red tiled roof.

Ten, maybe fifteen minutes pass and I know that I am wasting my time. There's no other way because I know that if I am to try and gain anything from any observation, it will need to be inside those gates. I exhale loudly and am about to turn the key when some movement in the rear view mirror attracts my attention. Two men dressed in track light coloured suits are walking through the car park, sports bags slung over their shoulders and playfully pushing at each other. I froze in shock and feel my chest tighten. The dark curly haired man with swarthy features, is in his fifties I guess, maybe five feet five inches tall and with an obvious beer belly and is more than likely Jo-Jo Docherty. I watch as Docherty points his hand at a silver coloured BMW four by four and from my off-side driver's mirror, see the lights blink on and off as the vehicle unlocks. The other man pulls open the passenger door and throwing his bag onto the floor, jumps in after it. Hardly daring to move, I see Docherty drive the vehicle out of the open gates and turn right. I watch the vehicle drive along the Strathblane Road then a short minute later, disappear from view through the gates towards the house I'm watching.

Now, you'll be wondering how I know the pot-bellied guy is Docherty? You don't need to be Sherlock Holmes to work that one out. It's an easy assessment to make, because the shaven headed-guy who was with him is a man I've followed and seen in all sorts of guises and is none other than Robbie Burns. I quickly jot down the details of what I have seen in my new notebook, surprised at how much my hand shakes and with nothing more to gain and in a state of high excitement, drive back to my parent's house. That is my first sighting of Docherty and I laugh out loud in the car, recalling his squat shape and pot belly and surmising that if he had spent any time in the fitness club it must be feeding the Mars bar machine. On the road back to my parent's house I think about the meeting with Docherty's squeeze, Ina. She had assured me that she didn't know where Burns was holed up, but if she is sleeping with Docherty and presumably at his place, then either that was a lie or Burns was just visiting Docherty at the house and is really living elsewhere.

As I drive, I know with certainty what my next move is. I have to get a closer look at the house to determine if Burns is living there and I sigh, because that means going over Docherty's wall.

Chapter 9

Captain Hook, or rather my dad holding a plastic sword with a handkerchief tied round his head, opens the door to me. From the front room I hear squeals as the girls, also wearing handkerchiefs on their heads and with eyebrow pencil used to draw moustaches on their upper lips, hide behind the couch from their nemesis.

"You okay Tom? You're looking awful pale," greets my dad.

I smile and pat his shoulder. "Pale or not dad, let me tell you I can't be happier."

This seems to satisfy him and he ushers me through to the front room where I pretend to ask where the girls have gone to and sniff at the aroma of a freshly baked apple pie that permeates throughout the house. The rest of the afternoon is spent playing games and to my folks delight, I suggest that maybe they can keep the girls overnight.

"Hot date?" jokes my mum, her hands in a basin of washing up water while I dry the tea plates, a smile on her face that quickly dies. "It's something else, isn't it?"

That's my mum all over, the most perceptive woman I've ever met. I smile in return and tell her it's nothing for her to worry about, but I just know that she and my dad must have discussed where I had gone that afternoon. I have never kept secrets from my folks; it wasn't how they raised me. Well, all right, maybe I was a little economical with the truth about my nearly relationship with Alice Foley, but there hadn't been much to discuss there. You see, believe me or not, I had told Gordon the truth that night at his home. I didn't sleep with Alice. Given the chance? Yes, I suppose I would have, but the opportunity just didn't arise. Makes me sound like a callous bastard, I know, me being married with two wonderful daughters. I did tell my parents part of the story, but not the full truth. I suppose to my credit I did make myself the bad guy in the failed marriage and whether they believed me or not, I don't really know, but they always loved Lisa and I didn't want to drive a wedge between them. It must have worked because every Christmas and on each of their birthdays, a card from her pops through the door.

"Look mum," I reply at last, wrapping my arms about her slowly expanding waistline, reluctant to tell her the truth, but not wishing to lie either, "There's a wee personal inquiry I'm making. It's nothing to concern you and dad and certainly nothing for you to worry about, okay?"

She reaches up and took my face between her hands, staring into my eyes. "If there's anything we should know ..."

"No, I promise. If there is, you're the first I'll tell," I smile at her.

I spend the early evening with the four of them and I am there to get the girls bathed and into their pyjamas and pretend that I don't know that the Saturday night nine o'clock bedtime curfew will likely be extended to ten. I kiss the girls goodnight and promise my folks I'll be back tomorrow morning when they return from church with the girls. That's the one thing neither Lisa nor I objected to, my parents bringing the girls with them to the Baptist church. Because I no longer believe doesn't mean the girls have to be denied a Christian upbringing and besides, I know the girls enjoy the singing and friendship they receive there.

As I drive back to my flat, my mind is again racing with what I'm planning for the dark night, turning over with what I'll wear and equipment I'll need. Maybe at this point you're wondering if I am considering that I'm some kind of Rambo person. Let me explain. During my time with the surveillance, I was one of a number of officers who were trained in what the police call CROP, that's an acronym for Covert Rural Observation Post; in essence, the training is designed for rural situations where conventional surveillance can't be considered. The types of situation where CROP officers will be deployed are farms and dwellings located in a rural environment. The individual training consists of camouflage technique using the darkness and available cover, such as shrubbery and high ground for concealment. You might recall the most notable and tragic use of CROP officers was back in the eighties, when Constable John Fordham, hiding in the large garden area and observing the Brinks Mat bullion robbery suspect Kenneth Noye, was stabbed to death. As you will gather, CROP training has moved on since then, but the job isn't without risk and invariably it's only the high profile criminals who are the subject of such operations. So ladies and gentlemen, that's my plan; get myself geared up with what dark clothing I have and I'm smiling at myself now, because I have virtually no equipment, but will make-do and I am determined to make a night-time visit to Mister Docherty's palatial fortress.

The question must also be in the back of your mind. If I find Robbie Burns there and the situation presents itself, what will I do? Honestly? I don't know, but what I do know is that I'll be taking the biggest fucking kitchen knife that I have.

I wisely decided to stretch out on the couch, my feet on the opposite arm rest and have a doze and now looking at my watch, see its one thirty in the morning. Having had dinner at my parent's house, I've supplemented that with a bowl of my own home made soup and a slice of bread, so I know that it's not hunger pangs that are causing the tightness in my gut. Tension I suppose, no other word for it. I shower and dress in the clothing I've laid out on my bed, the loose fitting, black corduroy jeans, navy coloured tee shirt and navy coloured woollen sweater, heavy duty black socks and my dark brown walking boots, a luxury I afforded myself with the intention of taking up hill walking, an activity which of course I never did. I carry the small, black coloured backpack into the kitchen that I occasionally use for taking my lunch into work. Into the backpack I stuff a small Tupperware box containing a thick, glutinous paste that I've made up consisting of a little water and gravy powder. CROP officers have access to the latest face creams, now made I believe by of all people the AVON cosmetic company, but I don't have this luxury so it's the home made stuff for me. I'm fervently hoping there is no Rottweiler's in the grounds to lick the gravy off my face before tearing my balls off and that's why I'm

also taking a half pound of link sausages to throw over the wall as a distraction. Before you ask, I've already made my mind up; any suggestion of dogs and I'm out of there. I haven't forgotten that there is a CCTV camera at the front gate and the need to consider the possibility there might be more cameras covering the grounds. The thing about CCTV cameras is that most householders use them as either a deterrent or to record incidents. Unless there is someone actually monitoring the cameras at the material time of an intrusion, they're as much use as a fart against a high wind. I'm gambling that if there are more cameras, Docherty probably installed them as a security measure, but probably doesn't employ anyone to monitor them and certainly not an outside security agency. If he is as high a profile drug-dealer as Gordon suggested, he won't want an outside company that might be friendly with the police, monitoring his home. And if activity is recorded by the cameras, what will they see? A dark clothed individual prowling about the grounds. One other concern I have is security lights of which basically, there's the two types; the conventional bulkhead ones that remain switched on during the hours of darkness, either manually or timed switch operated then there is the sneaky, photocell ones that activate at any movement in a dedicated space covered by their sensor arc. However, this type of light usually has an arc that limits its sensor and is sometimes set at a height of about two or three feet to avoid light being activated by cats and foxes and suchlike and prevents householders panicking every time an animal crosses their garden. The thing about security lights is with the type that is always lit ones, again someone needs to be watching while if the photocell ones aren't properly set, anything can set them off and householders usually tend to ignore them.
I also pack a damp cloth and small towel for cleaning my face off when I'm finished, simply in case I get a pull from the cops on the way home because it might be a bit hard to explain why I'm sitting in a Punto with a camouflaged face.

By now it's almost ten minutes to two; I go over my sparse equipment and clothing once more then, taking a deep breath, I select an eight inch, narrow, rigid bladed plastic handled kitchen knife from the knife block on my worktop and wrapping it in a couple of sheets of kitchen roll, stuff it into the backpack. I put both hands on the worktop and lean forward, my head down and take a minute to consider what I'm doing, the action I might have to take with the knife and wonder what the fuck I'm all about? I know I'm not a killer, so how the hell will I justify to myself shoving the blade into Burns, if he is there? Alice's face crosses my mind, her half smile and gentle eyes and I close my own eyes, savouring the image. The moment passes and I exhale loudly and gathering the backpack and putting on a black knitted woollen hat, lock the door behind me.

It's a cold, but dry night and my drive to Strathblane Road is uneventful. As I pass by the brightly lit grounds of the health club I see the car park looks to be empty. I am almost sure it is closed and the lights I'm seeing will be security lights, but consider there is likelihood because of its isolated location, there might be a nightshift security guard or at least, visits from a security company's vehicle patrol. For that reason, I've decided not to park the Punto in the deserted car park, but in the lane where I turned the car earlier that day. I pass by Docherty's house and see the gates are closed, but lights are on in the house. I'm surprised and pleased to see that the grounds don't seem to be too brightly lit. I arrive at the lane and as the road is deserted, slowly reverse the Punto down as far as I dare. I'm not worried about getting the car stuck or anything, because the ground is well compacted, but the last thing I need is to get back in a hurry to find a burst tyre. I rub the brown paste onto my face and neck, the front and back of my hands and for a brief second, risk switching on the interior light to ensure I've covered the whiteness of my face. The eyes that stare back at me seem oddly strange and again I wonder what I'm doing here. I lock the car, shrug into and tighten the straps of my backpack and check the rear wheels are okay. I need to pee and nervously urinate against a hedge, then hide the car keys on top of the back wheel on the drivers side and the last thing I do is jump up and down a couple of times to ensure that I'm not rattling and that done, I take a deep breath and set out for the house.

The night is cold and the moon has little chance of getting through the dark, ominous clouds. There's also a light fall of rain which is ideal, because Strathblane Road is poorly lit and any driver will be concentrating on the road rather than me walking beside it. Besides that, I've a clear view of approaching traffic headlights and continuously swivel my head to ensure nothing is approaching from behind. In any event, only one car passes from the direction of the city towards Strathblane and by the time it's parallel with me, I'm hiding in a hedgerow with my face turned away to protect my night vision. About fifty yards from the house, I get over the low, poorly maintained wire fence that borders the road and the nearby farmers field and almost immediately, trip in a furrow and fall flat on my face. I lie still for a few seconds, suppressing the nervous laughter that threatens to engulf me and slowly turn my head, knowing that nobody could possibly have seen or heard me, but reluctant to move until I am certain and also wiggling my toes and fingers to ensure I've not sprained anything, or worse. Pushing myself up to my feet, I gingerly step forward, aware now that if I have to move quickly, the ploughed field is hazardous, but grateful that even though it's raining lightly, the ground seems solid enough.

The soft lights emitting from behind Docherty's boundary wall beckon to me and I make towards the north east corner, my eyes and ears alert for any sound. The noise of a labouring diesel engine carries from the road that is twenty metres to my right, then fades in the distance and I'm guessing it is a private hire taxi. Suddenly, I'm at the brick wall and from my own height, judge it to be six feet high. I slip off the backpack and pick out the sausages from their greaseproof paper wrapper and fling them over the wall. Now before you wonder, this isn't James Bond stuff and I haven't laced the sausages with knock out drugs or such nonsense. Like I said before, the slightest hint of dogs and I'm out of here. I had left my watch at the flat and wait for what I reckon is five long, nerve wracking minutes and there's no sound. Paranoia kicks in and I'm now wondering if the wall is topped with broken glass, cursing myself for not bringing a blanket or something to enable me to pad the top. There's only one way to find out, so taking a deep breath, I reach up and easily grab hold of the flat brickwork, heaving a quiet sigh of relief that it seems to be just that - brickwork. I prepare myself and my right booted foot against the wall, bracing myself, slowly pull my frame up so that I can see over the top. I slowly inch my camouflaged face up then over the level of the brick and peer into the darkness of the garden. I can see the silhouette of shrubs and a couple of trees and on the house wall that faces me there is two darkened windows that peer like eyes from a lengthy, oblong face. I can't see the sausages, but neither can I hear any shuffling dogs, so decide to pull myself up and over the wall, gasping a little as my unfit muscles protest. I lie on top of the wall then quietly lower myself over, my boots scraping softly against the brickwork as I come to rest on the ground and think, so far, so good.

I pause, listening for any noise, quite prepared to scramble up and back over the wall at the slightest sound of alarm, but I hear nothing, only the pitter-patter of the rain dropping softly against the leaves of bushes. The wall has become my comfort blanket and I reluctantly ease myself from it and in a half crouch, carefully walk towards the building, toes pointed out to avoid tripping, each step tried before I put my weight on the foot. I hesitate when I hear a vehicle's engine and my eyes turn towards the front of the house where the gates are, but the vehicle, its headlights casting a ghostly hue to my right, drives past. I sigh with relief and concentrate on getting to the edge of the building, my confidence growing with each step. This isn't the first time I've been on a CROP job, though on the previous half dozen occasions, it was with a back-up team and sanctioned by the police management. If I'm caught here, I know it's at best arrest and at worse; well, I'd rather not think about that right now.

I'm at the edge of the building, my body merging with the shadow and surprised there is no security lights at all. I half consider that Docherty's arrogance, believing himself among his peers to be a top of the tree criminal, believes that nobody in their right mind would consider screwing his house and that he doesn't need security devices; that anyone stupid enough to break into his home will be found out and dealt with by him. I remember it's not an uncommon attitude among some of these bastards and on occasion, as a divisional CID officer, I dealt with seriously assaulted victims who had made the mistake of breaking into the wrong house and being summarily dealt with. Not one ever formally complained to the police.

From somewhere, I can faintly hear voices and feeling by hand, make my way past the edge of the house to the rear. Now I'm at the back corner and continue edging my way round. The first thing I see is light emanating from the house and casting a huge oblong square onto the garden. I realise the light is coming from a window and so the curtains must be open. This causes me to flinch, worrying that I might be silhouetted and making me even more cautious. The sound of voices and laughter is now a little louder and I recognise that it's the noise of a game show that's on the television. If nothing else, it confirms someone is at home. I'm now thinking that if whoever is there is at the room at the back of the house, maybe I can work my way round to the other side via the front. It's a bit riskier, but my CROP training gives me more confidence in my ability than perhaps I've realised. Decision made, I retrace my steps and go back the way.

It takes me about fifteen minutes; fifteen dry-mouth, sweaty palm minutes. The hardest part is crossing the area of the front door. A porch light was on and cast a semi-circle glow in a thirty foot arc and shone on top of an old style, light coloured Vauxhall Astra estate car. I sidled past and commit the registration number to memory; another entry for my notepad. Keeping out of the arc of light means my back is almost scraping the front gates. Holding my breath, I make it without any problem and continue round the house, passing on the other side of the building between an empty but open double door garage and the south side of the house. I stop, realising no BMW vehicle probably means at least Docherty probably isn't at home. By now I'm at the other corner of the rear of the house and again looking at the large square of light in the garden. I must admit to being surprised that for such a large house, there doesn't seem to be much ground round about it and surmised the farmer who had sold the parcel of land must have restricted the area. Saying that, what garden there is looks to be well tended. Right, here comes the tricky bit. I know that the amount of light shining from what now seems to be a panoramic window means there is likely no curtains obscuring the view so I'm now going to have a peek at what is inside the room. Don't think I've forgotten about Mister Burns. The knife I've brought with me is burning a hole in my backpack and slipping off the straps I fetch it from its sheath of kitchen roll and weigh it in my right hand. If you think that earlier my mouth is dry, I'm now so parched it's like my tongue is sandpaper rubbing my gums and though it is a bitterly cold night, a rivulet of sweat is running down my spine. I edge along the wall and just in time step over a plant pot with flowers in full bloom. I almost laugh out loud when I realise the bloody things are plastic and think to myself that you can take the man out of the housing scheme …. Unconsciously I glance around and it makes me wonder at the rest of the perfectly set out garden.

At the corner I take a fast peek and realise it is not a window, but a large set of solid looking French doors. I take a deep breath and pressing the front of my body against the wall at the window, prepare myself.

You probably know that if you are in a brightly lit room and the curtains are open onto a dark night, the window reflects the room light almost like a mirror, so unless your nose is pressed against the pane with your hands cupping your eyes and peering outside, it is extremely difficult to see into the darkness. A sudden movement in the dark might attract the attention of the periphery of the eye, but generally speaking, unless you are looking for something in particular, the reflected light is blinding. I rely on this to be true and as I cautiously turn my head and very slowly, peer into the room.

The first thing I see is bright, white painted walls and a large flat screen television set in the wall above a massive marble fireplace that is roaring out flames. I guess the room is very warm because there is absolutely no condensation on the glass of the doors. A pile of logs are neatly stacked against the wall. Two black leather easy chairs are placed side by side framing the fireplace and the back of a couch faces towards me. A dark haired woman's head lolls against the back of the couch, her face slightly tilted upwards as her attention is apparently taken with the game show on the TV. To her right hand, sits a small table with a half full wine glass on it. There doesn't seem to be any other occupants in the room. As I watch, the woman reaches out and takes hold of the glass and her head tilts slightly further back as she drinks from it. I quickly glance about me and am happy that nobody is sneaking up on me. There's that paranoia, again.

I assess what I have learned so far, what I have I achieved and frankly, in complete honesty, absolutely nothing. Yeah, I got into the grounds, but there is nothing to indicate Burns is holed up here. I decide to do a John Wayne and get the hell out of Dodge, but risk one more glance into the room. I shrink back because now there's a man in the room, standing in front of the woman, his finger pointing down at her and rage on his face. I risk watching, knowing there is just inches of me at the corner of the French door and confident they can't see me. The woman stands and turns her back on the man and towards me, her arms folded as she stares at her reflection in the window and even though I unconsciously shrink back an inch or two, I know she is unable to see me. My eyes widen with surprise. It seems evident she has been crying and the blackened eyes and swollen lower lip are testament to the beating she has endured. But worse than that, a cold shiver passes through me as I recognise her. Ina Carroll.

What was I to do? You know that feeling of helplessness that you sometimes experience, that murderous feeling when you wish nothing more than to beat the shit out of someone? It happens everywhere; road rage when driving; bad manners at a bus stop; grievance at a pub bar. Don't try to lie or kid yourself and tell me you know nothing of what I speak; we all have experienced that uncontrollable anger at some time in our life and some of us, more regularly than others. Well that's what I'm going through right now and believe me, nothing right then would have given me more pleasure than riding to the rescue, the White Knight charging in and saving the fair maiden. Only this isn't television or a film. This is me, a long-bladed kitchen knife in my hand, standing in the dark in the middle of the night in the private grounds of a house I've invaded without lawful authority, staring at a woman who is the bed-partner of a known and violent drug-dealing gangster. A woman who, by her own admission, knows the kind of company she keeps. I choke down the anger I feel and stare again at the man, his face vaguely familiar. The double glazed doors prevent me from hearing what's going on, but it seems patently obvious they're arguing. They stand facing each other, he finger-wagging as he rebukes her while with her hands held wide, she is gesticulating in anger. Her head is now down and she sits heavily back down on the couch and seems to be weeping. I can't stand much more of this and have to almost physically restrain myself from intervening. Besides, if the French doors are locked, how the hell am I supposed to get in?

I look again and Ina remains seated while the man is in the act of leaving the room and I decide that this time, I am going. I don't want to cross the expanse of light and quickly make my way back round the house, but when I get to the space between the garage and the house, I hear the sound of a car engine slowing and the headlight beam seeping through the cracks in the gates. I fall back into the even darker shadow and prepare myself to run at the nearest section of wall, to clamber over and take my chance in the darkness outside. The gates swing open on well oiled hinges and the blinding beam of a large vehicle slowly drives into the tar macadam area in front of the house. The engine stops and the headlights is switched off, Two men get out of the driver and front passenger doors and by the porch light, I can see it is Docherty and Burns. The knife is still grasped in my hand and an overwhelming urge to run forward and plunge it into Burns chest courses through me, but I'm not stupid. If he fights back, as surely he must, I will also have Docherty to deal with and I do not have the confidence to deal with two men. But the moment passes and they're into the house and with at sound of a door slamming, they are gone. I shiver as the adrenalin pumps into my veins and then, as though a switch has been thrown, I feel suddenly tired and wish nothing more than to go home and get to bed.

So I've maybe learned one thing; that Burns is for the moment anyway, staying with Docherty. I feel the knife in my hand growing heavy, but quietly smile. I might yet have another opportunity.

Chapter 10

I sleep through to just after nine o'clock on Sunday morning before I haul myself out of bed and into the shower. Sunday is my no-shave day, the one day a week I give my skin a rest. I almost laugh when in the shower, I see brown staining at my feet and realise I couldn't have wiped off all the gravy paste. Then I realise it's likely stained the pillow slips and sheets and sigh; so that's a bed change, then.

My first call is to my folks, confirming that I'll be up to collect the girls after they've attended church and though I already know, I'm pleased when my mother tells me they have been as good as gold. Towelled dry, I slip into my robe and with a coffee, sit at the table in the lounge and decide to update my notepad. I write a brief description of my night's adventure and include the registration number of the Astra, as well as adding the BMW plate number too. I describe Ina's injuries and am about to describe the man I saw speaking with her when I recall who he is. I sit back and smile at the small success, happy I have remembered. The last time I saw him he was pulling me a pint of Tennents in the Saracen Head pub; the Irish barman.

Then like a cold shower, it hits me. I figure he must be Docherty's man and probably reported Ina meeting Gordon and me, then wonder if he made us or even suspected us to be cops? If so, that no doubt accounted for the beating that Ina has suffered. I'm also thinking Ina didn't know the barman was reporting to Docherty or she would never have agreed to meet us there. What worries me now is what if anything she has told Docherty and Burns? It goes without saying they will have questioned her at length, as evidenced by her sore face, but if Burns is still living at Docherty's house, why hasn't he taken off like a scalded rat if he knows now that there is an interest in him being back here? Bloody hell! The only thing I can think of is that Ina hasn't told him, at least not yet and if she hasn't satisfied them bastards with a story, they might still be intent on having a go at her. Now I'm feeling pangs of guilt that I didn't get her out of there. I shake my head in frustration and decide that there is only one thing I can do. I have to send in the cavalry and by that I mean phoning the cops and getting them to turn Docherty's house over, telling them that Burns is back living there and Ina is being held against her will. It's the only way I can think of, if not to save her life then save her from more injury at the hands of those nutters.

I sip at my coffee and try to be logical, wondering if I might be over-reacting. Ina was sipping wine when I saw her. Yes, she had obviously been beaten, but would she still have the run of the house if she was a prisoner? The more I consider what I saw the more I convince myself that Ina has not told them I'm hunting Burns. Why else would he so openly allow himself to be driven about by Docherty, a known criminal who is often targeted by the surveillance units? I mean, Docherty can't possibly know when the surveillance might decide to …. I sat upright, an icy chill seeping through me as the thought strikes me hard, like a prop forward tackling a ten year old schoolgirl. I unconsciously gather the robe about me, my mind racing. Yes, it is a possibility, one that I hadn't and didn't want to consider.

I need to discuss what I have learned and what I now suspect with someone, giving in to the old adage that two heads are better than one. But glancing at the clock I rise to my feet and know that will need to wait till another time because right now, I have two bundles of joy to pick up from my parents house.

I get there early and when I open my parent's front door to greet them, the girls rush me and almost knock me off my feet in their enthusiasm. My mother and father squeeze past me to get the kettle on and prepare what has become a ritual; the Sunday brunch, a large fry-up, though the food is mostly grilled because my dad's cholesterol has been a source of concern these past few months. Mum is busy in the kitchen and I set up the gate-leg table and folding chairs in the lounge and lay five places, while dad, Sophie and Sarah cuddle on the couch as they watch the follow Jake and the Neverland Pirates adventures on children's TV.

"Did you get your business done, then?" asks mum.

"Aye, took most of the night, but I managed to get done what I set out to do."

"Don't suppose you want to talk about it?"

"Rather not, if it's okay with you mum. It's to do with an old case from when I was in the Force."

"About that wee lassie that was murdered, Alice, you mean?"

I've already told you how perceptive my mother is and if I've any detective skills, you'll have guessed from whom I get the gene. I take a deep breath and reply, "If I don't discuss it with you, mum I can't tell you any fibs, now can I?"

"Please yourself, then" she replies, trying to be huffy, but I know its concern for me that that caused her to ask.

"Gordon Roberts was asking for you at church this morning, Tom," said my dad at my back. "Told me you visited him a couple of nights ago and that he was right pleased to see you. Said to tell you that if you get the chance, you have to give him a call, okay?"

I nod and message delivered, dad rejoins the girls on the couch and groans theatrically as Captain Hook steals the treasure chest.

"Boo!" the girls scream at the television, then giggle as their grandfather squeezes them tightly.

After breakfast, I offer to help clear up but already know my folks won't have it and with kisses all round complete, pack the girls into the back of the Punto.

"How long you going to have the car?" asks my dad, nodding at it. "You can save yourself some cash if you want to borrow mine," he offers.

"Might keep it another day or two," I reply and politely decline his offer. My mother's arthritis has been playing up and in this weather, I much prefer she has a lift to the local ASDA than have to walk and carry her shopping.

I'm on High Street, waiting on the light changing to turn left into Duke Street when Sarah pipes up from the back, "Can we have some ice-cream please daddy?"

Though I'm not supposed to know, I'm aware that courtesy of my parents, they both have a packet of chocolate buttons in their small overnight cases; a secret not to be divulged and without turning my head, tell her no and remind them they have just eaten a big brunch.

"But Uncle Andy buys us ice-cream," she coyly replies.

I sit still, desperate to ask and yet reluctant to interrogate my six year old daughters. Andy? Who the hell is Andy? Like me, Lisa's an only child, so what we're not talking about a sibling here and unless my memory is failing, there's no 'cousin Andy'. The light turns to green, but I'm so preoccupied with the name Andy it takes the irate woman behind me sounding her horn to get me moving. The girls giggle nervously in the back of the car, uncertain what has come over their father. Andy?

I drive mechanically on Duke Street, my thoughts tumbling about as their names bounce about in my head, Andy and Lisa; Lisa and Andy. What right do I have to be concerned about Andy? I mean, Lisa and I are no longer an item, we're not a couple anymore, I tell myself. I turn left into Craigpark Drive and find an empty space a few car lengths from the close mouth and help the girls from their booster seats. They both run to the door as Iqbal comes out, laughing as he steps to one side to avoid the blonde avalanche.

"Mister McEwan, will I take those seats for you, sir?"

"Thanks son," I reply and grapple in my trousers pockets for some change, handing him a couple of pounds coins. "Tell your mum thanks and get yourself a comic or sweetie or something," I suggest. He raises his hands and smiling, tries to tell me there is no need, but I can see in his eyes he's grateful for the gesture and pockets the money.

In the flat, the girls insist on more TV and I capitulate then ask Sophie to come into the kitchen for juice to eat with their chocolate buttons. She pulls a face that I've guessed about the sweeties and follows me in. I lift her up and sit her on the worktop and take my time getting the plastic beakers from the cupboard. I love my daughters equally and while at six, they are far too young for guile, I know Sarah to be the questioning one while Sophie is more open and trusting.

"So," I slowly begin, pouring the squash into the beakers, "Uncle Andy buys you girls ice-cream, then?" Already I hate myself for what I'm about to ask.

"Sometimes," she replies, "when he takes mummy and Sarah and me out to the park and things."

"Is he a nice man?"

She nods rapidly, her focus now on popping some buttons into her mouth. "He kisses mummy," and puts her hand over her mouth as she stares at me and giggles, sharing a big, big secret with me.

I don't know why and I have no reason to be jealous, but that simple statement completely deflates me. As you now know, I'm no angel and since our split I've not played around or anything or rather, I remind myself, unless you include the two occasions with Cathy Williams. I try to convince myself sex with Cathy is irrelevant; a physical release with no emotional ties or come-back. But really, who am I kidding? I'm not a victim in the failure of my marriage, I'm the instigator and Lisa is quite right to get on with her life and if that means another man, well, I have absolutely no say in the issue. But it's hard to be philosophical about the thought of her being with another man and I sigh heavily and lifting Sarah down, watch as balancing the half full beakers she returns to join her sister and the Adventures of Scooby-Doo.

Maybe at the back of my mind, despite the turmoil that Lisa and I had gone through, I had some faint wish for reconciliation, but now this. Andy.

It's almost four-thirty and I'm nearly dozing on the couch, a tousle head against each arm and the television turned to the cartoon channel when I realise the time and scramble to get the girls into their coats. Lisa is the most punctual female I know and while punctuality and women is like a contradiction in terms, I don't want to be late and sour the relationship, as it is. I glance down to the street and see her Volvo semi-parked and through the front screen, her fingers drumming on the steering wheel. I organise the girls and accompany them to the close mouth and out into the pavement. I know Lisa would prefer I didn't approach and speak, so hang back ten feet from the car and watch as she emerges from the car and politely ignores me while she kisses and cuddles the girls, then helps them strap into the rear seats. That done she drives off, the girls frantically waving and Lisa staring straight ahead. Andy. Tempted as I am, it's not my place to interfere in her life, I tell myself. I've done enough damage and turn to walk back to the close when I see her standing there, casually leaning against a lamppost, one hand on her hip and small holdall type bag in the other. Her blonde hair is swept back into a ponytail and the dark coat buttoned to the neck against the chill of the day. She's wearing black denims and highly polished black boots.

"So, that will be the former Missus McEwan?"

"Hello, Cathy. I didn't expect to see you so soon. You get through your list of men quicker than you thought?" I ask, uncertain where the bitterness of my comment came from.

She smiles and I'm not sure, but is that a little uncertainty I see in her smile?

"I thought I'd move you to the top of the tree, Tom," she retorts and holds up the bag, swinging it slightly. "I've got the night off and it might be a very, very long night. You see, Tom, hubby is attending a conference in Liverpool So I thought you and I might catch up on a few things," and moves closer to me, close enough for me to get a whiff of her fragrance. "Wouldn't you like to know what kind of underwear I've got in the bag here?" she softly whispers and stares into my eyes.

A physical desire overtakes me and I catch my breath, all thought of Lisa and Andy dissipating at the fleeting vision of Cathy and her lithe, sensuous body lying on my bed. I try to smile and she recognises that as a 'yes', then turns and walks towards the close mouth. Wordlessly I follow her, the key in my hand and any intention I have of phoning Gordon Roberts vanish from my mind. Unlocking the close door, I half turn to see young Iqbal, curiosity written on his face staring at us from his front room window.

Chapter 11

A shuffling noise wakens me and drowsily, I turn and see on the digital alarm clock that it's just gone five forty in the morning. A crack in the curtained window allows moonlight to flood the room and I see Cathy in profile, slightly bent over as with one foot raised she carefully slips into her knickers, her loose hair and breasts hanging before her, the nipples protruding ripe and prominent from the chill in the cold room. I stare at her and feel yet another stirring in my groin as she half turns towards my movement and I can almost make out her smile as she gathers the rest of her clothing from the floor and pulls open the bedroom door. "Don't be late again this morning, Mister McEwan," she softly warns me, "I can't have people thinking I have favourites now, can I?" and slips through the door, gently closing it behind her.

I lie there, remembering with pleasure the evening and night before, idly scratching at my groin and half smile as I wonder again where I'm getting the energy to be aroused. A few moments later I hear the sound of the front door closing and with sudden memory cry out loudly, "Fuck!"

I've forgotten to get my door key from her and then inwardly grin at the vision of her, scantily clad in the lacy underwear she'd brought with her. Maybe Cathy visiting on a regular basis isn't such a bad idea, I muse.

I lie awake and consider my relationship – is that really the word? Am I having a relationship with Cathy Williams? I ponder that because, frankly, I have no emotional feeling for her. I certainly don't love her, not like I love …. No, loved Lisa … or Alice? Did I love Alice, I ask myself. I squirm in the bed, all the memories flooding back in a jumble. Maybe I should say, not like the protective feeling I had for Alice. And right there, in the darkness of my room, a few hours after I have made love to a woman that I barely know, I finally and at last come to terms with my feeling for Alice Foley. I desired her, wanted to keep her safe, but didn't love her. Not the way I loved Lisa. Shit!

I close my eyes tight, making fists under the duvet cover, trying to drive the thoughts away. I don't want to accept what in my heart, if not my head, I know to be true. I love Lisa still and Alice was a beautiful distraction, nothing more. I've messed up my life because of an infatuation. God, what am I to do? I tossed the cover aside and naked, stood in the chilled room, all thought of sleep driven from me. I don the my robe and walk through to the kitchen, filling then switching on the kettle for coffee.

I opt for a bath rather than my usual shower, figuring I've plenty of time before I depart for my work and decide to walk, the morning again bright if cold. No sense in taking the Punto because parking in the city centre at any time is a nightmare and I absolutely refuse to pay the extortionate costs of the high rise car park.

The walk to Bothwell Street is invigorating and I arrive twenty minutes early, greeting Gerry Higgins who is again sitting at his desk. I sometimes wonder if Gerry has a camp bed behind there for he always seems to be on duty.

I'm not surprised to see Cathy already there, dressed in a sober, navy coloured trouser suit, hair in a ponytail and walking into her office, her head down and concentrating on a sheaf of papers held in her hand, then closing the door behind her. I see there is a few people already at their desks, but first stop for me is the kettle where I make myself a coffee and accept nods from then half listen to a couple of young guys discussing their weekend. If they are to be believed, every young, short skirted, big-titted woman in the bars and clubs they frequented was gagging for sex from them both. Call me Mister Cynical, but as I listen to their increasingly juvenile patter, trying to outdo each with their sexual exploits, I'm grateful for the maturity age brings and inwardly smiling, return to my desk to find old Archie winding his way towards me.

"Morning Tom," he greets me and then nods over his shoulder to Cathy's office. "The wicked witch is in early right enough. Word is that some of the subscriber checks for the phones landed on her desk this morning and she's been instructed to speak to the staff about it." He cackles like the old gossip he is and adds, "Wouldn't be surprised if some of these young buggers have been phoning their aunties in Oz. Heard that it's in some cases it might be a sacking offence, if you get my drift."

I place my coffee on the mat and sit down. "But you'll be all right, won't you Archie?"

"Oh, aye, worst I do is call the missus and that's easily explained. I'll just tell them it's a domestic issue and that I need to keep in touch at home. Probably get my knuckles wrapped and that will be the end of it." He taps the side of his nose with a nicotine stained finger. "Too long in the tooth to catch me," he smirks. "Oh, oh, she's out and about. Better scoot," he whispers and scuttles back to his desk.

I watch as Cathy walks towards to a young girl and catching the girl's attention, beckons with her forefinger to her office, then see them both disappear inside with the door closed behind them.

I begin catching up with my weekend mail when ten minutes later, Cathy's door opens and the girl comes out. It seems obvious she is crying as she makes her way to her desk.

During the course of the morning, the whole floor watches as a further five staff are called into Cathy's office of whom four return to their desk while the fifth, a heavy-set woman of about forty who I know only as Maggie and who is known for constantly whining, storms out and slams the door behind her, then clears some items from her desk that she shoves into a large, canvas handbag and finally with a loud crash, sweeps the desktop computer to the floor. The staff around her sit stunned as red-faced and ignoring everyone, she makes her way to the lifts that open to reveal Gerry Higgins and another commissionaire inside, apparently summoned to escort Maggie from the building. Like everyone else, I'm watching the spectacle when the phone on my desk rings. I answer mechanically, absorbing the drama playing out as Gerry and his colleague, hands raised, are subjected to a torrent of abuse from the enraged woman.

"So Mister McEwan, how was last night for you, then?" asks the calm and silky voice of Cathy Williams, no hint or trace in her tone of the argument that must have ensued just minutes earlier in her office. Startled I unconsciously glance about to ensure I'm not being overheard. "Thoroughly enjoyable," I reply, then cheekily add, "I didn't realise you were so agile."

She softly laughs and says, "Well, get ready for an encore, my hubby is detained another night in Liverpool." I'm about to protest that I've something else to do, when she adds, "And it might also give you and I the opportunity to discuss your Spanish telephone call. So, I'll be waiting for you."

I softly exhale, knowing that she's got me by the short and curlies and rather than an embarrassing summons to her office, she's covering for me. Or, you if prefer, blackmailing me for sex. I inwardly smile, but sex with benefits for us both. Then it strikes me what she said. Waiting for me? Of course, I remember as I chew my lower lip again, she has my spare front door key.

I take my lunch break walking down to the Mitchell car hire premises and extend the hire of the Punto for one week. I'm giving much thought to what my next move is and to be honest, my resolve to murder Robbie Burns weakens by the day. As I walk through the lunchtime pedestrian traffic, I assess what little I've achieved so far and what I intend doing. You will realise by now that I'm not a killer. A cowardly idiot whose boss is shagging him and fearful if he says no, he'll lose his job? Yes, shamefacedly, I'll put my hands up to that. A stupid bugger who threw away a good career and an even better marriage? I plead guilty again. So, regarding my one-man hunt or vendetta, whatever you wish to call it, for the elusive Robbie Burns, I've pretty much made my decision.

I'm confident that Ina has not told her boyfriend Jo-Jo Docherty nor Burns who Gordon and I really are and probably made up some story that earned her a beating, but thankfully no worse. I'm also satisfied from my nocturnal visit to Docherty's house that if Burns even suspected for a second that his hiding out there is compromised, he would be on his toes and gone to pastures new. What I can't get my head round is why Burns is so openly living there, even happy to use the nearby health club and be conveyed by Docherty round the city when both must know that Docherty is frequently the subject of police surveillance. But as I walk, I shake my head, for I suspect that I already know the answer to that question.

My next move has got to be a meeting with Gordon. A phone call is no use; it has to be a face to face because after what he has done for me, I owe him at least that. First thing will be to apologise to him for not getting back to him sooner then tell him of my CROP visit to Docherty's house. I know I'll need to be careful how I break the news of Ina's sore face, for if I know the big guy, retired or not, he'll want to rush up there and kick the door down and hurt anyone who gets in his way and when I say hurt, that doesn't even describe him in a rage. Logically, the meeting should be tonight, but let's not beat about the bush here. Cathy Williams knows about my Spanish phone call and frankly, I have no business excuse for the call so if I piss her off, I could be looking at unemployment and convince myself that, just as the lovely Scarlet O'Hara says at the closing of 'Gone With The Wind', tomorrow is another day.

I see Cathy depart her office just before three o'clock and as she walks past me without even a glance, I find myself becoming aroused and resist the temptation to turn and stare after her. God knows, though she's a controlling bitch and whether I like it or not, the woman is having a powerful effect on me. The remaining two hours pass ever so slowly and at last it's time to power down my computer and shrug on my suit jacket and anorak. With the other staff, I make my way to the lift and listen as they discuss the day's events and the final tally of eight staff members disciplined and the sacking of Maggie, who though previously was described as a back-stabbing, whining cow by most, is now evoking sympathy and has graduated to become 'poor Maggie'. Needless to say, the disparaging comments about Missus Williams range from evil to worse. I dread to think what my colleague's attitude will be if they ever learn that I'm shagging 'That Vile Tart', as one young woman describes Cathy and likely if that is ever disclosed, I'll be forever known as the spy in the camp.

It is cloudy and overcast, but the rain has stayed away as I hurry through the city, deciding to walk home and forego the bus, wondering what Cathy will be wearing when I get in. I smile to myself and hope it's the black coloured Basque and seamed stockings from the previous evening. The very personal striptease she performed to music for me was every heterosexual man's secret desire and I half thought she enjoyed the teasing of me as much as I did.

It's dark when I finally arrive at the close mouth and glance up at the light emanating from my first floor flat, confirming that Cathy is there. I won't say that my hands are shaking when I insert the key into the close door lock, nor did I race up the stairs, but I will admit to a sense of expectation and again chastise myself for not keeping a toothbrush and paste in my desk at the office. I hesitate at my front door and hear the strains of Mick Hucknell's new album coming from inside. I considered making some jokey comment when I get through the door, something Like "Honey, I'm home," and am almost embarrassed to admit that I even quietly practised it when I walked along Craigpark Drive, but thought it too stupid. So instead will simply go in and see what pleasure awaits me. Should I have got some food, I wonder? I shrug and suppose that if it comes to that, I can always order in.

I insert the key and push open the door, guessing that she's waiting for me in the lounge. I hang my anorak and jacket on the hook by the small hall cupboard, loosen my tie then unbutton the top of my shirt. Through the open bedroom door, I see her holdall lying on the floor and her business suit jacket and trousers she'd worn that day at the office lying abandoned across the chair in the corner. I lick my dry lips and slowly walk towards the lounge, my breathing slow as I push open the lounge door that is slightly obstructed by my robe lying abandoned on the floor.

Cathy, her blonde hair about her, is lying on her stomach on the couch wearing as I had hoped the black coloured Basque, a thin, black laced thong that shows off her perfectly rounded and unblemished buttocks and seamed stockings, each seam straight and aligned on her well toned, athletic legs with one ankle daintily crossed over the other. Her right arm hangs loosely by her side, the fingers of her hand trailing on the small rug and the left arm provocatively on the armrest. Her head is turned slightly to one side with her eyes closed, her small, dainty tongue protruding slightly from her open mouth.

I might have been excused by believing she was asleep, but the only problem is I'm also seeing the dark, haemorrhaged arterial blood that has cascaded from the horrific, gaping wound at the back of her skull, for Cathy is very, very dead.

Chapter 12

Even in death, she is startling beautiful and after sitting on the chair for about five, full minutes staring at her and in my defence, probably suffering from shock, I decide there is nothing else I can do and call it in. I don't bother with the local office for these days all calls are routed through a police call centre and I go straight for the good old traditional 999. The unnamed operator talks me through my name and address and conscious that the call is being recorded, I am as specific as I can be, telling him that I have just returned home to find my friend, I describe her, lying murdered in my front room.

"How do you know she has been murdered?" he asks me.

I want to scream at him that she has a got a fucking great bash in the back of her head, but realise the guy is only doing his job and describe the wound.

"Is there any trace of a pulse?"

"Believe me, pal. She is dead."

"Yes, but have you checked for a pulse?" he asks again.

"I've checked," I lie, "No, there is no pulse."

"Right Mister McEwan, if you please remain where you are, I'll get someone with you as quickly as I can. Are you able to stay on the line?"

"I'll leave the line open, but I'm putting it down on the side table. You will be able to hear everything that is said when your cops arrive," I reply and set the mobile down on the small, pseudo walnut table by the television.

The operator's promise of "... *as quickly as I can*" is almost ten minutes, during which time my training as a police detective kicks in. Without touching Cathy or the rug where her blood has dripped and congealed, I can see whatever caused the wound was heavy and sharp, but there is neither any sign of a weapon that caused such an injury nor can I think of anything that I own that might have been used. I sudden thought strikes me and I check to discover all my kitchen knives are neatly stacked in the wooden block on the worktop, including the one I returned with from my night prowl. That would suggest her killer brought and took away the weapon. I'm guessing that whoever had struck her on the back of her head would undoubtedly be blood spattered as was the couch and even some of the furniture, indicating to me it was at least one, solid and fatal blow. Back in the lounge again, I lean over and see something that disturbs me. I know she was fastidious about her hair and could see that the way it was tangled at the back perhaps also indicates that she had been held firmly by her hair. Look, I know I'm surmising here, but what the hell. If she, as I suspect, answered the door to her killer, it's possible she was forced to walk from the front door by her killer who was holding her by the hair. Another thought strikes me. Cathy wasn't a big woman, but trust me on this and I almost blush as I tell you; she was fit and very, very agile so, if my theory about her being held by the hair is correct, whoever did this has to be a strong person. I take a deep breath and leave her untouched and walked through to my bedroom where I find her black leather handbag lying next to her holdall. I open the handbag and ensure her pursue, with money and credit cards intact, is still inside then replace them for the police to examine. The money and cards apparently rule out theft. I examine the front door and it seems to be okay, not forced, which would also seem to indicate Cathy let her killer into the flat.

I'm just about to pour myself a glass of water when the front door gets thumped and a young voice shouts loudly, "Police!"

I take a deep breath, then snatch open the door. The young tall, lanky cop who looks like a sixth former is about to again bang on the door, but takes a step back, his pale face staring at me as he fumbles at his issue utility belt. I realise he is reaching for his CS gas spray, but before I say anything, a female Sergeant, in her mid forties I'm guessing, puts her arm across her partner and stares at me.

"Mister McEwan?" she at last must realise I'm not a threat and smilingly asks, her voice rasping and sounding like an advert for forty fags a day. "I'm Sergeant Kennedy. You phoned to say you've a dead woman in your flat here?"

I nod and invite them in. I courteously stand to one side and allow the cop to walk past me, but the Sergeant isn't stupid. She stops, continues to smile and says, "After you," that I take to mean, 'There's no way I'm turning my back on a possible killer'. It didn't escape my attention either that her fingers were playing a tap dance on the handle of her metal baton. In the hallway, I turn to the Sergeant and explain that Cathy is in the front room.

"Look," I begin to tell her, "Firstly, I found Cathy where she is lying. Secondly, I'm no threat to you. If you agree I'll stand in there," and point to the kitchen doorway. "There's a window, but it's too wee to jump out of and if you stand your cop at the door, I'll wait till you examine the lounge. I haven't touched the body and because you will likely find out later anyway, I am a former cop and with respect, can I suggest that as it's a murder scene, you might wish to stand at the door of the lounge. You'll be able to see what you need from there and there's little likelihood of you contaminating the locus.

Her eyes narrow and I see the faintest of nods, then she turns to the nervous looking cop and tells him, "Ewan, stand by that door and if Mister McEwan should try to escape, you have my permission to batter him to death, okay?"

It was a bad joke that I got, but I don't think the cop did. If anything, he turned a whiter shade of pale, if you forgive the pun and nervously glances rapidly from his Sergeant to me. I watch as the Sergeant took a pair of thin Forensic gloves from a small pouch on her utility belt and indicated for the young cop to do likewise then I turn and walk in to the kitchen and stand with my back to the worktop, head bowed and arms folded. I've missed something, but for the life of me I can't think what it is.

A few minutes later, I hear the sound of voices at the front door and then two young guys in suits are at the kitchen door, almost rudely ushering the cop out of the way.

"DC Craig," the shorter of the two introduces himself, hands on hips and legs astride, his obese waistline threatening to erupt over the top of the trousers of his cheap, chocolate brown suit trousers. "You McEwan?"

"Mister McEwan," I politely reply, staring at the brown sauce stain he'd missed at the lower right hand side of his cream coloured shirt and probably can't see because it's under two rolls of fat. Already I'm peeved that this arse thinks he can dominate me simply because he's CID.

"Aye right, *Mister* McEwan," he replies, his voice oozing with sarcasm and already alienating me without even having conducted an initial interview. His pal isn't much brighter; his jaw working overtime as he chews gum like some poor mans parody of a detective from an American cop show. Hands in trouser pockets, the younger detectives' inexperience seems obvious by the way he lounges against the door frame, trying to pretend he has seen it all.

"So, *Mister* McEwan," asks Craig, "did you kill the bird in there then?"

The bird in there? I can't even summon up the energy to respond to such a stupid question and at first, simply stare at him. He stares back than hooking a thumb over his shoulder, says, "Patsy tells me you were in the job. That right is it?"

"If by Patsy you mean the Sergeant, then yes. That is correct and can I suggest that as she certainly seems a lot more professional than you, maybe she should be the one that is conducting this initial interview and not you two fucking Muppets."

I hear a choked laugh from outside in the hallway and know I've maybe hit a home truth. Craig turns white, then red, his fists clenching back and forth and eager to come at me, but uncertain of his ground. His partner stands staring at him, waiting for some instruction.

"I could arrest you right now!" threatens Craig.

"No you can't," I lazily respond, smiling at his reddening face and watching a bead of sweat forming on his brow. Having worked him into a rage, I'm content to keep winding the bastard up and if the situation had not been so serious, I might even have enjoyed myself. "For one, I called you to report the murder. That for the minute makes me your number one witness. Two, other than the fact Missus Williams was discovered in my flat, there is no evidence I committed or am involved in the murder. Three, if you were any kind of police officer, let alone a detective, you would have some professional dignity and refer to the lady as the deceased, not 'that bird' and finally, put some fucking gloves on. You are contaminating the locus."

Now, as I stare at him, it occurs to me that I might end up having to perform CPR on the fat bastard because he starts to shake with anger and I know, just know, I'm looking at a premature heart attack victim. He was saved from any further indignity by voices at the front door and he turns away to be replaced not by the cop Ewan, but Patsy the Sergeant.

"Play nice, Mister McEwan," she quietly suggests to me, with the faintest trace of a grin, "the fat bugger can't help being a wanker." I smile at her and watch as a hand taps her on the shoulder and moves her aside and who should be standing there, but the duty Detective Inspector, my former surveillance team member, Graeme Fleming. "Hello, Tom," he greets me, "long time no see."

There's no offer to shake my hand and I merely nod. If nothing else, Graeme was a more than capable Detective Sergeant and quite possibly what I will describe as the consummate professional police officer when we worked together, so at least now I can trust the inquiry will be conducted properly. Don't get me wrong, though. Like the rest, he turned aside when I needed a friend, so I have no reason to trust him anymore than any other police officer, but my opinion of him doesn't mask the fact I believe him to be very competent. While others like me settled down into police work and regarded it as a job, Graeme considered it almost to be a calling. He steps into the kitchen and with his back to the cooker, folds his arms and stares at me for a few seconds, then asks, "Maybe give me a brief summary before we head to the office?"

"You haven't cautioned me," I remind him.

"Do I need to formally caution you?"

I offer him a grim smile and shake my head in reply. So I summarily tell him that Cathy is, or rather was, my boss, that we had a drunken fling at the office Christmas party, that she visited me here at the flat last Thursday night at which time we had sex and again last night when she stayed till the early hours of the morning, that she had my flat key, though I didn't tell him how she acquired it, believing that it wasn't relevant. I finish my narration by describing how she had decided to leave early, that I saw her later in the day at the office and we had arranged that she be here when I got home.

"The way she is," he hesitates then softly continues, "… attired. I presume it is or was I mean, a current sexual affair you and she were conducting?"

I nod and for the first time since discovering Cathy, a wave of emotion sweeps through me.

"I see she's wearing wedding and engagement rings. I also presume she is married?"

"She has, had," I correct myself, "a husband and two teenage sons, at least as far as I know. I really have no knowledge of her personal life and she seldom spoke of it. If anything, that was a part of her life she kept very close to herself. She told me that her husband had travelled on business to Liverpool and is again there overnight. It'll be easily checked, I suppose."

"You think he might have been responsible for her murder?"

I shook my head and with some hesitation, reply, "No, I don't suppose, but no, I just don't know. "

"You know I have to ask this, Tom. Did you kill her?"

I vigorously shake my head and tell him, "No, no and no again. I realise you'll want a full statement and I will cooperate in everyway possible with your inquiry. Have I any idea who might be responsible? No again. What I do think, if you're interested is that she let the killer into the flat. Cathy had the key to get here first and my robe is lying on the floor in the lounge. I'm guessing she used my robe to cover herself when she answered the door and it has dropped off her when she was forced into the lounge."

"Forced?"

I exhale softly and explained my theory, that whoever had killed her had forced her into the lounge, probably by seizing a handful of her hair and propelling her in front of the killer.

"Something to consider," he concedes, his brow furrowing. "I'll have Forensics check if there are hair follicles on the floor. If she has resisted at all, she will have lost some."

"She was a fit girl," I told him. "Cathy wouldn't have just given in without a fight. It wasn't in her nature. She was a strong and assertive woman." I don't know where it came from, but tears form in my eyes and I suddenly feel the room sway. Graeme reaches out and taking my elbow, helps me sit at the small stool I keep by the larder, then turns and fetches the water in the glass I had almost used before the arrival of the uniform cops. "Here, drink this," he instructs and places the glass against my lips. I gulp down the chilled water and exhale loudly. "Sorry," I stammer.

"Don't be silly," he replies, his concern sounds genuine. "You've had a shock. Who says that cops are supposed to be immune to death?"

I smile at that. 'Cops', he says, probably unaware he is including me in his Band of Blue Brothers.

"Any idea who might want to set you up? I mean, leaving a dead woman in your flat?"

I stare at him. I'm so wrapped up with Cathy's murder, her being the victim that it never occurred to me I might be the subject of the killer's attention.

"Boss?" the younger of the two detectives interrupts my thoughts, "That's the casualty surgeon and the Scene of Crime arrived. How do you want to handle it?"

Graeme turns away from me and instructs that the casualty surgeon first pronounce life extinct, then have the SOC tape off the room, adding he wants the place hovered for hair and fibre and particularly the floor at the lounge entrance before anything else is done, including the removal of the body. "There's been too much foot traffic through the hallway and it's probably contaminated by us and the uniform cops, so leave that for now Morris. Then you and Peter get round the doors, starting with downstairs. No need for statements at this time unless the residents have something definite to offer."

"What about the removal of the," Morris glances at me, "the deceased?"

"The lady has nowhere to attend right now, Morris and I feel certain she would trust us to get it right and if that means lying on the couch for another few hours, I'm sure she won't mind."

The young detective nods and was about to move away, when Graeme calls him back. "I fully realise how this might seem, Morris. The apparel she is wearing," he adds.

Morris seems confused by apparel, so Graeme explains, "The way Missus Williams is dressed. We will maintain professionalism and the lady will not be the subject of solicitous gossip. Are we clear on that?"

Eyes widening, the detective nods his head and disappears.

"Thanks Graeme," is all I can manage.

"Now, Tom," he adopts a formal voice, "I feel certain that you will wish to voluntarily accompany me to the station where I can obtain your statement, DNA and fingerprints for elimination purpose."

"As a witness?"

"As a witness," he confirms.

I have no complaint about how I am treated at the London Road police station. Graeme leads me to the uniform bar where as a matter of course, I am asked by the Duty Inspector to sign a Voluntary Attendance form. Though technically I am a witness, I understand Graeme's logic in that if it should later transpire I am in some way suspected of being involved in Cathy's murder, he can truthfully present in evidence that I was not at all coerced into providing a statement, that I had willingly attended with him and signed my name to a document that clearly stated I agreed to be at the police office. But conversely, such a document is also in itself, clear and unequivocal evidence of my desire to assist the police in the brutal murder of Cathy Williams.

I knew London Road office from the many inquiries I had previously worked on and after a civilian bar officer electronically takes my fingerprints and swabs my mouth for DNA, I follow Graeme to an interview room where over the course of the next two hours, he laboriously writes out my statement and concluding, requests I read and sign it. I had known Graeme to be a family man and believe he still is and I am pleased that he doesn't dwell on the sexual aspect of my relationship with Cathy.

So, watching me sign the statement Graeme sits back in his chair and folds his hand behind his head.

"Now that the formal part is over, do you mind if we have a wee off the record chat, about Cathy?" he asks.

I nod and he asks me what she was like as a person. I describe her as a smart and worldly-wise, a martinet at work, intolerant of subordinates and keenly ambitious, but curiously, she didn't seem to have any close work friends. That is, I shrug, apart from me but, I tell him even our brief relationship was sexual, not sociable.

"However, she did take an interest in you?"

"I can't explain that," and again I shrug my shoulders, "but I suspect that Cathy had more irons in the fire than just me. She was a lady who liked to tease and well," I half smile, "she was very difficult to resist."

"Ah, yes. I suppose she was. So you think that there might have been other men she was seeing outwith the marriage?"

Over the course of my time in the surveillance unit, I had attended a few functions where Graeme was also present and I can't recall him ever taking an interest in any women other than his wife, so figure that he's a pretty straight guy and the idea of a man or woman cheating on their spouse doesn't find favour with him. I can almost read his thoughts. He is considering that Cathy's killer is either a jilted or jealous lover. The next half hour of informal chat continues with Graeme asking further questions about Cathy, some of which I can answer and others I can't and confirm what I'm thinking, that Graeme's line of inquiry will concentrate on Cathy's extra-marital affairs, that she was the killer's target and not me and though it sounds callous to admit it, this suits me to and lets me get on with my own investigation. Investigation? Listen to me, sounding like I'm still on the Force.

A sudden knock on the door is followed by the tousled red-haired head of a female detective who asks Graeme to step outside. He returns just over ten minutes later, a statement form in his hand.

"That was one of my Sergeants," he begins. "I'd sent her to your place of work and she spoke to the late shift commissionaires there. They in turn put her in touch with the dayshift man, a former police officer ....." he glances at the statement in his hand, "Gerald Higgins?"

I nod and experience a sense of anticipation. "That's right, Gerry Higgins."

"Mister Higgins confirms that Missus Williams departed just after three o'clock this afternoon and he saw her hail a black hackney cab outside the building. Says that you didn't leave till shortly after five o'clock, so we'll speak with your colleagues and if they can confirm you were at your desk during that two hour period and you called us shortly after you arrived home, added to the attending doctor's assessment that Missus Williams was dead for at least two hours, that more or less takes you out of the time frame to have committed the murder."

I feel a sudden burst of relief and can only dumbly nod at him. He leaves to fetch me a glass of water and I sit back, thinking of what he had said when he read from Gerry Higgins statement. Cathy had caught a taxi to my flat and I realise that is why there was no car keys in her handbag when I searched it. Car keys. I close my eyes in sudden understanding. There had been no reason to inform Graeme that I had rented the Punto and I then know that is what had bothered me, the thing I couldn't quite recall, for when I had hung up my anorak and jacket on the hook next to where the keys hang, the Punto car keys weren't there. They were gone.

It is past midnight when Graeme informs the Duty Inspector that my Voluntary Attendance is concluded, that I am free to go. He walks me to the front doors of the office and asks me to sit for a few minutes, that he has a couple of phone calls to make and that he will shortly return. After the warmth of the interview room, I shiver slightly in the glass enclosed area, my mind whirling as I tried to assess why the killer would take the keys and presumed the car is also now gone. It wouldn't have been hard to find it. Thirty yards either side of the close and pressing the remote locking control button will have identified the Punto when the flashing indicator lights activated. I contemplate telling Graeme, but considered that it might mean another couple of hours in his office explaining why I hadn't mentioned the car and right then, all I want to do is get out of there.

"Sorry to have kept you, Tom," he says, pushing through the security door. "I just wanted to ensure that Missus Williams body has been removed. She's now at the mortuary. I've had her husband contacted at his hotel in Liverpool by colleagues from Merseyside and informed of her death." He takes a deep breath and looks me in the eye. "Mister Williams, according to the Inspector at Liverpool I spoke with, wasn't alone in the hotel room. He's driving back home as we speak. I'm afraid your flat has been given the once over by the Scenes of Crime," he said, handing me the flat keys, "so it's a bit of a mess. Have you anywhere else you can stay tonight?"

"Are you finished with the flat?"

"For the meantime, yes, I don't think there's any need for us to be back at your flat for now. My two lads told me that the door to door in the close didn't produce anything and the guys at SOC tell me they've done as much as they can and I should get the results some time in the next day or two."

An awkward silence falls between us and I realise he is uncomfortable, then he says, "Sorry to be meeting again under these circumstances. Back then, I didn't stand up and say what I should have. No excuse. We let you down, Tom, all of us and most importantly, the job. I can only think that we were confused, that we needed to vent our anger against somebody and because that bastard Burns got away, you were the one we turned on. At least he finally got what he deserved. It doesn't help now, but for what it's worth," he stuck out his hand.

What can I say? Graeme Fleming is one of the bastards when my so-called team-mates rallied together against me and now here he is, sheepishly apologising and wanting to shake my hand.

I shook my head and thought 'Fuck it', grasp his hand in mine and walk through the glass doors towards the patrol car he has arranged to take me back to my flat.

The two cops hardly speak to me during the trip to Craigpark Drive, more intent on discussing the upcoming unification of the eight Scottish police forces to become one, single Force. They drop me off at my close mouth and I watch as they drive off, ensuring they are out of sight and the street deserted before I hustle over to where I had parked the Punto. To my surprise, the car is still parked exactly where I had left it. I try the driver's door, but it's locked and walk to the rear, where I'm even more surprised to find the keys in the boot lock, particularly as it's not unknown for the streets around here to be targeted by opportunist car thieves and can only assume that in the darkness, the keys weren't that visible. Added to this, the rear of the Punto is only eighteen inches from the front of the car behind it, so I'm supposing passers-by probably didn't give the boot a second glance. Now, I know it wasn't me that left them there because quite frankly, I haven't yet bothered or needed to open the boot. Licking my lips, I slowly unlock then quietly raise the boot lid, uncertain what if anything, I'll find there. The raising of the lid operates a small bulb on the side that casts a beam of light across the carpeted interior. Empty. I frown, because I know that whoever took the keys must have had a purpose for doing so. I reason the boot must be deeper than what I'm seeing and guessing that is where the spare tyre will be located, I lift the carpet by the edge and pull it back. And there it is, wrapped in one of my blue coloured, bathroom hand towels, the murder weapon, a large, wide bladed, wooden handled machete of the type that is issued to the British military. Not hard to come by and available in most Army & Navy stores or at a number of stalls at the Glasgow Barra's and certainly very, very dangerous in the wrong hands. I recognise it for what it is simply because I've seen a number of them seized by the police after gangland violence. I lean into the boot and without touching the wicked looking thing, by the small light I can see what looks like blood staining on the blade. I shake my head and leaving the machete there, quietly lower then lock the boot, but on this time the keys go into my anorak pocket.

As I walk back to the close mouth I think that whoever planted the machete in the car obviously reckoned I will have mentioned the Punto to the cops in my statement which would then of course as a matter of routine, be searched by the Scenes of Crime officers. I know from my CID days that it is highly unlikely any fingerprints will be found on the wood and I just know the killer will have wiped the blade before using it on poor Cathy. No, the circumstantial evidence will have hung me out to dry. The car is hired to me and the keys left in the boot will easily have been explained, that in my panic to dispose of the machete, I inadvertently left them in the lock; so simple but so very effective. If nothing else, the finding of the machete in the car and the rather make-shift and crude attempt to set me up settles in my mind what I already have guessed, that Cathy wasn't the target for the murderer; she simply got in the way. No, the killers target was and is still likely, me.

The only question that remains now is who and why and already my mind is working on a suspect.

Entering the flat, I switch on the lounge lights and see the confusion that was once my orderly and tidy room. I balk at the staining on the couch and rug, closing my eyes against the horror of Cathy's death and know that no matter how hard I try, the room will never again be entirely clean. I open a sash window a few inches to let the night air in against what I know will be the rancid smell of blood staining. Fingerprint powder used by the SOC officers is all about the floor and elsewhere and will take sometime to clean up, but right now, I'm exhausted and wish nothing more than to fall into bed.

I'm too exhausted to even undress and it's ironic that even as I collapse fully clothed on top of the duvet, I smell Cathy's fragrance on the pillows and tears bite at the back of my eyes as mercifully, I fall into a dreamless sleep.

Chapter 13

I had forgotten to draw the curtains and am awoken by the winter sun and the rain beating a tattoo against the single glazed bedroom window. The room is chilly and it's almost eight o'clock and my mouth feels like I've swallowed two day old socks. My bladder reminds me it's time to get the hell up and I stumble to the bathroom, fumbling with my trouser zip then unleashing a stream into the bowl that seems to go on forever. I close my eyes but the one name haunts my thoughts. Cathy. I try to shake my head clear, but consider that two Paracetamol and strong coffee might be a better solution. In the kitchen, regardless of the cold I tear off my shirt and throw it into the plastic washing basket then switch on the kettle. The small radio is set to Clyde 2 and I catch the news on the hour. The third item, behind a gas explosion and a football result, reports the police in Glasgow are investigating the discovery of a woman's body in the Craigpark Drive area of the city, but her name is not being released till the family is informed; the stock answer the Force provide to nosey journalists, but my experience is that usually somebody will get a back-hander for giving the press what they want. The kettle's boiled and I gingerly pour the steaming water into the mug over the coffee granules, surprising myself that my hand is shaking slightly.

I almost take my coffee into the lounge, intent on switching on the twenty-four hour BBC news channel, but at the door I again see the staining on the couch and rug and I falter and decide instead to sit on my bed. Drinking the coffee gives me time to think. I can't go to work today, so that will mean phoning in sick, then I remember that my mobile is sitting where I left it on the small table in the lounge and likely still switched on from when I spoke with the 999 police operator. I sit my mug down and try not to look at the blood stains when I fetch the phone that, as I thought, is out of battery life. I plug the phone into a socket in the hallway and almost immediately, a text message is received and I see it is from Gordon Roberts and was sent about an hour previously. The message simply reads: Call me g.

I think that maybe if I had been stronger yesterday and did as I had planned, met with Gordon and not been so concerned with keeping my job …. But as they say, hindsight is twenty-twenty vision and if I'm totally honest, the thought of again bedding Cathy was too powerful an incentive to meet her at the flat.

I make the decision to get cleaned up, first phone into work sick and then call Gordon.

Half an hour has passed and I'm feeling better. Shaved, showered and wearing a plaid casual shirt, black cargo pants and with a bowl of cereal in me, I use my now charged phone to call the company HR department and I speak to the laconic sounding Louise, telling her that I'm unwell and listen to her reciting the statutory regulations that I have to adhere to when off work and which she quite obviously is reading from a prepared script. Then she stops speaking and there is a slight hesitation in her voice.

"Tom, it says here that your home address is at 76 Craigpark Drive in Dennistoun, is that right?"

I'm immediately suspicious, but if it's in front of her on her screen, I can hardly deny it. "Is that a problem?" I ask, my throat tightening.

"Eh, no problem, but that's where the radio says that a woman was murdered last night," and I can hear the excitement in her voice. "Is that near where you live?"

"No, sorry, I didn't hear anything about that, but it's a long road Louise. Anything else you need from me?" I ask, keen to terminate the call without prompting further suspicion.

"No, you're all right, that all I need," she replies and I know by her voice that I haven't convinced her, that to use the old Glasgow vernacular, by lunchtime 'I'll be the talk of the steamie' or simply put, I'll be the top gossip item in the building, so God alone knows what they'll think when it emerges that Cathy Williams is the murder victim.

I phone Gordon Roberts and ask if he's free to speak and he tells me to give him a couple of minutes, that he'll call me right back. I wait patiently and within minutes, he's on the line and I'm guessing he's taking a walk round the building because I can hear traffic in his background.

"Sorry, Tom, I was in the office and had to take a walk," he confirms to me, "Am I hearing the right story? The Chief's twenty-four hour bulletin lists the murder of a woman in what I'm guessing is your flat. That can't be correct, surely?"

I hear the shock in his voice and take a deep breath. "Her name was Cathy, Cathy Williams. She was my boss at work. We were having, well. Let's just say I was seeing her."

"Are you a suspect?"

"Not as far as I'm aware at the minute, but you know the polis," I joked, "if they can't find the real killer, I'm sitting on the sub's bench. It's a DI called Graeme Fleming who has the inquiry and he's taken a statement from me."

There's a definite pause as Gordon digests what I've told him then he asks me, "The other business, is there any movement with that issue?"

"I'll need to speak with you about that Gordon. The only thing is I don't want to put you in a position where you might get yourself into bother…" but I might as well have saved my breath.

"Bollocks!" he berates me. "Remember this young Tom, the polis is the hunters not the hunted, so don't try to be teaching me what I already know, okay?"

I grin into the phone and we agree when his shift finishes we'll meet at the Wetherspoons on the corner of George Square and St Vincent Street. "I'll be wearing a red rose in my lapel," he quips and hangs up.

I stand for a minute, preparing myself for what I know I have to do and reach into the cupboard under the sink for a large, black bin bag, a spray bottle of bleach solution and a pair of Marigolds. The lounge window I opened has allowed a draft of cold air into the room so the sweet smell of dried blood, well known to operational police officers, has in the main dispersed. The first thing I do is dispose of the rug into the bag, feeling slightly guilty as if I'm throwing out Cathy's lifeblood, then I liberally spray the couch and with a torn hand towel, rub hard at the stains till at last the leather is clean or at least as clean as I can get it. I must have done a good job because the wide area I've rubbed with the bleach solution is actually a little lighter than the surrounding leather. The rag and Marigolds go into the black bin for dumping later. The second hand Hoover I bought at the Sally Army shop deals with most of the SOC fingerprint dust and after a hard hours graft, I'm as satisfied as I can be that the room is back to normal. Normal? What am I saying? The fucking room will never be normal, it's the place where Cathy was murdered and I sit wearily down on one of the armchairs and stare helplessly at the couch, knowing I've really no choice. I fetch my mobile from the kitchen and phone the Council cleansing department to arrange a street-side pick-up and told Friday at the earliest, that all I have to do is get the couch downstairs to the pavement before nine in the morning. I grab the bin bag and head downstairs, dump the bag in the bins at the back then knock on the Ahmed's door. Missus Ahmed, eyes betraying her nervousness, smiles through the crack in the door and shouts young Iqbal to come and translate.

"Actually, it's you I'm looking for son," I smile at him. "Can you give me a hand to bring a couch downstairs? I want to get it to the pavement to be collected by the cleansing on Friday."

Iqbal utters something to his mother then walks with me upstairs and I know he's desperate to ask. I pre-empt his questioning look by commenting, "You know the police were here yesterday?"

He nods, his face betraying his curiosity. "They not arrest you Mister McEwan?"

"No Iqbal. There was a lady killed in my flat, but it wasn't me who killed her and the police will investigate. You understand investigate? Ask questions?"

He nods, but something in his eyes betrays his apprehension and I can't quite put my finger on what it is. He's a bright lad and I suspect he'll tell me in his own good time. I lead him into the front room and his head swivels on his shoulders, the relief on his face evident and with a jolt, I believe it is him seeing that the body is gone.

"Right, son, think you can manage this?"

He smiles and flexes his muscles or what passes for muscles, because I've seen thicker knots in thread. Between the two of us, me taking the weight of the couch on the down stair side, we hump the couch to the first landing, take a break and continue to the ground floor landing where we again take a break and sit on the couch armrests. I glance at Iqbal and see he's itching to ask more questions, so smile and ask him what's up?

"The detective, he say to me that you are killer, that you kill girlfriend and if we don't watch out, you will kill us all in the close," then screws his face up into a grin and continues, "but I do not believe him Mister McEwan. I think he make it up to scare us only."

I almost know before I speak, but ask anyway. "What did he look like, this detective?"

Iqbal puffs out his cheeks and extended his arms to each side, indicating the girth. It has to be DC Craig, the fat bastard.

"Are detectives not supposed to write things down, Mister McEwan?"

"Why do you ask, Iqbal?" I nod for him to again lift his end.

"When I tell the detective about the woman, he did not write it down. Should he not maybe write it down, Mister McEwan?"

I felt a chill run through me and almost drop my side of the couch, but instead I stop and forcing myself to smile, lower my end, indicating Iqbal should do the same. "What do you mean, telling the detective about the woman, Iqbal?" He slowly lowers his side of the couch and a sudden fear appears in his face. I put my hands up and continue to smile in an attempt to reassure him. "Its okay son, don't worry. You're not in trouble or anything. No one will know what you tell me, I swear. We're friends aren't we Iqbal? Good friends?"

He glances at his front door and I'm afraid that he will run through it, that I won't get to hear what he has told Craig, but he remains standing and fearful, his eyes wide-eyed as he stares at me. I need to gain his trust. I again sit on the couch armrest and try to give the impression I'm relaxed and not a mad killer like Craig has portrayed me.

Soothingly, I ask again, "What did the detective say to you, Iqbal?"

"The fat detective man, he not really listen to what I say. He tells me that the case is over, solved I think he says."

"So what did you say, Iqbal, what did you tell him?" I urge.

"I tell him that I see the woman. She get out of taxi and come into close door. I do not see her after that."

I relax, realising that what the lad saw wasn't really of evidential value for after all, nobody disputes that Cathy arrived at my flat and when the Hackney taxi driver is traced, the record of the trip will confirm the drop-off time.

"And the man, I see him when he leave, but not see him arriving."

There's that cold chill streaking down my back again. Any more shocks like this and I'll need to wear a fucking vest. I swallow hard and quietly ask, "What man, Iqbal?"

His brow furrows as he concentrates and replies, "I don't know him, Mister McEwan. He not live in close. I'm at window watching for mother and sisters to arrive from ASDA to help with the shopping, you understand? I hear close door bang and a big man come out. He leave the close, but at first I did not see where he go."

"Did you see the man's face at all? Can you tell me what the man looks like?"

He shakes his head and repeats, "Big man," extending his hands to show wide shoulders. "He have his back to me." His brow furrows then he excitedly says, "He stopped at the path onto pavement. He bends his head down," and shows me what he means by almost bowing, "and he does something with his hands, but I not see what."

I'm thinking that the man was pressing a car key remote, the Punto car key remote.

"Then he walk that way, fast," says Iqbal and with his arm extended, indicates to the left and coincidentally, where the Punto was still parked twenty yards away. "Then he come back fast and get into car, a dark car."

"What kind of car was it Iqbal? Can you remember the make of the car or what kind of model it was? Or the colour or anything?"

"No, I not recognise the car," he replies and his face screws up as if in surprise. "That is funny for me."

"When was this, Iqbal, can you remember the time?"

"It was just when Mastermind was beginning on TV and that start at four o'clock," he proudly tells me.

I smile in return, but the enormity of what Iqbal has witnessed is just hitting me. The lad has likely seen both the arrival of Cathy and the departure of her killer. And all this, I grimly consider, was told to a police detective who dismissed it because he has decided that I'm the number one suspect and the case is already solved. Bastard! But I can't disclose this information to Graeme Fleming because to do so would not only identify Iqbal as a witness, but if the killer learned of Iqbal's sighting, it might put the lad in jeopardy and right now I have a strong suspicion that the killer just might have access to every facet of the police intelligence network.

"Right," I wink at Iqbal, as an idea crosses my mind, "let me see if you can earn yourself a couple of pounds by helping me get this couch out of the front door and into the street and then I want to show you something on my laptop."

I arrive early for my meeting with Gordon Roberts at the palatial former bank that is now Wetherspoons and find an empty table in the crowded bar that gives a good and unobstructed view of the entrance. I like Wetherspoons for a number of reasons, but primarily because the bar staff are usually very friendly and they serve drink and food at an affordable price and don't rip off their customers like other city hostelries. I've left the Punto in Craigpark Drive and treat myself to a pint of a particularly, potent real ale and order a double Glenmorangie, no water, for Gordon. He arrives a few minutes late, apologising and explaining that he had been caught up in a flap at the office, but doesn't disclose anymore.

"The lassie that was found murdered in your flat, Cathy Williams. More than a friend from what I'm hearing," he begins and gives me a knowing look.

I nod and sipping at my pint, wonder at the police gossip machine then spend the next fifteen minutes giving him a second by second account of my leaving the office and expecting to find Cathy in my bed, but instead discover her murdered. I relate the circumstances and the subsequent arrival of the police. I leave out nothing and conclude with my interview by DI Graeme Fleming, who isn't known to Gordon, though he recognises the name from the police bulletin that passed through his office. I continue with my realisation that the car keys had been stolen, presumably by the killer and the finding of the murder weapon in the boot of the car and my unshakeable belief that Cathy was murdered to frame me. Gordon is shocked and I see concern etched in his face, the question forming in his mind as to why I haven't disclosed the finding of the machete?

"For one simple reason, Gordon, because I believe that your mob, police intelligence I mean, is compromised."

He stares wordlessly at me then slowly shakes his head. "I can't possibly vouch for everyone in my department, Tom and to be frank, some of them are asses, but what you're suggesting is criminal activity. So, how do you arrive at this conclusion?"

The next ten minutes is spent telling him about my clandestine visit to Jo-Jo Docherty's house, but without the boring details of me falling on my arse and wearing gravy on my face. When I relate seeing Ina and her badly beaten face, Gordon is holding his whisky glass and I'm watching his knuckles turn white and almost afraid that the glass will shatter as his fist tenses.

"I think Ina has been forced to disclose who we are, Gordon and that is why I was targeted for murder. Docherty and Burns now know we're not cops and probably aren't too worried about us, particularly if they thought I was getting the jail for murdering Cathy," I bitterly burst out.

A couple of pensioners at the adjoining table turned to stare at us, but merely smiled when Gordon tells them, "He's always talking about killing that wife of his."

"Sorry," I mumble to him as he gives me a reproving glance.

"So, what makes you think there's a leak in the Intel department?"

"It stands to reason, doesn't it?" I hiss at him, conscious now that I should really be keeping my voice down. "Burns feels safe being driven about by Docherty because either he or Docherty knows when the surveillance will be targeting Docherty. Ina has never met me before, but somehow or other, they get my address and either one of them or someone they send comes after me, but kills Cathy instead, then tries to set me up. They've obviously believed if I'm arrested for murder then who is going to listen to my fairy-tale about a dead man living with Jo-Jo Docherty."

He slowly shakes his head and replies, "You have to admit Tom it's a bit tenuous, is it not? I mean, you can't surmise there's a leak based on just that."

I sit back and stare at him. "How else would you explain it then?"

"I admit, the bit about Docherty running around with a wanted man in his car when at any time he could be subjected to surveillance, there's some credence there. But how would they get your address? I send you a Christmas card every year and I have to refer to an old diary that Wilma keeps. And by the way," he points a forefinger at me, "I don't get one back."

"Sorry. About the card, I mean. Look, I can't explain the address thing, but with the network the police have, it can't be that difficult, can it?"

I sit finishing my pint while Gordon brings another round.

"You know that it is unlikely that Burns will be staying at Docherty's place and that he'll have got out of there pronto if he knows you're still kicking about?"

"The thought has crossed my mind," I reply, nodding my head in agreement. "He'd be an idiot to hang about now." I take a sip at my pint. "One thing that puzzles me Gordon, the question we've not asked ourselves. Why is Burns back? If memory serves me correctly, he isn't married though I recall he was fond of the birds, he hasn't any kids that I know of and his parents are both dead, so it's not as if he's homesick. I'm guessing that when he was robbing security vans he made a pile of money and I suppose he stashed some of the money away, but when you're on the run, that will soon fritter away on high living, expenses and accommodation. Burns got out of the country in a hurry and he couldn't have had the opportunity to take much with him, so whatever money he did take with him must have been used by now. But to come back here when he knows he could be recognised and arrested? That's just plain madness unless he's now so desperate for cash, he's returned to his old hunting ground where he knows the area and where he will be protected and hidden while he's committing crime. To your knowledge is there any Cash in Transit robberies in the recent past or maybe something along those lines?"

Gordon slowly nods and sips at his whisky, smacking his lips together, his eyes narrowing as he considers my question. "We've had a spate of post office cash delivery hold-ups in the last month, four if I remember correctly that were spread out across the West of Scotland region; two in our area, one in the Central Scotland Police area and one in the Lothian & Borders area. We were thinking that it was a new team. There's two of them, well organised. The main man wields a sawn-off to threaten the cash couriers. A second man grabs the cash cassettes and nearby, there's a get-away car parked with the engine running. My boss, DI Danny McBride is coordinating the Inter-Force inquiries, but to be honest," he gives me wry grin, "Poet Burns would never have been considered a suspect. After all," he chortles, "the man's dead, isn't he?"

We sit for a few minutes in comfortable silence then Gordon asks me, "So, what's your next move Tom? Are you still intent on tracking down Burns on your own? Or will you consider some professional help from the Force? You know I'm more than willing to back you in anything you decide, but with this new development and you a possible target for murder, my advice has to be that you tell the cops what you know and let the polis deal with tracking him down."

"Maybe," I reply, "but before I make that decision, how exactly do you contact Ina?"

Chapter 14

I catch a taxi home just ten minutes before nine PM that evening, two and a bit pints of the strong ale under my belt and more sober than tipsy because I'm now worried that having failed to kill me, I might still be a target. I have ignored Gordon's protest that I either stay with my folks or go back and use his spare room. Nonetheless, my decision to return to the flat doesn't mean that I won't take precautions and I get the taxi to drop me off at the corner of Duke Street and Craigpark Drive, then take my time walking in the drizzly rain to the close mouth, alert to any movement within the parked vehicles or anyone standing loitering. As it happens, the road seems clear of maniacal killers lurking in the dark and I breathe a sigh of relief when I insert the key into the lock and let myself into the chill of the close. I stand and listen intently, my heart racing in my chest, but there's no sound and I climb the stairs ready to either bolt or defend myself against unexpected attack. But there's nobody there. I check the small, unobtrusive wedge of paper I left jammed low down in the hinge side of the door and see that it's not been disturbed. Why, you may ask? It's because I know that the spare Yale key Cathy had pinched and used to get in yesterday was not among her possessions, leading me to conclude that the killer has taken the key along with the car keys, when he has made off. I ease open my front door and let myself in. The flat sounds ominously quiet and just to be sure, I check each room and satisfy myself that I'm alone.

First stop is the kitchen where I boil a pot of water and prepare myself a ready-mix pasta dinner. The radio is playing classics from the eighties and I hum along to the tunes, trying to block the image of Cathy from my thoughts. You might think I'm heartless, that within a single day I've moved on and already dismissed her from my mind, but you can't be more wrong. I lean on the worktop and first my hands, then my whole body involuntarily shakes. I tense myself, recognising that I'm about to weep but whether its grief or me being maudlin because of the alcohol, I'm not certain. I smile when I remember the first time I took Lisa to meet my parents, my mother embarrassing me by telling her that I used to cry at the slightest thing and in particular sad films. The memory seems to

calm me and I'm no longer shaking. I finish making the meal and pouring a glass of milk, take them both into the lounge and switch on the television. I try to ignore the space where the couch had been and which now sits forlornly on the pavement outside the tenement. The BBC Scottish news broadcast doesn't come on till almost the half hour and rather than suffer the antics of some overpaid celebrities discussing themselves, I spread the local 'Glasgow News' on the low coffee table and read as I eat. Cathy's murder is on page two and her face stares at my from a good sized photograph, captured with her husband at a function. I guess that some friend or neighbour has earned a back-hander for providing the reporter with the snap. I stare at them, both dressed in evening wear and smiling for the camera, surprised that he is almost as handsome as she is lovely and wonder what their relationship was like. The article by the News' chief crime reporter Alistair 'Ally' McGregor begins with an overall view of Cathy's home life, that she was much loved by her businessman husband and two teenage sons, aged thirteen and fifteen years, then read with increasing anger that Cathy is described as a woman who reputedly had multiple affairs, that police suspect a jealous lover killed her and the Craigpark Drive flat she was discovered in is rented by one of the lovers, a work colleague and former police officer.
Great!
The bastard stopped just short of naming me. Of course, while I suspect there is a strong likelihood that someone in the Force tipped off McGregor, the reporter has fallen back on the standard phrase much loved by all the Press, the mysterious and unnamed 'police source'. I sweep the paper off the table in disgust, yet worried that I'll be plagued by reporters looking for the inside story, as they call it. I'm just about to start my meal when the front door is knocked loudly. I take a sharp intake of breath and wonder who is calling at this time of night, suddenly thinking that it might have been prudent to keep a large and heavy stick beside the door. I leave the hall light switched off and tip-toe to the front door, lowering my head slightly to peer through the eyepiece. I'm stunned when I see who is standing there and take a second look, just to convince myself. The stair head light illuminates Lisa, whose fist is raised to knock again when I jerk the door open.

"Well, hello, this is a surprise," I tell her, inwardly cursing myself for coming out with such a stupid comment. Her hair is tied back and she's wearing a warm, dark grey coloured polo neck sweater, navy blue jeans and short, black leather ankle boots, a black leather handbag slung across her left shoulder, carrying a waterproof jacket across her arm and seems to be clearly ill at ease. "I drove by earlier, just after seven, but your front room light was out and I didn't think you were home."

"No, I only got in half an hour ago. I was meeting Gordon Roberts," I explain, wondering why I feel the need to do so and thinking that she could not have looked lovelier than she does right now.

"Ah, yes. How is Gordon these days?"

"Fine," I reply then shake my head and self consciously smile. "I'm sorry, Lisa, I wasn't thinking. Please, come in," I invite then close the door behind her. She stands nervously in the hallway till I point her towards the kitchen and follow her in. I've chosen the kitchen because I'm reluctant to take her into the lounge, where it happened. I switch on the kettle, taking it for granted she'll at least wait for a coffee.

"My father was at the golf club this afternoon. Spoke to one of his police cronies and couldn't wait to get home to tell me about..." she paused, then grimaced, "about what happened. How are you?"

"Not great, but maybe better than I deserve," I reply, surprising myself with my own honesty.

Her eyes narrow and she leans back against the worktop, arms folded and asks, "How do you mean?"

"The woman who was murdered here, Cathy Williams. I don't think it was Cathy the killer intended to kill."

Lisa's face pales and I can see she is shocked. "But the newspaper said ...."

"Yes, I'm aware of what the papers said," I bitterly retort, then immediately regret it. "Look, I'm sorry. I'm not getting at you. There will probably be a load of shit bandied about in the papers in the next couple of days, but believe me, it will be nothing like the real story."

The kettle clicks off and I turn away to pour the water into the mugs and give me the opportunity to gather my thoughts. I stir the mugs and offer Lisa hers.

"So, what is the real story, Tom? Was she a girlfriend? Or was she more than that?"

I smile without humour and wonder why it is that women have this need to put labels on relationships?

"Cathy and I worked together or rather, she was my boss. Last week, she took an interest in me and we met a couple of times."

"Here?"

I nodded. "Yes, here."

"The papers say she was married."

"I knew that, but she didn't talk about her marriage." I almost add that we didn't talk about anything, really, just shagged each other like rampant bunnies, but right now, Lisa is the one person I don't want to piss off. "She kept her private life. Just that," I diplomatically tell her, "private. The relationship was ..." I search for the correct word, "physical."

"Physical," she repeats and softly exhales through gritted teeth, then takes a sip of her coffee. "Like Alice?"

She doesn't sound bitter, but then again, what do I know about women and I have to admit I didn't see that one coming and decide on some more honesty and a little humility. "Look Lisa, I don't have to explain myself to you any more," I begin, not intending to but hearing my voice rising a pitch or two, "You've moved on and you have your own life to lead, as you've made that perfectly clear to me."

I decide not to mention this guy Andy, knowing that will be a step too far and leaving me open to accusation that I'm asking the girls about their mother's male friends and I don't want my comment about 'not having to explain myself' thrown back at me. "Alice was someone that I thought I cared for. I realise now on hindsight, I was mistaken, that I completely misjudged my feelings for her and any feelings I had were based more on sympathy than, than ..." I falter, not wanting to use the word love. "I confused my sympathy for genuine feelings and I've paid the price. It cost me more than just my job."

She glances away rather than look at me, then says, "And this woman Cathy?"

I shrug and sip at my own coffee, trying to find the right words to explain. "Cathy was someone that needed me more than I needed her. I was a distraction for her, nothing more."

She softly smiles and shakes her head. "I've called you a few choice names in the recent years, Tom McEwan, but I've never thought of you as a distraction."

We stand facing each other in silence and I sense that like me, Lisa is unwilling to start a war.

"I'm grateful you came by," I break the silence. "It was kind of you."

She half turns to place her mug on the worktop and again shakes her head. "I didn't want to tell you on the phone, thought it better if I visit personally, but I don't think it's a good idea the girls visit you here, at least not for the foreseeable future."

I nod in agreement, but don't tell her that had also been my thought. The last thing I want is my daughters caught up in a confrontation between me and a killer. "You won't mind if I maybe collect them from you, somewhere you're happy to hand them over and for me to take them to my parents?"

"I'll be happy to drop them at your mum and dads house, if it makes it easier for you," she suggests.

I agree that will be helpful and we lapse again into silence.

"How dangerous is the risk to you?" she unexpectedly asks and I'm surprised because I see what looks like concern in her eyes. I don't want to tell her the whole, sordid story yet I'm reluctant to end the visit, so I summarise, instinctively knowing I can trust her. I tell her about meeting Mike Farrell and seeing Robbie Burns, whose name she recognises from the aborted robbery and murder of Alice. I tell her about meeting with Gordon Roberts who in turn arranged the meeting with Ina and her confirmation that Burns is alive, but not of my night-time visit to Docherty's house. I tell her of Cathy visiting me and stealing my house key, then returning finding Cathy dead in my flat, but not how she was dressed. That might be just too much information, I reckon. I tell her of my interview by Graeme Fleming, another name she recognises from my surveillance days and before I know it, an hour has passed and I'm offering her another coffee.

"No, thanks, it's late and I'm working tomorrow," then slipping her bag strap over her shoulder, turns to walk to the front door. I grab at my anorak from the hook and she stares curiously at me.

"Call me old fashioned," I smile at her, "but I'll be happier if you let me walk you to your car," I grin at her rather than suggest there might be a murdering psycho waiting outside with a replacement machete. I pull open the close door and walk out in front of her, then decide to go for it. Ask the question that has been bugging me. "So, anybody in your life right now?"

"Andy's just a friend, Tom. We've dated a couple of times and that's it."

"Andy?" I reply, feigning innocence but I know she's seen right through me.

"We're raising two smart young girls, Tom. Think they didn't catch on when they mentioned his name and you got all curious?" But she's smiling and I'm relieved that she's not angry, but I don't understand why I should be so pleased she's not annoyed. She gets into the Volvo and lowers the driver's window, but I'm eager to keep the conversation going and ask how the old bus is doing?

"Dad's a pain in the arse about it, keeps urging me to upgrade to a new car, but it's comfortable and I feel safe driving it. Yes, its doing okay," she says, patting the steering wheel then stares quizzically at me. "What did you mean, earlier on when you said that your mistaken sympathy for Alice cost you more than just your job?"

I stare at her, having forgotten how Lisa was always able to so easily blindside me and grope again for the correct thing to say. I shake my head and once more decide on honesty. I shake my head and finally admit to her, "It cost me you."

She doesn't respond, just stares back at me.

"Right," I stand up and slap the top of the car, "I'd better let you get going then."

She reaches through the window and gently massages my arm.

"Don't ask me why I should worry, you two-timing sod, but please be careful. Take care of yourself. The girls need their dad," then wound up the window and drove off.

I stare after the car and I'm thinking to myself, but what about you Lisa? What do you need?

As you will have guessed, the pasta is congealed and beyond recovery, so I make do with some toast and cheese, maybe not the best thing to eat last thing at night, and a refreshed cup of coffee. I intend catching the late night news and absent-mindedly check my

mobile phone to discover there's a new text message that reads:
7pm meet at same plce as 2nite. G
So, he managed to contact Ina. I'm pleased and hoping that
Docherty doesn't have a barman working in Wetherspoons too.

Chapter 15

I don't know if it was the cheese or my conscience catching up
with me, but the night is punctuated with bad dreams, the worst
being a scantily dressed, Cathy, her face dripping blood and
reaching out to me, panic in her eyes as Lisa pursues her with a
large machete. I wake up in a cold sweat and stumble to the
bathroom to urinate. Curiously, though I'm shivering I need a glass
of water to cool me down.
The morning light wakens me before the alarm clock and I lie for
half an hour, turned away from the window, my eyes closed tight
and try to sleep, but to no avail. Reluctantly, I surrender and get up
feeling cheated and fetch a coffee through to the lounge to catch
the BBC 24 News Channel. More unnecessary deaths in
Afghanistan, rioting in the Middle East and a multiple shooting in
Florida dominate the news. I switch to the eight AM local news, a
two minute summary that begins with allegations of further
corruption in Scottish politics and the Edinburgh nearly-tram
system, but nothing about a poor unfortunate woman who met her
demise in a flat in the East End of Glasgow. It seems then that
Cathy Williams is no longer newsworthy.
The mobile phone rings, but I don't recognise the incoming
number.
"Hello?"
"Mister McEwan, its Louise from HR. Are you free to speak?"
I recognise Louise as the girl I spoke to when I called in sick. I'm
immediately suspicious because of the formality, recalling the last
time we spoke she called me Tom. "Louise, what can I do for
you?" I pleasantly ask her.
"I'm sorry to have to tell you," she begins, her voice betraying her
nervousness and in a rush tells me, "I am instructed by the HR
manager to inform you that in light of recent events that occurred

and featured in the media and the involvement of the police that you are hereby notified as of today's date that the company is suspending you without salary, pending further inquiry and a letter to this effect will be posted to you outlining the circumstances of your suspension."

I listen and am of the opinion she is reading from a prepared script. I keep my cool and my voice level and ask to speak to the HR manager who I suspect is sitting beside her and coaching her through the call.

"Sorry, but Mister Henderson, the manager is unavailable," she replies.

"Okay Louise," I reply, "I know that you are only doing your job and I have no issues with you personally. However, will you please inform Mister Henderson that as he is the company representative who is seemingly instigating the suspension and under whose instruction you are issuing me with the suspension, that subsequent to this call it is my intention to visit my lawyer and relate the circumstances of your call. Please also inform Mister Henderson," I continue, my blood now racing through my veins and my head pounding and suspecting Henderson is probably listening in with a headset, "that I am a vital witness in the police inquiry being conducted to trace the killer of our mutual colleague Missus Williams and I intend instructing my lawyer to issue a writ against both the company and Mister Henderson as an individual for defamation of my character by suspending me when clearly, I have done nothing wrong."

Okay, I know I'm maybe overstepping the mark about a 'writ' and me being a 'vital witness', but if it puts the shits up these buggers, then it will give me some satisfaction.

I hear what sounds like a distorted cry, then Louise, sounding like she is stifling a giggle, says, "I'll pass your message on, Tom," and I just know the story will be round the office within the hour.

I'm about to press the red End button when Louise quickly whispers, "It was the polis that was here that told them you killed Missus Williams, Tom, a fat guy with bad breath. He tried to give me a line of patter, so he did and him wearing a wedding ring too. Oh, oh, better go," then the line went dead.

I'm angry, really angry and feel like throwing the mobile through the window, but stop. Of course, I don't have the money to hire a lawyer to fight my case against an large organisation like the company, but then a thought strikes me and I fetch the card that Mike Farrell gave me from the inside pocket of my jacket. 'Martin McCormick & Co. Legal Services' reads the card with a Glasgow telephone number. Seems that I might have use for Mister McCormick after all, I muse.

I call the number listed on the card and speak to a young, cheerful sounding woman who informs me that Mister McCormick is at court, but takes my number and promises she will get him to phone me back.

I sit and stare at the phone, still angry that I'm suspended and decide a bath might be the answer to my headache.

I might be living alone, but it never ceases to amaze me that the house can get so untidy and the rest of my day is taken with washing clothes and general tidying up. It is when I'm stripping the bed I again I smell a hint of Cathy's fragrance and feel a little guilty when I stuff the duvet cover and pillows into the washing machine, imagining that in some way I'm washing her from my life. Stupid, I know but when you are alone with your thoughts, a million little things that seem to be petty cross your mind.

My chores completed, I sit with a coffee and consider tonight's meeting with Gordon and Ina.

I make the decision to get there early and find myself somewhere to sit and watch for Ina's arrival and try to clean-sweep her. I know it's unlikely that I will recognise anyone tailing Ina who works for Docherty, but after seeing the Irish barman at Docherty's house, I'm trusting that my instinct for noting anyone who seems suspiciously like a bad guy might kick in. If nothing else, it's worth a shot.

The only other thing I worry about is that Gordon's trust is misplaced and that Ina herself is a bad guy.

What, with the washing and ironing, the morning soon passes and it's just gone three in the afternoon and I'm catching up with Sky Sports when the mobile rings.

"Hello?"

"Mister McEwan, its Martin McCormick. Is that the same Tom McEwan that Mike Farrell spoke of?"

"Mister McCormick, it is and thanks for phoning back," I begin, but he cuts me short and tells me to call him Martin.

"Did Mike tell you that I'm expanding my business and looking for someone to do a bit of legwork? Witness tracing, statement taking and I understand you have some surveillance experience?"

"Yes, he did say, but to be honest, employment wasn't the reason I called you today. Is there any likelihood I might pop by and seek your advice?"

I sensed some hesitation and he stuns me by replying, "Yes, of course. Would this be related to the unfortunate death of the lady in your flat?"

"You're very well informed Martin," I reply at last. "In a way it is. I'm not a suspect, you know that?"

"So I hear," he replies. "So, can you give me a brief outline of why you wish to see me?"

"My company have likely read the reports and been visited by my former colleagues, put two and two together and made five. I received a call early this morning suspending me without pay. In short, they've convicted me on the basis of media gossip."

"I sense some litigation here and I presume that you are seeking equitable remedy?"

"If you mean do I want reinstated and my salary refunded, yes."

"Give me a second," he tells me. I listen to the shuffling of some paper and then he says, "Tomorrow, ten thirty at my office? The address is on the card Mike gave you."

"Thanks Martin, I'll be there," I confirm and end the call.

I remember that Ina was early for the meeting in the Saracen Head and catch a passing bus on Duke Street that drops me in Ingram Street just after six that evening from where, with my anorak collar up against the drizzling rain, I walk the short distance to the corner of Queen Street and George Square and purchase a 'Glasgow News' from the vendor there. The wide and brightly lit entrance to Wetherspoons is on St Vincent Street, just off the Square and I find a doorway thirty yards away on the opposite side of the road. Commuter traffic at that time of the evening is heavy and the blanket of night has fallen, but I'm reasonably confident I will be able to identify Ina when she arrives. The problem is,

Wetherspoons is a popular venue with a stream of punters coming in and out of the entrance and I reluctantly concede I'm not in a good position. I change my mind and decide instead to try and find somewhere inside where I can better watch the coming and going of the patrons. Besides that I think, as I give an involuntary shiver, it'll be a lot warmer.

I get a pint of Tennents and decide to loiter on the side of the bar away from the toilets. Experience has taught me that the vanity of women arriving at a venue usually means they make a bee-line for the Ladies to find a mirror to repair the ravages of travel before they settle themselves at a table. I don't want Ina to greet me before I have the opportunity to check if she has acquired a tail. A couple vacate a table and I grab it before three young business suited women, who flash me huffy glances and pretend indifference as they retreat to a corner, their eyes predatory as they scan for a free table.

The 'Glasgow News' headlines are full of the usual stories of inner city mayhem and on page five, I find a quarter page paragraph by the reporter Ally McGregor that includes an appeal from DI Graeme Fleming for any information on Cathy's murder. My stomach clenches and the memory of it still hurts, finding her the way I did. I will have to accept that no matter what else occurs in my life, the memory might fade but will never go away.

It's now just gone six-thirty and the waiters are working like beavers, trying to keep up with the demand of customers who are filling the place as I watch. I see Ina, wearing her dark coat appear at the top of the entrance stairs and with a quick glance about her, predictably makes her way to the ladies toilets. Like a smart-arse, I inwardly smile with satisfaction at my assessment of women in general, but keep watching the entrance. A few minutes have passed and I'm still watching and see nobody that either I recognise or seems suspicious, when a hand taps me lightly on the shoulder.

"Hello Tom, got here before me then?"

So intent on watching the doorway I failed to see Ina approach me and I stand and pull out a chair for her to sit down. "Had time to kill, so thought I'd catch up with the news, Ina," I explain to her, pointing to the folded paper. "Can I get you a drink?"

"If you don't mind, I'll wait till Gordon gets here," she replies, leaning over and smiles as she taps me on the knee. I see fresh lipstick, her eyes are bright and she seems pretty animated. However, I can't help myself and stare at her face. Try as she has with women's war-paint, the bruising still shows through and the pupil of her left eye is bloodshot. I pretend shocked surprise and ask what happened to her?

"I had an argument with a door," she half laughs and cups her hand as though holding a glass and shaking it. "Stupid really, had a couple of wines too many and tripped going to the loo."

I weakly grin and smile as though believing her. We sit and chat about nothing in particular, waiting for Gordon who arrives a few minutes later, his face red from hurrying.

No greetings. No "Hello Ina" or "Hello Tom". No. His voice raised, he launches straight into it like a Scud Missile. "Look at your face, hen! Did that bastard Docherty set about you?"

I close my eyes and slowly shake my head, grateful that I'm not Jo-Jo Docherty and envisage the pain that Gordon has planned for him.

Ina, so composed up to now, bursts into tears and the crowd nearby quieten with a few angry stares directed at me and the enraged Gordon, who is completely oblivious to the hostility that now surrounds us as it seems the punters suspect we're to blame for Ina's distress.

"It's okay," I manically grin at the punters and think on my feet. "She's upset because she is going through a recent bereavement," I call out, thinking to myself I might not be too far off the mark if Gordon gets hold of Jo-Jo Docherty. Quick as a flash, the crowds' attitude changes and comments of "Poor soul," and "Shame for the lassie," are tossed at us then the crowd go back to their pints and halves.

Being the considerate gentleman I am, I produce a newly washed and ironed that afternoon handkerchief and Ina dabs at her eyes while Gordon fetches both of them a drink from the bar.

Ina sniffs, takes a deep breath and a long pull at her vodka and coke and thus once more composed, is ready to be grilled. I deflect Gordon's anger by changing the subject, telling him and Ina that today, I've been suspended from my job, but intend seeing a lawyer tomorrow morning. Gordon nods in understanding, but my employment problem washes over him and I can see he is still angry and turns to Ina.

"So tell us," asks a slightly more sedate Gordon, pointing at her face, "who did this to you?"

She shrugs and turns slightly to face him. "That night we met in the Sari Heed, it turned out the barman, Connor McLaughlin, worked for Jo-Jo and saw us talking together. When I got back to the house, Jo-Jo got a phone call from McLaughlin and asked me who the two punters I was drinking with were and then, out of the blue, smacks me one to the face and accuses me of touting to the cops. Sorry, boys," she smiles apologetically at us, "I get really frightened when he gets one of his rages on and I told him you were ex-polis and trying to hunt down his pal, Robbie Burns, but that I told you I didn't know where Burns is."

"He didn't believe you, then?" I pointed to her face.

"No, not at first, but I'm a tough old bird. He's not the first man to use me as a punch bag, Tom," she replies, almost with a hint of pride at her resilience. "He kept punching me, on and on while his fucking pal Poet sat in the chair, watching and egging him on," she spat out. "The only thing is, I had to give them something and I told them your names. I'm so sorry, Gordon," she reaches out for his hand as though seeking forgiveness.

He smiled at her, his face etched with concern and pats her hand in return as though calming a small child. "Don't you worry about it Ina. Tom and me, we're big boys now and we play by big boy's rules. So, what else did he want to know and what did you tell him?"

"He wanted to know how you had found out that Burns was back here and if you have told the polis, but I said I didn't know anything about that. He also asked me how I knew you two. I told him that when you were younger and worked the beat in my area, you had a wee fancy for me and that's how you knew me," she laughs at Gordon's reddening face. "I said that somebody must have given you my mobile number, that you had phoned me to ask for a meeting and that you wanted to see me about something important, but that I had no idea what it was and I went along, you know, for old times sake and because I was curious. I said that when you wanted to know about Robbie Burns, I couldn't tell you anything because I just didn't know anything."

I glance at Gordon and his eyes agree with me. Ina didn't give me up to Docherty and also likely didn't associate the murder of Cathy Williams with me. After all, how could Ina possibly know my home address? At least, she didn't at first, but then in a low voice I briefly tell her that the murdered woman in Craigpark Drive flat was my friend. She stares at me aghast. "Did he ask you anything about where we live?" I ask her, just to be certain.

Her face registers her surprise and I instinctively know she is telling the truth. "No, he didn't, honest to God Tom, nothing like that. Why would he want to know where you live?" then her eyes narrowed as if in understanding and she put a shaking hand to her mouth, "Oh, my God," she almost cries out, "oh no. The woman who got murdered? You think that Jo-Jo had something to do with that?"

I shrug and leave her to make the connection herself.

Again I glance at Gordon and it's the crunch question. I don't want to disclose to Ina that I saw Burns at Docherty's house because it will remind her that when we first had met with her at the Saracen Head, she claimed she didn't know where he was staying

"Do you know where Burns is staying now?" asks Gordon and I hold my breath, awaiting her response.

She throws back the rest of her drink and shakes her head. "He was kipping occasionally at Jo-Jo's the odd night here and then and when I saw you boys the last time, I couldn't say for certain where he was staying. Since that night Jo-Jo gave me a beating, when he heard you were looking for Burns and you took an interest, he stayed that night, but now he's left. But I think Jo-Jo took him somewhere else, somewhere safe."

The answer seemed to satisfy Gordon and in fairness to her, I suppose previously she didn't want to commit to saying he was at Docherty's. At last, not staying there full time as it where.

"Would you be able to get an address for him?" I ask.

She smiles humourlessly and leans slightly toward me. "Look at my face, Tom. I'm visibly battered. Do you want you want to come with me to the ladies and I'll take off my blouse and my bra and give you a Technicolor show of my tits that would put a rainbow to shame? I survived one kicking from Jo-Jo, but I'm not sure if I might survive another."

I swallow with embarrassment and shake my head. "Sorry Ina, I don't want to put you in any further danger. Honestly."

As she did with Gordon, she reaches out and clasps my hand. "I know, son, I know."

It's in my mind to ask why she stays with someone who beats her, but like I said, I have never understood women and Ina isn't the first that I've met who has remained with an abusive partner. Gordon insists on getting another round and while he is at the bar, I ask her, "Any idea what Burns is doing for money? Is Jo-Jo subbing him while he's back?"

She shakes her head. "Poet's got money, there's no doubt about that, but it'll not be Jo-Jo he's getting it from, for he's so tight that he doesn't give anything away and has to ask himself for permission to take a shit."

Her crudity causes me to laugh, or maybe it's the beer. "What about Jo-Jo. Is he up to anything in the recent past?"

She rubs at her chin and replies, "That's the funny thing. He isn't afraid of the polis and he doesn't seem to be bothered by them either. I heard him a couple of months ago talking on the phone and he was talking about a deal," she put her hands defensively up in front of her, "and before you ask, I don't get involved in his business. But whoever he was speaking to, I heard Jo-Jo tell the guy that there would be nothing doing on the Tuesday through to the Friday because the manky mob," she interrupts and smiles at me, "that's you lot I think. Anyway, what was I saying? Oh aye, that you lot were on the job and that Jo-Jo would phone the guy to tell him when it was safe to come on up. From England, I suppose he meant," she shrugs her shoulders.

My mind is spinning with all kind of thoughts. If what I'm hearing is correct, Ina has heard Docherty warning an associate that surveillance were operating on Docherty or his team on those particular days and that could only mean he was being tipped off and by someone with Intelligence knowledge of the operation.

"That's very useful, Ina," I tell her. "Thanks for that. But do you know if Docherty has any other houses or flats? Anywhere else that he owns that he might let Burns use to hide-out?"

Gordon returns and sets down a fresh drink in front of her. "Use? Rent, you mean," she snorts as she takes a swig of her drink and I realises that she's becoming slightly tipsy. It occurs to me then that

Ina might not have been completely sober when she arrived and is topping up her previous alcohol intake, as it were. "No, Jo-Jo doesn't do favours for nothing. If he's helping Burns to hide anywhere then he's getting something out of it. They might act all palsy-walsy, but," she replies at last and for the first time I notice she is slurring slightly, "they're not that tight. No, I can't think of anywhere else that Jo-Jo owns."

I'm thinking it's a dead end, that Burns must have made his own accommodation when Ina then adds, "Unless you count the caravan of course, but that will be closed up because Jo-Jo didn't pay the site fees this year. At least, that's what the miserable bugger told me."

Gordon's whisky is halfway to his lips, but he stops and stares at me. Caravan, I see in his eyes. What caravan?

"So, where exactly is this caravan?" he asks her.

"Well, when I say caravan, it's not got wheels any more, one of they, what do you call them, mobile phones?"

"Mobile homes," I correct her.

She giggles like a schoolgirl. "Aye, that's right, mobile home. Mobile phones, listen to me, I must be getting pissed," she giggles again.

Gently, Gordon probes again, asking where the caravan is located. "Down by the water, down past Gourock, what do you call the place again? The bay, you know, where you get the ferry over to Rothesay. Weymss Bay, aye, that's it; in the caravan site down there."

"There are quite a few caravan sites down that way Ina," Gordon comments and I'm happy to let him continue. "Can you recall the site name?"

"Eh no, sorry, but I've only been there once before Gordon and that was over a year or two past. All I remember is there's a turning off the main road before the ferry terminal and we went under a bridge and it's next to the water, along the shore road."

That is enough for me. It's a starter for ten, as they say and if the caravan site is there, I'll find it.

Gordon is worried that Ina might be getting drunk and smoothly suggests that as he hasn't had dinner yet, he order some food from and indicates with me to walk with him to the bar. Leaving Ina at the table, he pretends to read the menu, while asking me, "What do you think? Poet's holed up in Weymss Bay?"

"Possibly," I agree, "but certainly worth a wee run down there to find out."

We're interrupted by a smiling young girl to whom Gordon provides the table number and orders a meal each for Ina and him, as well as a strong pot of coffee.

"I think this is a job for the polis, Tom. You can't be risking yourself any further. Let me speak to my boss, Danny McBride. He's a good guy. Danny will organise a team to check the place out. If Poet is down there, there is a real likelihood he'll have a shooter with him and we both know he's fond of a sawn-off. Danny will be able to draw up an operational plan using me as the informant and I'll simply say it was a former tout that provided the information. That way, you get to stay out of it and don't run the risk of getting yourself killed. Besides," he grins suddenly, "you're in enough shite trying to extricate yourself from the lassies murder in your flat and if as you suspect you are the real target, who's to say they won't have another go at you, so you'll be as well to keep your head down meantime. Talking sense, aren't I?"

Of course he is making sense, but am I listening? No, I'm not because don't forget, I've made myself a promise that for what he did to Alice, Burns will pay and I also haven't forgotten what both he and Docherty, whether personally or by hire, did to Cathy. Have you thought I'd forgotten that?

So, I tell Gordon a barefaced lie by agreeing with him and arrange with him to be introduced to his boss, DI Danny McBride the following afternoon. Gordon is pleased and I feel guilty for deceiving him as he arranges to call me in the morning to firm up with a time and rendeavous for the meeting.

Paying for the food, we return to the table to see that Ina is making eyes at a couple of guys at the adjoining table and I realise yes, she is pissed. I'm worried that when she returns to Docherty she might be vulnerable to his questioning and express my fear to Gordon, who likewise is also worried Docherty might give her yet another beating.

"I know, I know. I can't let her go home to Docherty in this state," Gordon hurriedly whispers, glancing at Ina as he sits down, "so I'd better get her filled with coffee. As far as I'm aware, she still has her house in Balornock. I'll get her home to there and if I have to, lock her in for the night till she sobers up." He turns to me, "What about you? You'll be all right, I mean, you'll go straight home, but you'll check the place out first, right?"

I nod, pleased and a little touched with his concern for me and promise that when I'm safely locked in the flat, I'll text him. I leave the two of them, laughing together over a private joke and head into the rainy, damp night.

The flat is dark and cold and the first thing I do is turn on the central heating, shivering as I hang my anorak up behind the door. At least there isn't anyone with a weapon waiting to bludgeon me. The couple of pints I downed haven't really affected my judgement, but have sharpened my appetite and the fish supper I bought is now tantalising me. I zap it for a minute in the microwave and forget my upbringing as I attack it with my fingers. I burp and remember I've to text Gordon and send him a quick message. The digital clock in my bedroom tell me it's gone ten o'clock and I decided an early start tomorrow morning for my meeting with the lawyer means an early night and, making sure the door is secured and the key in the inside lock, I tumble into bed.

Chapter 16

The sound of mail being delivered wakens me and with a furry tongue and a full bladder, I realise I've slept well and thankful that I'm feeling relaxed. The mail is mostly the usual junk with a reminder my TV licence is due, but includes an envelope bearing the company logo inside of which is the letter confirming my suspension that informs me 'due to circumstances that bring the company into disrepute'. I slip the letter into the inside pocket of my jacket to ensure I don't forget to take it with me when I meet Martin McCormick later in the morning. That done I head straight for the bathroom, shave and brush my teeth while I'm showering. Me being a news-junkie, I keep meaning to get myself one of those waterproof shower-radios, but of course the road to hell is paved with good intentions. Dressed now in a clean, light blue shirt, navy blue tie and dark pin striped suit, I switch on the kettle and television in that order and turn to Sky news. As usual, international news takes precedence, but the report of a murder and attempted murder in Glasgow attracts my attention as a wet and bedraggled reporter standing outside what looks like a council tenement building in the north side of the city, vainly trying to keep an umbrella upright and wiping her wet hair from her face, grimly relates the discovery of a woman's body and a seriously injured man. The kettle whistles and I nip into the kitchen, but by the time I've returned to the lounge, the story has ended and we're into sports.

I leave the flat just after nine o'clock and decide that as long as I'm paying for it, I'll take the Punto and besides, I've a trip to make to Weymss Bay when I'm done with the lawyer. I drive to the Pollokshields area on the south side of Glasgow where the business card indicates Martin McCormick has his office premises and discover the place in what seems to have once been two shops, now knocked together, in the ground floor of a tenement building in Albert Drive. The freshly painted exterior seems to indicate the business is doing well and I'm mentally practising my speech to Martin McCormick when I push through the glass doors. I'm greeted by a young woman, dressed in what looks like a multi-coloured bell tent and seated behind a desk and whose smile is nearly as wide as her ebony face. Funny that, I'm thinking, just when you believe you are in complete control, how a smile of welcome can disarm you.
"Let me guess," she grins at me, then in what sounds like a sing-song Jamaican accent, says, "You'll be Mister McEwan for the ten thirty appointment?"
I must look surprised because Martha, telling me her name, then says I look like a policeman and asks me to take a seat and would I like tea or coffee?
"No thanks," I reply, smiling back at her and can't help notice that extremely rotund as she undoubtedly is, there is something very attractive about Martha.

I hear her speak into the intercom and inform McCormick I'm here, then his voice asking her to send me through. I'm pointed towards a door at the back of the office that in turn leads to a short corridor with three doors to offices off the corridor and an open door at the end of the corridor that I see leads into a brightly lit kitchen. McCormick stands at his office door, jacketless and shirt sleeves rolled to his forearms, wearing a red tie over his white shirt and a grin on his face. He is my height, short dark hair and clean shaven with piercing blue eyes and if his nose and athletic build are any kind of hint, I take him to be a rugby player.

"Pleased to meet you, Tom," he says and shakes my hand while offering me a seat with the other.

He sits behind his desk, a jumble of files to one side and a large mug on the other. I see the mug has a fair haired woman and two kids embossed on the outside. He catches me staring at it and says, "Helen my wife and our two tearaways, Philip and Paul and on that point, coffee or tea?"

I'm feeling relaxed and ask for a strong coffee, milk only. McCormick, or Martin as he insists I call him, presses the intercom and asks Martha to stick the kettle on. "So Tom, you said on the phone that you have been suspended. Have you received any official confirmation of the verbal notification yet?"

I hand him the letter that arrived this morning and he skims through it. His face is expressionless and I'm uncertain if I have a case. He audibly sighs and tosses the letter onto his desk.

"Standard scaremongering tactic, beloved by al companies," then explains, "bringing the company into disrepute. How the hell can you bring the company into disrepute if you haven't done anything?" He stares right through me. "I mean, you haven't done anything, have you Tom?"

I vigorously shake my head. "Cathy Williams, my boss. The deceased, yes, we were having an affair, if you call three liaisons an affair. But no, Martin, I'm not involved in her murder." Then an idea occurs to me. "As of now, will you consider me to be a client?"

"Of course."

"So, that means that anything said between us is subject to client confidentiality?"

"Yes," he slowly replies and leans forward, his hands flat on his desk and those blue eyes staring into mine, "but understand this, Tom. If you tell me anything that I deem to be outwith my jurisdiction as an officer of the court, I mean, if you suddenly here and now confess to a criminal act, I am duty bound to report it. So, before you say anything else that you might later regret, do you understand that?"

"Completely," I reply, "but relax. I'm not about to make a confession or anything, but I do wish to make you aware of circumstances that might later be used in evidence."

He sits back, his expression puzzled and clasps his hands behind his head. "Shoot," he says.

I start from the beginning and during the next hour, punctuated only by Martha bringing us two coffee's, describe my time in the surveillance unit, the disastrous operation that resulted in Alice's death and the ending of my marriage, my drumming out of the Force and subsequent employment with the insurance company, my first sexual encounter with Cathy Williams, my sighting a few short days before of Alice's murderer Robbie Burns and my phone call to the Spanish police and my attempts to track him down. I tell him of Gordon and our meeting with Ina Carroll and curiously, I see his eyes narrow, but he makes no comment and I continue with my narrative. I relate my night-time visit to Jo-Jo Docherty's house and my confirmation that Burns is alive then why, I can't explain it, but I'm conscious of my voice dropping almost to a whisper as I tell him about finding Cathy's body. I pause and finish my coffee, strangely affected by the retelling of the discovery. I continue with the interview by Graeme Fleming and he nods, commenting that he knows Fleming. He makes a notation on a notepad when I relate the discovery of the murder weapon and stops me to question why I didn't report the finding of the machete, but I can't look him in the face and don't have the courage to tell him that it is my intention to use it on Robbie Burns.

He makes further notes when I tell him of my suspicion that I was the intended victim of the murder and poor Cathy was simply in the wrong place at the wrong time. I finish my narration telling him about last night's meeting with Gordon and Ina, who admitted the beating she had endured from Docherty and Gordon and my suspicion that Burns is hiding in a caravan in Weymss Bay, of

Gordon's insistence I let the police handle it from this point forward.

He licks his lips, like people do when they are about to impart bad news. "Your friend, this woman Ina Carroll. What's her home address, do you know?"

I shake my head, puzzled by his question. "All I know is that it's in Balornock somewhere. Why do you ask?"

He pauses and a feeling of dread sweeps through me.

"This morning, the local news reported a woman was found murdered in the Balornock area. A man who was with her and is described as a former police officer was brutally attacked and taken to hospital. I know it might be coincidence," he says, reaching for a phone. "Give me a minute. I've a contact who might know more."

I watch as he dials a number then asks to speak with DCI Lynn Massey. A minute passes then he says, "Lynn, Martin here. Sorry to bother you at work, cuzz. Are you able to speak?"

I remember then that Mike Farrell told me that Detective Chief Inspector Lynn Massey is Martin's cousin.

He listens then asks, "The couple that was attacked last night in Balornock. Do you happen to know the man's name, by chance?"

Massey speaks and I hear him say, "It's to do with a client of mine," as he stares at me, "but trust me, please. It won't interfere with the inquiry and if anything, I'm certain if my client has any information about the attack he will be more than happy to impart it to you, but first I'd like to discuss it with him. Yes, yes, I see."

He frowns as he listens then thanks the Massey and hangs up, takes a deep breath and tells me, "I'm sorry to have to tell you this, Tom, but the woman that was murdered was Ina Carroll and your friend Gordon Roberts is currently in a coma at the Southern General Hospital."

I hang my head in my hands, unable to believe what has happened. Ina murdered and Gordon in a coma? I know that the Southern General Hospital is the Scottish centre for excellence for head trauma and only the most serious patients are treated there, so reason that his injury must be life threatening. My hands shake and I'm aware that Martin has left the office and returns with a glass of water. "Here, drink this," he orders and I throw the water down my throat and spilling some on my chin, the sudden chill making me gasp.

"Did she, your cousin, I mean, did she say if anyone is arrested?"

"No, all she said is that it's an ongoing inquiry and of course, as you heard, asked what my interest is. She's a good cop," he adds. "It might be worth taking her into your confidence. If you have a clear suspect, Tom …"

"But that's just it," I burst out and jump to my feet and knocking my chair over onto the floor, an uncontrollable rage overcoming my emotions. "I know, just know it's that bastard Burns and his sidekick who are involved. But did they kill Cathy? Did they kill Ina and hurt Gordon? Of course they did, but what proof have I got and believe me, the fucking polis, they'll ask because they need proof!"

But I don't need proof, a sudden clarity hits me. I've got a big fucking machete hidden in the boot of my car that doesn't need proof. All I need is to be within striking range of either of the bastards and they are getting it – straight between the eyes!

"Calm down, Tom," I hear a voice saying. It's Martin, his eyes betraying his alarm as the door bursts open and his secretary Martha, large as life and wielding a baseball bat in her podgy hands, fills the doorway. "You okay Martin?" she shrieks, looking from one to the other of us and clearly uncertain what to do.

"It's okay, Martha," Martin tells her, waving his hands to calm her, "It's okay. Tom here has just had some bad news. Honest, we're fine," then turns to me, "We are, aren't we, Tom? We're fine?"

I'm breathing like I've run a fast hundred yards and nod my head, the madness departing me as quickly as it arrived. "Yeah," I agree, "Yes. We're fine. I'm okay, honestly," then sheepishly bend to right the overturned chair. "Sorry," I awkwardly tell them both, then repeat, "Sorry."

We're standing there, the three of us and all I can think about is getting the fuck out of there, driving to Weymss Bay and finding Burns. Two minutes with him, that's all I'll need. Two minutes. Just me and Burns and the machete and I'll have the truth from him. Two minutes.

"Get the kettle on," Martin tells Martha and I turn to leave, but she stands firm in the doorway and the baseball bat is raised, a clear and visible warning that I'm going nowhere. At least not till Martin says so. I turn a questioning eye towards him and he shrugs. "You're my client now, Tom. Like I said, I'm an officer of the court so I can't condone you leaving here and committing a crime now, can I? And don't give me that look," he grimaces. "I'm too long in the tooth to ignore what's on your mind."

Suddenly I'm tired and just want to sit, so I do, heavily and wearily into the client's chair. Over my shoulder, I hear Martha close the door behind her and Martin sits down to face me.

"There's nothing I can do or say that will make this better, but if you take the law into your own hands, Tom, you're as bad as the bastards that hurt your pal. Take your counsels advice and let the police handle this. They have the resources and the intelligence network. You could not only get yourself hurt or worse, but if you interfere in an ongoing police inquiry, you might find yourself locked up."

Martha, using a well rounded buttock, pushes open then backs through the door and is no longer the friendly young women from when I arrived. She eyes me like I'm about to explode as she enters bearing a tray with a pot of tea and curiously, two china cups on saucers and a small plate of tea-biscuits.

"You calm down now, Mister McEwan?" she asks me.

I try a smile, but it's not returned and I simply nod my head.

"That is good, Mister McEwan. Martha very fond of Mister Martin here and I no like the thought of having to crack your head open," she tells me, then thrusting her nose in the air and her chin out, serenely wobbles her way out and closes the door behind her.

I stifle a grin and comment, "I don't like the thought either of her cracking my head open."

"Yours wouldn't be the first," Martin dryly replies. "Not all my clients behave themselves. So what's your next move Tom? Will you consider letting me call the police on your behalf?"

"Let me think about that," I tell him, slowly rising to my feet and trying my damndest not to project any kind of threat because the last thing I need is Martha coming to get me. Martin shakes his head and sits back in his swivel chair, both hands again flat on his desk.

"All I can do is caution you that if you take the law into your own hands, you will face the consequences. As you have so kindly appointed me as your legal representative," he says and without any kind of sarcasm, I'm pleased to note, "I will do my best to represent you if you do fall foul of the courts, but take note, Tom. I won't cover for you if you decide to tell lies. That's not the way I work."

"Noted," I reply and almost as an afterthought, say, "and thanks. For taking on the employment issue, I mean. Anything else, I'll give you a call."

Outside in the fresh air, I take a deep breath and consider whether to go straight to the SGH or travel to Weymss Bay. I don't even remember getting into the car, my head pounding with what has happened. I'm trying to come to terms with Gordon being at the SGH, blaming myself for involving him in this madness. I think about phoning Wilma, but know she won't be at home, but will be by his side at the hospital and I don't have a mobile number for her. Fuck me, but the more I think about it the more it seems to me I've become a character in some sort of low budget American gangster movie. But this isn't fiction, this is real. One of the few friends I've got left might die and the thought horrifies me.
I can't do any good at the hospital, so that leaves me just one course of action.
I'm going to find Robbie Burns.

Chapter 17

The rain stays away and the drive to Weymss Bay is uneventful and I slow down as I approach the area. I had already examined my trusty Glasgow A to Z, but the mapping didn't cover that far west and the local map on the Internet wasn't as specific as I had hoped. Ina had said that the one time she had visited the caravan site Docherty had turned off the main road, travelled under a bridge and the site was on the shore road. I'm travelling in a parallel route with the River Clyde to my right, so reason the shore road must also be on the right. The railway line that terminates at Weymss Bay ferry terminal also runs to the right of me, so again I reason I must pass under the railway line. I've passed through Weymss Bay a few times through the years, but really don't know the area that well and I happen upon a road on my right and drive into what seems to be a large and modern private housing estate. I spend about ten minutes slowly driving around looking for a tunnel, but the railway line passes to the north of the estate and there is no tunnel. Other than attracting some suspicious glares from residents, I learn nothing and backtrack to return to the main road. Then I spot a fallen traffic sign opposite the junction that informs me I'm turning onto Shore Road. I slowly continue towards the ferry terminal and see that the next right turn takes me onto a narrow road that suddenly dips low and almost immediately, I'm going through a short tunnel with the railway line passing overhead. The road is well maintained and a warning sign tells me 'Children Playing' and not to exceed ten miles an hour. A further larger sign welcomes me to the "Sunnyside Caravan and Leisure Park' with a list of tariffs and rules underneath and I convince myself this is the place. I drive through the narrow entrance into a neat, tidy and well laid out park of static and towing caravans and some that look like they are almost permanent homes. By that I mean the absence of wheels as they seem to be sitting atop small dwarf walls. I'm guessing that most of the owners have locked and packed up their caravans for the onslaught of winter, for there are few cars around and even fewer people. As I pass by, the office and shop premises at the entrance seemed to be closed, though likely visited daily. If Burns is here I'm thinking, he will have to use the entrance, particularly if the shop is closed and he needs to purchase groceries and decide that is my best option, to try and find a parking spot where I can watch the comings and goings from the site without attracting attention to myself. The car clock says it is almost two o'clock and I decide I'll find a shop in the small town and grab some water and a sandwich. I turn the car in a lay-by and drive out of the park towards Shore Road. I'm approaching the tunnel when I see a young guy on a bicycle coming toward me. The road leads nowhere but to the park and knowing I'm respectably dressed, I make the decision to speak to him. But before I flag him down, I wrestle a precious tenner from my wallet and turn on my brightest smile.

"Hello, there, I'm wondering if you could assist me please."

"Yes mate, what can I do for you?"

The kid's about seventeen years of age, lanky blond hair and dressed in jeans and an old khaki coloured work shirt and trainers that a poverty stricken third world teenager would have thrown away.

"I was in the park looking for a resident who owns a caravan there, but I'm afraid I don't know the pitch number and was wondering if you might assist. You do work there, yes?"

He slowly nods and I can see it in his eyes that he's slightly suspicious of me. "I'm not supposed to talk about the residents, mister. It's Data Protection, you know," he says with a hint of officialdom.

I'm thinking that he probably can't spell 'Data' let alone 'Protection' and reluctantly decide to give up my ten quid for a good cause. Then I remember what Ina had said about Docherty's failure to pay his site fees.

"You seem to be a smart young man, so I'll take you into my confidence," I softly whisper to him and almost laugh as he leans forward, his mouth and eyes widening and certain I'm about to impart something juicy. "I work for a debt collection agency and the person I'm looking for owns or rents a caravan here. His names in Mister Joseph Docherty, do you know him? It's worth a tenner if you do."

His eyes nearly pop out of his head, but whether at the mention of Docherty's name or the tenner, I'm not quite sure. However, he replies, "You mean Jo-Jo? Aye, mister, I know him. And you're right. He owes my boss money too. But he's not here the now. Well, I don't think he is, because I haven't seen his big motor at his pitch," he shakes his head, "just the other car."

I swallow hard and try not to show my excitement as I ask, "Other car?"

"Aye, a Ford Focus. A black one, a hire job I think. It's some old guy that's using the caravan. I don't know his name and the only time I saw him was when he came into the shop to get a Calor Gas replacement."

I'm guessing that anyone over thirty years will be an old guy to this kid.

"What number is Mister Docherty's pitch, son?"

"It's number one-one-nine, mister. It's down Cherry Tree Lane, third turning on the left past the office."

I'm about to thank the young guy when I see he's peering at the tenner in my hand and as I hand it over, I remind him, "This discussion is confidential, okay?"

"No problem, big man," he says, cheerfully tucking the money into the breast pocket of his shirt. "I don't like Docherty anyway, the guys a miserable bastard."

I smile because he's not the first to have told me that and as he cycles towards the park I drive away towards the village to collect what I need before I find somewhere I can hole up till darkness arrives.

A small grocer's on the main street does takeaway sandwiches and I buy a pack, some chocolate, a bottle of water and a local newspaper. On the counter is a small, cheap, plastic torch that comes with free batteries. Free because frankly the torch isn't worth what I pay for it.

The car park beside the ferry terminal is three quarter full, but still plenty of spaces available and I settle down with the intention of reading the paper, but I can't concentrate and worry about Gordon and what action I'll take when I face down Robbie Burns. As dusk settles about me, I decide to call the hospital and dial the phone inquiry service, then note the number. I'm about to dial when the bloody thing chirrups with an incoming call. The readout tells me it's Gordon Roberts. With relief I answer, "Hello, Gordon," but get no further because a man's voice interrupts and says, "Tom McEwan? Sorry, but I'm not Gordon. I'm using his phone that's how I got your number. Please listen and don't hang up."

I draw breath and the voice continues, "My name's Danny McBride. I work with Gordon. Hello? You there, Tom?"

"I'm here."

"Good. First things first, Gordon is stable at the minute. The neurological consultant has seen him and reckons the blow to Gordon's head narrowly missed a vital artery and tells me there is every likelihood he will pull through, but the damage is significant and he will require surgery. His wife Wilma and son and daughter are with him as we speak. Do you understand?"

"I get that," I reply, then ask, "but who did this to him? Who killed Ina Carroll?"

"I was kind of hoping you might have an idea about that," replied McBride. "I know that Gordon was meeting you last night. He didn't give me much detail, but said that he hoped to persuade you to meet with me, that you might have information for me."

"Did Gordon tell you what that information is Mister McBride?"

"Danny," he replies. "No, just hinted that he would need your permission before he could say any more, but if it is why he's been attacked and the woman murdered, then I really think you and I should meet Tom and the sooner the better."

I think fast, aware that if McBride has my phone number, technology these days is such that the longer he maintains contact with me might provide the police the opportunity to triangulate my signal and trace my location. But is my revenge worth what happened to Gordon and Ina, I ask myself? Am I so focused on getting Burns that they have become innocent casualties? I exhale loudly and remember that Gordon trusted this guy and if that is good enough for my pal, then it must surely be good enough for me.

"Mister Mc- I mean Danny. Does the name Robbie Burns mean anything to you?"

I hear a sharp intake of breath and then he says, "I know who you are Tom. I know about the operation when the young cop was killed. Burns was your target that night, yes?"

"That's right. After the murder he was reported to have fled to Spain and we, the police I mean, received word that he died in a car accident in a small town called Badajoz. Only he didn't. I saw him last week in a car in St Vincent Street. With Gordon's and Ina Carroll's help, I tracked him down to a house on the Strathblane Road owned by Jo-Jo Docherty. I presume that is a name known to you?"

"Oh aye," he replied then in a weary sounding voice, says, "Mister Docherty leads a charmed life."

"Probably because I suspect he is getting information from someone in your Intelligence network," I quickly respond, suddenly and unaccountably angry at this complete stranger. Or is it the police in general I'm angry with? I can't quite make my mind up. There is a slight hesitant pause then McBride asks, "You know this for a fact, Tom? Or is that speculation?"

The seconds are passing and I'm keen to end the call. "Something Ina Carroll told me, the night before she died," but I decide to keep this little gem to myself for really, though Gordon trusts this guy, I have no idea to whom McBride might pass this information and reason that in good faith, he might inadvertently tip off the bad guy.

"Do you know where Burns is right now, Tom?" he cuts into my thoughts.

I smile and think about the machete nestling the boot of my car. "I believe so, Danny and I'm about to go and have a little chat with him," then press the red button to end the call.

I drive slowly into the mainly darkened caravan park with just my side lights on and guided by the eight foot high lampposts, of which it seems only every third one is lit and presume this is to save power. I park the Punto on Cherry Tree Lane just short of the junction that will take me down to pitch number one-one-nine. I exit the car, stick the torch into my anorak pocket and retrieve the machete from the boot. Okay, you're wondering now, am I going to kill Burns or just cut him up a little? To be honest, I have no idea, but I do know I'm still inwardly carrying a rage and whatever I decide, he is about to suffer one way or another. I creep down the gravel slope as quietly as I can towards the caravan and using the shadows cast by its unoccupied neighbours, arrive unseen at the adjoining mobile home. The outline of a Ford Focus sits outside one-one-nine next to a small square of decking and the caravan front door is closed over. I crouch low and carefully make my way to the side of the caravan, working at controlling my breathing. I see lights are on inside, but the windows are covered by closed curtains and I can't hear any noise from within. I stretch to my full height and try to sneak a look through a crack in the curtained window, but all I see is someone, a man I think, lying down, his face turned away from me and apparently sleeping on the bench type seat under the opposite window. A fitted table top beside the man's feet is littered with beer cans and some newspapers. Being unable to see his face is frustrating, but I have to assume the man is Burns. The absence of noise convinces me that he is the caravan's only occupant and I make my decision. I will grab open the door, scream blue fucking murder to disorientate him and wave the machete to terrorise him. I'm annoyed that I didn't think to bring some plastic ties to secure his wrists, but there's no time to collect some now and I tip-toe onto the decking, hesitating as a loose plank squeaks under my feet, but still, there is no noise from within. Taking a deep breath, I try the door handle that easily turns and snatching open the door, thrust myself through while waving the machete in my right hand and scream, "*DON'T MOVE YA BASTARD OR YOU'RE GETTING IT!*"

The man doesn't move, doesn't even flinch. Then the sweet, sickly smell of blood assails my nostrils and in the poor light of the caravan, I see the massive head wound at the back of his head, the white of bone and grey brain matter splattered across his dark coloured polo shirt and the caravan wall.

The tension of the last few minutes, the adrenalin rush and the unexpected sight of his injury combine to nauseate me and I run outside and drape myself over the rail of the decking and vomit into the grass. After a minute or so, the wave of nausea passes and shaking, I wipe my mouth with a handkerchief and walk unsteadily back into the caravan. I try to turn the dead man onto his face, but the narrowness of the bunk means that his body weight carries him to the floor and he falls onto his back. Some of the blood and brain matter splashes onto my lower trousers and I stumble back, more with disgust than shock. I shake my head and stare into the open-eyed, surprised face of Robbie Burns and I'm now feeling completely deflated. There's nothing I can do for him and as another wave of nausea hits me, I stagger back to the door and out into the decking, the machete still hanging loosely by my side. A sudden movement twenty yards away attracts my peripheral attention and I stare at the young guy I had met earlier that day and who had cost me a tenner. He in turn stares at me, holding the machete and takes off into the darkness like a startled deer and whether by accident or design, I realise with a touch of irony that I have just become the number one suspect for the murder of the former deceased Robbie Burns.

Chapter 18

It takes me seconds to realise the predicament I'm in and within minutes I'm on the Shore Road and heading back towards Glasgow. Less than five minutes after I began driving a marked police car, its blues and twos flashing and sounding passes me in the opposite direction and it's a fair guess where it's heading. I don't know if the young guy has noted my registration number and while it's unlikely he did, it is likely he will be able to tell the police what kind and colour of car I'm driving. I'm fortunate that the Fiat Punto is a popular make of car and quite common, so it's not as if the car will be a huge stick-out in the metropolitan area of Glasgow. Don't ask why, but as I'm thinking about the Fiat Punto, something resonates in my mind, something that I've missed. I know, I know, I've said it before, but if I ignore what's bothering me, sometime later I'll remember. All I have to do is give it time. As I drive, I'm constantly keeping one eye on the rear view mirror and consciously keeping my speed within the limit while my thoughts concentrate on who murdered Burns. Undoubtedly, the same killer is responsible for attacking Gordon and killing Ina and probably Cathy too. But why, I ask myself. Jo-Jo Docherty has to be the prime suspect. Ideally, I would like to sit down at a desk, relaxed with a coffee and a large notepad and make notes as I think, piece things together as it where. But I don't have this luxury for like it or not, I'm currently a fugitive and will soon be identified for the murder of Burns.

Right now, my first priority is to find somewhere to hide and gather my thoughts. Somewhere the police won't come looking for me. Though it is painful to admit, my social circle was mainly cops and when I was drummed out of the Force, most of them dropped me faster than a Blythswood Square tarts knickers. The few that kept in touch like Mike Farrell would be useful, but to contact Mike now might implicate him and leave him open to a charge of collusion with a murder suspect. I already feel responsible for Gordon's condition and there is no way I'm dragging another faithful friend into this debacle. I should really call my parents and explain because I have no doubt they will be getting a rapid knock on their door, but to do so will only prematurely worry them to death and with my dad's cholesterol condition, that last thing he needs is stress. As if that isn't going to happen, I sigh to myself.

I'm on the M8 motorway approaching the Glasgow Airport and as I glance over to the terminal building, part of it is hidden by the huge newly constructed hotel and I smile. Perhaps the one place that is open to me at the minute is a hotel where at least for a day, maybe two, I might be safe. I know that my finances won't cover me for an extended period at a hotel and anywhere outside the city might attract undue attention, particularly as I don't have luggage with me. By this time I'm passing Ibrox, home of the once might Glasgow Rangers football team, now struggling to retain even their name. As I approach the Kingston Bridge, I smile and take the Charing Cross off-ramp. Behind the Kings Theatre in Bath Street is a multi-storey car park where I can safely dump the Punto and within a short walk from there is a Premier Inn hotel. For now, I breathe a sigh of relief for it seems my immediate problem is solved.

The young Polish receptionist gives me a professional smile and hardly glances at me and if he wonders at my lack of luggage, he makes no comment. As it is my own credit card, I've no option but to book in under my own name, trusting from memory that the cops don't have sufficient resources available to immediately start canvassing local hotels when searching for me.

The double room is clean and tidy and more functional than comfortable I surmise, probably because the hotel is more used to stop-over businessmen than holidaying couples. I check the bathroom and I'm pleased to see there is complimentary soap and shampoo and I run a bath. I undress and with one of the small bars of soap, tackle the body fluid staining on my lower suit trousers that was caused when I flipped Burns onto the caravan floor. I know they look and seem clean, but realise that without professional cleaning, they will never stand up to a Forensic test. I use more soap to rub clean my underwear and socks and wring them as best I can. The trousers I drape over the suit press while the underwear and socks are placed on the bathroom towel rail and left to dry overnight. My shirt will need to stand up for one more day as it is. While the bath water runs, I saunter into the bedroom and switch on the kettle. I hadn't realised how hungry I am and soon demolish the small wafer thin buscuits, washed down by two cups of coffee.

The bath relaxes me and I go over the evening's event again in my mind, trying to piece together what I know so far. Fall out among thieves, I wonder. Is it Jo-Jo Docherty taking some sort of revenge against Burns, perhaps? But why, I ask myself and honestly can't make a connection other than maybe Burns killed Ina and injured Gordon, but is that enough provocation for Docherty to kill Burns? I argue with myself, defence and prosecution. From what Ina had told Gordon and me, Docherty had no emotional feelings for her, other than proprietarily and she did say that he was a tight bastard, that he never gave anything away. Did that include her? I shake my head, knowing that it is unlikely that Ina would be any kind of excuse for Docherty to take the chance and face a murder charge.

I'm beginning to feel sleepy and pull the plug, stand and dry myself with the large towel and am about to step onto the mat when I hear the mobile phone chirruping in the bedroom. Naked and still dripping, I get to the phone just as the message service is about to kick in and glance at the strange number on the screen. "Hello?"

"Tom its Danny McBride. Don't hang up," he says at a rush, "I'm calling from another phone. Gordon's phone was seized as a production by the murder inquiry team, but not before I noted your number. First, Gordon's in surgery as I speak so don't ask, I haven't got any kind of update. Second, I'm making this call without any kind of authority, so don't worry about any trace. Let's just say if I'm caught talking to you, I'm in the shit much like you seem to be, okay?"

"Okay," I slowly reply, but can't avoid the suspicion in my voice.

"I don't want to know where you are right now, but are you in a position to speak?"

I glance down and smiling at my nakedness, sit on the edge of the bed. If he only knew, then hear him say, "Yes please, a cuppa would be great love. Sorry, that's my wife Brenda I'm speaking to," he explains and I realise he must be calling from home. If he is, then it is likely as he said, his call is without any kind of authority and my trust in DI McBride fractionally increases.

"They found Robbie Burns body tonight in a caravan down in Weymss Bay, Tom. A witness says that he spoke with a guy in a

Fiat Punto motor car earlier on that was asking about Jo-Jo Docherty and later this evening saw the same man at the murder caravan holding a great big knife. That wouldn't happen to have been you, was it?"

I sigh and reply, "That was me, Danny. But I didn't kill Burns. Don't get me wrong, the idea had crossed my mind more times than I can admit, but somebody got to him before me."

He pauses before he answers and for a brief few seconds, I think the connection has broken.

"I'm afraid to tell you that right now, Tom you are the number one suspect. However, there are a couple of things that I don't quite understand. Will you stay on the line while we discuss these?"

"I'm listening," I reply.

"I spoke to the Senior Investigating Officer, DI Pete Murray who's at the scene. It seems that Burns was initially identified as, wait a minute," and I hear the rustle of paper and presume he is reading from notes, "a William Arthur McDade because of a passport that was found in the caravan, but on closer examination while the deceased looked remarkably like McDade, it isn't him. The murder team also turned up a bag hidden in a panel that might have contained a gun. They believe this because they discovered a loose shotgun cartridge at the bottom of the bag. They also discovered hidden in a panel in the caravan kitchen a bag full of money that is still being counted. The SIO got in touch with me to inquire if McDade is known to us and when I did a check I find that he is previously recorded for minor stuff, but has been off the grid for the last few years. More interestingly, his antecedent history records him as a cousin of one Robbie Burns. Now, call me old fashioned, but that's too much of a coincidence as far as I'm concerned and being privy to the information that you and Gordon turned up, I suggested the SIO send the deceased's prints to the Records Office only to discover that because Burns was previously reported as having died abroad, Robbie Burns fingerprints and DNA have been wiped from the database."

"Is that normal procedure?" I ask.

"No, it's not because it's not the first time that a deceased person has after his or her death, been identified as the culprit for a cold case inquiry."

"Who authorised the deletion of the prints and DNA sample?"

"It seems the authorisation has also been deleted," he dryly replies and I'm guessing from the tone of his response he isn't happy about this.

"So, how will you prove it's Robbie Burns?"

"One way is for you to give yourself up and tell everyone," but to my relief I realise he's joking and he then adds, "I had some of your original surveillance team members race down to the mortuary at Greenock police office and they have visibly confirmed the deceased is Robbie Burns."

He must have guessed what I am thinking and I suggest, "The guy that died in the fireball accident in Spain. Your thinking it was this cousin of Burns, this guy McDade?"

"Aye, that's exactly what I'm thinking. Because we have no record of McDade being dead, I'm presuming his prints and DNA are still on file so I have every expectation that we will be requesting an exhumation of the body and samples taken for comparison purpose. Thanks Brenda," I hear him say, then, "What, no biscuits?" Whatever her response is, it causes him to laugh and he then speaks to me. "Sorry," he apologises, "We're not that long married, but standards have already dropped."

"Anyway, getting back to you Tom, who do you think murdered Burns?"

I'm startled that he asks me this and I wonder at his presumption that I might not be the killer. It doesn't stop me asking him, though. "Given what seems to be overwhelming evidence that I killed him, how can you be so certain that it wasn't me?"

"Couple of things strike me as in your favour. One of the Detective Sergeants at the scene used his I-pad to e-mail me the initial statement's from the young lad that saw you today the caravan park and also the statement of the attending casualty surgeon who attended to formerly pronounce life extinct. The young lad, Johnston is his name, was on his way to check some path lights that needed bulbs replaced when he came across your Punto. He didn't recognise the car as being one of the regulars in the park and thought it might be thieves screwing the empty caravans. He says in his statement that he touched the bonnet and even though it was a very cold night, it was warm and concluded that whoever had driven the car into the park had just arrived within the preceding five or ten minutes. He seems to be a smart lad."

A lot smarter than I took him for, I'm gratefully thinking.

He continues, "Added to that, the doctor's statement suggests by the lividity of the body and the temperature conditions in the caravan, he's estimating that the deceased had been dead for at least twelve hours and that takes the murder to a time that was well before this lad Johnston says you even arrived at the park."

I sat forward, unable to speak, my mouth suddenly dry.

"Tom? You still there?" he asks.

"Yes," I manage to say, but a wave of emotion and a sudden weariness overtake me. "Does this mean I'm no longer the SIO's number one suspect?"

"Whoa, there laddie," he replies. "I haven't spoken with the SOI, just one of his DS's that I know. You've got a mass of questions to answer and you did flee the scene of a capital crime. Like I say, I can't speak for the SOI, but if he is worth his salt as a detective, he will need to consider that the evidence speaks for itself and pursue all alternative theories."

I hear an intake of breath when McBride mentions the SOI, but I can't imagine why.

"We both know too many mistakes have been made in the past by detectives who jump at what seems to be obvious conclusions and then the truth comes back to bite them in the arse. Sorry love," he says as an aside to his wife who must be in the same room and can hear him. "Brenda's an analyst in my Department," he explains to me, "so I don't get away with anything."

"Danny, can I call you back? I'll save this number and be about ten minutes."

"Okay, buddy," he replies, "I understand."

I can't explain why, but I believe he does.

I hadn't realised the passage of time and the digital clock by the bed reads almost ten PM. I rub vigorously at my body, but not so much to dry myself as to keep awake. As I rub I think about everything McBride has told me and I am relieved that at least I have fighting chance to clear my name. Yes, I know. I've made a lot of mistakes, beginning with keeping Cathy's murder weapon in the boot of the Punto. The thought of the Punto brings back the thing that is haunting me, the issue at the back of my mind that I can't recall and what I believe is important, though I can't explain why.

But it'll come, I just know it will.

I check my mobile and see I have just over one bar of battery life, then slip into the hotel bathrobe and dial McBride's number. He answers almost immediately.

"Before we begin, there's still no change in Gordon's condition, Tom. I'm sorry because I know you guys are close."

"Thanks for that. How are Wilma, his son and daughter holding up?"

"I haven't spoken to her and I don't know her as well as you do, but I understand she's a strong woman. My wife Brenda is driving over the SGH right now, taking some sandwiches and a flask of soup. It's not much, more to show support more than anything."

That simple statement spoke volumes about the kind of couple McBride and his wife is and together they climb even further in my esteem.

"When we spoke earlier today, you alluded that there might be a leak in the police Intelligence network. Given all that has occurred today, are you able to tell me any more?"

"Last night," I begin, finding it hard to believe that so much had happened since then, "when Gordon and I met with Ina Carroll in Wetherspoons in St Vincent Street, she told us that she had some months previously she overheard a one-sided conversation Docherty had with an associate. Ina wasn't specific about the date and I can't recall word for word what she said, but the sum of it was that between - I think she said it was between a Tuesday and the following Friday - Docherty was confident that the police, though Ina said he used the phrase 'manky mob' were conducting a surveillance operation against either him or his team. Ina wasn't sure which. In essence, he told the person on the other end of the line not to 'come up', was the words she heard used and her opinion was that the person was in England, but that was just what she thought and she wasn't certain. If I read her information correctly, she's overheard Docherty imparting a warning and probably relaying information that he had received from his police informant."

"Was it a landline or mobile phone he used?"

"She didn't say. Why, is that important?"

"If it was a landline we could always try for back-billing of Docherty's number and see if we can pin down any numbers that we might have recorded, but on hindsight, I don't suppose that is really any use. I mean, even if a number did turn up that is known to us, he could easily have been calling about the football or it might even have been a social call. The time and date is the important thing, but with the poor woman murdered," I hear him sigh, "that information is lost to us."

"What's my best move do you think, Danny?"

"You're asking advice from me?" he half laughs. "Right now, I don't know where you are and I'm quite happy with that. The murder inquiry team will be looking for you, but you already know that. I expect Frankie Jackson, oh sorry, he's my boss, the Detective Chief Superintendent …"

"I know who he is," I interrupt.

"Well, I expect Frankie to be calling on me first thing in the morning. He's one of the good guys and will want updated on not just the Robbie Burns murder, but the woman's murder and the attempt on Gordon's life. From what you've told me, it doesn't take a genius to work out that they seem to be related and we probably have a psychopath on our hands. I don't like using the term serial killer, but how else am I to explain the two killings?"

"Probably three, Danny if you include the woman in my flat, Cathy Williams."

"Aye well, right enough. At least that bastard Burns has finally answered for the police woman's murder, Foley her name was I think?"

"Alice Foley."

"Right, Alice Foley," he repeats. "I'm sorry. I'm forgetting that you were partnered with her that night." There's an awkward pause and ne says, "I remember now. There was some talk about you two." I can almost hear him wincing. "Trust me Tom if I'm going to put my foot in it I do it properly."

"Water under the bridge," I tell him. "I took the fall and lost my job, my wife and almost my kids, but Alice lost her life so I've nothing to whine about."

I pause and recall him telling me about the discovery of a bag that might have contained a gun. "You mentioned the recovered cartridge and money that was found."

"Yeah, what about it?" he asks.

"Last night, when I asked Ina if Burns had money, she said he had but, because Docherty is such a tight-arse, she was certain that he wasn't subbing Burns and didn't know where Burns was getting the money. I asked Gordon if there had been any Cash in Transit robberies. He wasn't certain, but did mention some Post Office security vans across the region getting hit. What do you think?"

"There might be something in that," he slowly replies. "Some of the notes stolen were serialised and it shouldn't be difficult to check it out." He half laughs. "How I'm going to explain Frankie Jackson where I'm getting this information, God alone knows."

A thought crosses my mind. "Before you go Danny, as the DI in charge of the Intelligence department at headquarters, do you have access to all the police surveillance operational logs?"

"Yes, the hard copies are filed at Meiklewood Road, but my department are e-mailed the day to day logs and we store them on a secure Intranet hard drive. Why?"

"Who has access to these logs?"

"To be honest, any number of personnel who are positively vetted by the police Vetting Department and that includes my Department staff, senior management, SIO's, analysts, surveillance officers and Divisional Collators. I can't think of a figure off the top of my head, Tom but we're talking dozens and dozens of personnel, both police and civilian staff."

"If I remember correctly from my time in surveillance, it is standard protocol for a team leader to sign in with your Department what days that team will be deployed on a particular target, is that right?"

"You're right. The purpose of that is to avoid two teams from different agencies operating against the same target and maybe compromising each other. So, what's your interest in the administration of the operations? What do you have in mind?"

"One of the ways we as a team would identify a stranger in a targets vehicle was to get a traffic car to give the target's car a pull. If Burns was in the car at any time surveillance was on Docherty, it might be worth checking the logs to see what name he gave. I suspect he's produced William McDade's passport you spoke about."

"You're right. I'll get onto that in the morning. Right now, I suggest you get your head down and if you don't mind, I'll give you a call in the morning."

"It might be a short call. The battery life in this phone is low and as you'll have guessed," I grin at the mobile in my hand, "I'm not at home at the minute so don't have access to my charger."

"Okay, got that. One last thing, if there is any news about Gordon, I'll bell you. Right, goodnight, Tom," he signs off.

I close the phone and place it on the bedside cabinet, thankful that I now know I'm not alone in this nightmare.

Chapter 19

The digital clock radio startles me and I silently curse because I didn't set it. It seems the room's previous occupant must for some God-forsaken reason have wished to be woken at six-thirty. I lie there for another half an hour, my bladder reminding me it needs emptied, but my mind numb from the preceding evening's discovery of Robbie Burns' body. Danny McBride will not know, but his reassuring phone call last night lifted a dark cloud from me and the morning, tired though I feel right now, seems a lot brighter. I sit naked on the edge of the bed and bemoan the fact I've used both coffee satchels. So, tea it is then, regretting that I didn't have the foresight to purchase one of the continental packs of bread, jams and coffee so beloved by the modern overnight hotels. The small kettle quickly boils and I decide to treat myself to another bath. I've no shaving kit and rub my fingers along my jaw line. Maybe stubble is in, I tell myself. While I drink the tea and wait on the bath filling, I know I have a decision to make. Do I stay one more night or surrender to the police? The decision can wait till I bathe and dress.

My mobile informs me a text message has arrived. I see the incoming number is Danny McBride's and open the text that reads: No chnge Grdon. Case meetng 11am at hq re turning ovr jojo's pad. Will you attnd meetng? Chnce you mite get the jail. Considr it as option 2 come in & bettr than being arrested. Balls in ur court. D

I read the text twice and realise that he is giving me the opportunity to voluntarily surrender myself as a witness rather than being apprehended and treated as a suspect. I sit and ponder for a few minutes then decide, what choice do I really have? But before I do anything, there's one guy I need to speak with.

I'm leaving the Punto in the high rise car park, deciding that I'm better off travelling on foot. Glasgow isn't downtown New York or Los Angeles where the American police issue BOLO's, their Be On the Look Out' to all their vehicles. While I know it's unlikely that a popular car like the Punto will attract much attention, it's simply not worth me taking such a risk and I'm also mindful that it has the murder weapon again secreted in the boot.

I get off the bus in Albert Drive and pushing open the door of McCormick and Co, I'm greeted by a grim faced Martha who stops typing and sternly stares at me. "Mister McEwan," she greets me, "you not going to upset my Mister Martin now, is you?"

I smile reassuringly because I haven't forgotten that this attractive but extremely large and no doubt powerful lady has a baseball bat sitting somewhere handy. "Sorry to arrive without an appointment, Martha," I tell her, closing the door behind me and apologetically raising my hands because I don't want her to even consider I might be any kind of threat, "but is Martin able to see me right now?"

She grunts and without taking her eyes from me, presses the button on her intercom. "Mister Martin, I got that Mister McEwan here in the front office. You able to see him or will I just toss his sorry ass out of here?"

McCormick's voice cackles on the intercom, instructing her to send me through.

"You heard the man," she says then waves a warning finger at me, but you be good Mister McEwan else Martha might have to hurt you, understand?"

I nod and head towards McCormick's office.

He's sitting behind his desk and beckons me to sit ain the chair in front of him. "If it's about your employer, Tom I've only sent the letter and …."

I shake my head and tell him, no, that I need his help and immediately. Then I launch into my narrative about travelling to the caravan park in Weymss Bay and discovering Burns body. The more I retell the story, the less innocent I sound and he slowly wheezes as I finally finish my story, telling him of the last text I received from DI Danny McBride. I can't imagine why, but he suddenly grins at me.

"Bloody hell Tom, no half measures with you, is there? I might end up shutting up shop and making you my career. Right, to business then," he picks up a pen and prepares to take notes, "How well do you know McBride?"

"I don't know him at all, but Gordon trusted him and that is good enough for me," I reply with more confidence than I really feel.

"The weapon, this machete knife thing that was used to kill Missus Williams, it's still in the boot of the Punto?"

"Yes."

"So, at the very least, you are facing one charge of concealing a vital piece of evidence when you are aware it should be surrendered to the police. And that's just for starters," he grimaces. "This DI McBride, he informed you that the time-line evidence seems to indicate you might not be responsible for the murder of Robbie Burns?"

"That's what he says," I nod my head.

"Well, if nothing else, I agree with DI McBride that you should consider surrendering yourself rather than wait to be arrested. That at least indicates willingness, albeit a little late if you ask me, to assist the police in their inquiries."

"That's my intention, Martin and why I've come to see you. I'd like you to accompany me to police headquarters. I'm figuring that if they decide to arrest me, then I keep my mouth shut but if they have any sense at all, they will consider treating me as a witness and I might be able to add valuable intelligence to their inquiry. I don't think that McBride will have disclosed how he can by the information I gave him because if he did, it will almost certainly put his own head in a noose for not giving me up."

He smiles and shakes his head. "And I suppose you want me there to ensure that however they treat you, it's within the parameters of the judicial code that in the Glasgow polis parlance means you don't want to find yourself fitted up with Burns murder?" He shakes his head and grins at me. "If nothing else Tom, you've got some balls, I must say." He leans forward, resting his elbows on his desk.

"You said that McBride's boss is Frankie Jackson. If it's the same guy, I've met him. My cousin Lynn speaks highly of him and says he's a very fair man and a good cop, so let's find out, eh?" and with that, lifts the desk phone from its cradle and dials a number. I listen as he gives his own name then ask what sounds like an operator if he may speak with Detective Chief Superintendent Jackson. There's a slight pause, then he presses a button on the phone and returns it to the cradle. I hear the phone ring and realise Martin's activated the speaker.

"DCS Jackson," says the voice.

"Mister Jackson, Martin McCormick sir. I wonder if I might have a couple of minutes of your valuable time. I'm at my office with my client, Tom McEwan who I understand the police wish to interview regarding the finding of a body in the Weymss Bay area sometime last night."

"That's correct Martin and will I also be correct in recalling that you are Lynn Massey's young cousin?"

Martin smiles and confirms this, then adds, "I have learned that the police intend holding a conference today, that you might be linking the murders of Robbie Burns, Ina Carroll and the attempted murder of one of your own, Mister Gordon Roberts."

There's a pause and I'm guessing that Jackson must be wondering how the hell Martin knows this.

"I won't ask for your source, at least not now and I presume from the echo in your background that I'm on a speaker-phone. Not very fair of you, Mister McCormick if, as I suspect, you are calling me to make some sort of arrangement for Mister McEwan."

"Of course, you are correct sir. The speaker-phone is to allow Mister McEwan to listen in and I assure you, there is no recording device in operation. It's simply to permit me to move things along without the need to relay our discussion in the third party to Mister McEwan."

"Okay, I accept that. Now, Mister McCormick, what can I do for you and your client?"

"Mister McEwan, Tom if I might call him by his forename, has instructed me to inform you that last night he discovered the body of the deceased Robbie Burns, but circumstances that preceded the finding of the body and which he is willing to impart, panicked him into fleeing the scene. He is now quite contrite and more than willing to come forward as a witness and provide you the police with certain information that is known only to him. I know it's a little unusual, but he asks if you might consider his attendance at your meeting where as a witness, he can provide you with this information that includes the whereabouts of the weapon used to murder his friend, Missus Cathy Williams."

I hadn't given any such instruction and was about to protest when Martin raised his hand to stop me and from his expression, made it more than clear I am to shut the fuck up.

"Are you seriously asking that I include Tom McEwan in a briefing at police headquarters about a series of murders that might possibly result in him being arrested for at least one of these murders? You have got to be joking!"

"No, sir, I'm very serious," replies Martin. "I believe that Tom's information might just tie in your murder inquiries and might I also add that Tom has a strong suspicion that you Intelligence network might be compromised so I strongly urge you to consider my proposal. I understand you might wish to consider my suggestion and will wish time to reflect on this, but before you go can I have your assurance that there will be no officers kicking down my office door in the interim? After all, Mister Jackson, one willing witness with information is likely preferable to a suspect who I will certainly instruct to tell you nothing."

"That sounds like a veiled threat, young McCormick, your cousin Lynn told me that you are good, but didn't mention you're a blackmailing bastard," though in fairness I don't hear any malice in the comment. Through the speaker, I hear Jackson sigh and he says, "Very well. Give me ten minutes till I think about it and I'll get back to you," then an audible click indicates he's hung up. Martin stares at me for a few seconds then exhales with relief. "Don't think that went too badly, eh?"

Just under five, long, nail-biting minutes pass then the desk phone rings and I watch as Martin snatches it from the cradle to his ear. "Yes?" I hear him say, then, "Eleven o'clock. Yes sir, I'll certainly accompany him there and Mister Jackson, thank you sir."

Jackson says something else that makes Martin frown slightly and he reaches down and hits the speaker button and I hear Jackson say, "…. so under no circumstances will I give any kind of guarantee that your client will not be arrested, Mister McCormick. Are we absolutely clear on this issue?"

Martin turns to me, his eyebrows questioningly raised and I nod my consent. "Absolutely clear," he repeats.

The speaker is still switched on and Jackson tells Martin, "As we agreed earlier, Mister McCormick, the circumstances of your client attending this meeting is unique and I'm making this decision based on your statement that your client will provide an insight into the ongoing inquiries and who he believes might be leaking confidential information from my Intelligence Department." I almost hear him growl when he concludes, "And I strongly urge that your client does not make me regret my decision."

Martin smiles at me as he presses the End button on the phone cradle and says, "This could prove interesting. Maybe we've just time for a cuppa then," and shouts out very loudly, "Martha, get the kettle on!"

Chapter 20

It's just gone ten o'clock when Martin leads me out of the office to his car that is parked round the corner in Glenapp Street. He presses the button on his key fob and the indicator lights flash on a top of the range Audi estate car. I climb into the passenger seat and can't help but notice the two child car seats fastened in the rear, but if that isn't a giveaway, the toys and sweet papers scattered about the floor is.

"Charlie's four and Lynn's almost two," he grins at me. "My wife Agatha," then grins again and explains, "Her parents had a sense of humour. She's a part-time nursery teacher and the days she's at home, I get the car."

"Lynn?" I ask, but guessing what he is about to tell me.

"After my cousin, Lynn Massey," he confirms as checking over his shoulder, he smoothly pulls away from the kerb. "She's been like a big sister to me and in my early days, kept me on the straight and narrow."

"A bit like Gordon Roberts," I tell him, but don't go into a lengthy explanation.

He negotiates the car through the Pollokshields area and we're travelling north on Shields Road when the in-car phone connection activates. I turn to see him smile as he hits a switch somewhere and a woman's voice says 'Hello." From the discussion that follows, I realise it's his wife and of course, there's nowhere for me to step away from the conversation, so I politely turn my head towards the passenger window. Martin apologises and tells her he has a client with him and will call her later.

"Sorry about that," he smiles without turning his head. "Sometimes these new cars are so full of gadgets it's like sitting in my office."

I smile in return, thinking back to when Lisa and I first started out together, me rejecting her father's offer of a loan for a new car and instead going through a succession of bangers till at last we could afford something decent. Of course, I was a bit petulant, but I just couldn't abide the thought of being in debt to the obnoxious bugger.

I think that's when it hit me, the thing that has been bugging me. It was the discussion of cars that did it and I inwardly smile. Not with pleasure, but with relief for finally I know I'm really on to something. I glance sideways at Martin, but don't believe this is the time or place to disclose what I know. Intelligence or as we said when we were kids in the playground, 'My ball, my game' gives me the advantage that I just might need if Frankie Jackson decides I'm more of a suspect than a witness. I can't explain it, but an unusual calmness comes over me and I'm no longer feeling the same fear of attending this meeting that I previously did.

We arrive at the front door of Police Headquarters to be met by the commissionaire who after we give our names, smilingly points towards a man lounging against the reception desk.

"Danny's waiting there for you, gentleman."

McBride came forward and I judge him to be in his late forties, about my height, slim build and with light grey coloured eyes. He wears a dark grey two piece suit, white shirt and what looks to me like some kind of regimental or club tie. I suddenly remember that I'm wearing a day old shirt and my attempt at laundering my smalls in the hotel room doesn't hide the fact that I feel uncomfortably dressed and it takes me all my energy to refrain from sniffing at my armpits. We shake hands all round and McBride asks Martin if he can have a private word with me.

I glance at Martin and nod and see him turn away to sit in the reception area while McBride and I walk the short distance through the glass security doors and stand in the corridor by the lift area.

"First," he raises his hand, "I know that you will be anxious, but I have no good news about Gordon. Wilma is still at the hospital and promises to let me know as soon as there is any change, okay?"

I sigh in understanding and he continues, "This won't be easy, Tom. Frankie Jackson is no fool and when I told him this morning about the possibility of a connection between Robbie Burns and the Post Office robberies, he didn't ask, just accepted that it is credible information, but he musts suspect we've already been in contact. And on that point, the check on the serial numbers is still to be resulted to me. So, how do you wish to handle it? Do you want to admit we've spoken?"

"Will it damage your career or land you in trouble?"

"No more than usual," he grinned. "It's not the first time I've been subject to a rubber heels investigation."

Startled, I remember then who he is and my mouth hung open and I'm gaping at him like some sort of idiot. Danny McBride. The Detective Sergeant who pursued a killer to the top of a multi-storey building somewhere over in the south side of Glasgow and the story that was widely reported, if I recall correctly, is the killer dragged McBride's Detective Inspector over the edge of the building to his death or something like that. Details at the time of what really occurred were a bit sketchy and there was whisper of a cover-up, but I took that to be the usual police 'two and two make five' gossip machine.

"So," he repeated, "how do you want to handle this?"

"Gordon Roberts speaks highly of you and I know that you are his boss. If anyone asks, are you willing to say that I contacted you with information and that I drip-fed it to you without disclosing where I got it or where I was when I contacted you?"

He slowly nods and must realise I'm doing this to protect him then smiles as he replies, "Well that much is correct. Where were you anyway?"

I smile and nod through the building westwards. "I was staying in the Premier Inn hotel at Charing Cross. The Punto is parked up in the multi-storey car park behind the Kings Theatre."

McBride's eyes narrow. "I know the car park," he slowly says. "Before we married, my wife Brenda worked as an analyst in the Department and she was mugged there."

Not much I can say to that and I watch as McBride summons Martin through the glass door and leads us for the next few minutes through a succession of corridors to a conference room that is located on fifth floor at the west side of headquarters.

In all my time in the Force I had never had the opportunity to attend at the any of the conference suites on the fifth floor and entering the large, imposing room wondered why the senior management bothered to pay for conference facilities at swanky hotels when they could easily utilise this place. But then again, they say power corrupts so I'll let you work that one out yourself. Three men were seated at the highly polished wooden table and stood when we entered. I recognised Frankie Jackson and Graeme Fleming, but the third man, in his late twenties, tall and athletically built with jet black hair expensively styled and wearing a three piece, charcoal grey suit, with a light grey shirt and mustard coloured tie and looking like a male model from a catalogue wasn't immediately familiar. His face did strike a chord and it was only when Jackson introduced him as Detective Inspector Pete Murray and I see him glare at me that I recalled I had met him some years previously. He was a Detective Sergeant then when we were on a one-day Intelligence course being instructed in Organised Criminal Enterprises, or OCE's as the polis like to term them, at the police training college in Fife. I nearly smiled when I recalled his nickname. He might look the part, but behind his back, Murray was known as Gillette, a complete contradiction of his ability because he was the dullest tool in the box and rumour had it his promotion through the ranks was credited more to his in-law's political contacts in the local council than his ability. I also recall that he has a big mouth, but it doesn't work in conjunction with his brain. The formality of hand-shaking is dispensed with and I'm guessing from his scowl that he already has me arrested, tried and convicted.

Jackson informs Martin that Graeme Fleming is the SIO for Cathy's murder and Pete Murray is the SIO for Burns murder, then invites us to sit and hands clasped on the table in front of him, commences what I think is a prepared speech. The SIO for Ina Carroll's murder and Gordon's attempted murder, Jackson informs us, is detained at the High Court on an unrelated case.

"First things first, Mister McCormick," he begun, "I want to make it absolutely clear that what I said on the phone stands. Your client here," he inclined his head to me without taking his eyes off Martin, "does not have a blank get out of jail free card. I've discussed his presence at this meeting with my Detective Inspectors and agreed that though the final decision is mine, Mister McEwan might still be subject to arrest at the end of this meeting. To this end, I instructed that your client is not at this time issued a formal common law caution and therefore I am willing to treat him in the first instance as a witness, so we will note what he says and dependent on his responses to our questions or whatever information he cares to make known to us will determine our ..." he pauses, "my decision. Are we clearly understood on this issue?"

"Understood," Martin nods in reply. "However, what I will ask is that my client be treated with consideration for frankly, Mister Jackson," and smiling I can see he's enjoying himself, "he doesn't trust the police."

"I just want it to be recorded, sir," interrupts Murray, "that I don't agree with your decision. I am of the opinion McEwan should be arrested."

A palpable silence descends on the room and Jackson audibly takes a deep breath.

"Your concern is duly noted, DI Murray," he replies and I see that he doesn't even glance towards him. He then looks quickly from Martin to me and asks, "To continue. Care to explain your mistrust?"

I shrug and relate, "You'll be aware of the discovery of my friend, Cathy William's body in my flat. My youthful neighbour, spoken to by one of DI Fleming's detectives, can verify that when he was very briefly interviewed by the detective, he was told in no uncertain terms that the inquiry was complete, that I had been identified as the killer. That coupled with the fact that the man, who I believe to be the same detective officer attended at my place of employment in pursuance of the inquiry and apparently also made it known to my management that I am the culprit. As a result, I am currently suspended from my job and denied my income. The employment issue is being dealt with by Mister McCormick here," I turn towards Martin.

"And are you the killer, Mister McEwan?"

I see Graeme Fleming turn pale and decide a little bonding is required, not so much to save his arse, but more for my own credibility regarding what I am about to disclose to them.

"No sir. I believe that DI Fleming has evidence, both Forensic and time related, that exonerates me from involvement in the murder. However, I would also like to add that DI Fleming there, as far as I am aware and believe, has no part in this false allegation against me and truth be told, he treated me fairly and honestly. I am of the opinion that the detective who accused me acted without DI Fleming's knowledge."

I don't look at Graeme, but imagine I hear an audible sigh of relief from across the table.

"Is that your purpose for coming here today, Mister McEwan? To make a complaint about one of my officers because let me tell you …"

I raise my hand up to halt Jackson in mid-flow, surprising even myself that I'm being so bold as to interrupt the man who was not only so far removed from my own rank in the Force as a general is to a private soldier, but might also be the man who determines whether I remain free or am arrested.

"That's just part of the story, Mister Jackson. You see, when DI Fleming interviewed me, he was unaware that I had the use of a hired vehicle, a Fiat Punto from Mitchell's …."

"The car you escaped in after you murdered my victim," scoffed Murray from across the table. I turned to see a gloating Murray staring at me and to my surprise I think that he's losing his self-control.

"Maybe we should let Mister McEwan finish his tale, Mister Murray," interrupts Jackson and I interpret that as not a request, but an order.

"The day Missus Williams was murdered in my flat, I had left the car parked in the street outside the building because parking where I work is a nightmare. The keys for the Punto were left hanging on a hook by my front door ..."

"Where Missus Williams took your spare key from?" asks Graeme Fleming and with those few short words, I realise that Graeme believes me, that he is confident my statement to him was true. Only now I am about to sow in his mind the seed of doubt.

"Yeah, exactly," I reply, turning my attention again to Jackson. "DI Fleming arranged for a lift to get me back to my flat and when I returned, I discovered the car keys were gone. I knew that the CID hadn't removed the keys because I would have been questioned about the car and it would have undoubtedly been searched."

Jackson gives me an almost imperceptible nod, agreeing with me.

"I then thought maybe the car had been stolen and went down to check on it only to find that the car was still locked and secure, but the keys were inserted in the lock of the boot."

"What, you mean that whoever took the keys simply left them open for everyone to see, stuck in the boot lock?"

I kind of smirk and stare at him. "Not for everyone to see, Mister Jackson, for you guys to find. The murder weapon was wrapped in one of my towels; a machete."

You know the saying you could cut the atmosphere with a knife? The room was suddenly silent and I held my breath, because I am committed now and there is no turning back.

Jackson asked, "Where's the weapon now, son?"

"Still in the car, sir and before you ask, the car is parked on the second flight in the multi-storey car park behind the Kings Theatre. It'll be easy to spot; it's black coloured and will have half a dozen parking tickets on the windscreen," I quip, but he didn't laugh or even smile.

"Keys?" he held a large hand out to me. I hand them to him across the table and watch him pass them to Graeme.

"Do you think that this detective officer you are accusing is responsible for planting the weapon in your car?"

I took a deep breath. "No sir, I don't believe that at all. If that was true," I wiggled the forefingers of both hands in the air and said, "it would have been discovered that night and I would have been challenged about the car by DI Fleming and likely charged with murder. No sir, I believe whoever killed Cathy Williams was in fact out to kill me, but discovered her in my flat and in an attempt to implicate me in her murder planted the murder weapon in the belief the attending officers would discover the machete in the boot of the car."

"And the reason for implicating you is ....?"

"To get me out of the way, sir because I think ...no, I'm certain ... I am a threat to someone who is an associate of Robbie Burns and Jo-Jo Docherty. This person learned from Docherty that I was convinced Burns was alive and back in the country and it's this person, this third party who believes me to be a threat, but I'd like to explain that statement as I go along."

"Okay, Mister McEwan, we'll come back to that at a later time, though obviously I'm curious as to the identity of this ... this third party. So now you have my full attention, tell me, what exactly did you intend doing with the machete after you discovered it? Hand it over to DI Fleming?"

Here we go, I'm thinking to myself. It's all or nothing now. "No sir, it was my intention to bury the fucking thing in Robbie Burns head."

This makes the big guy sit back and he stares at me. "We might be able to manage without the expletive's young man. Now, what exactly do you ...." but he is interrupted by Danny McBride's mobile phone chirping in his jacket pocket. We all stop and stare at McBride who glancing at the screen says, "Sorry, I need to take this," and rising from his seat, hurriedly leaves the room and shuts the door behind him, but not before I just catch him saying, "Hello, Wilma?"

I can't help myself. I'm anxious for my big pal and I turn back towards Jackson, but there is something in his eyes and he raises his large hand and tells me, "We'll give DI McBride a minute, if you don't mind."

We sit in silence for what seems a tense eternity. McBride opens the door and I can tell almost immediately its good news. He sits down and smiling, addresses Jackson, telling him, "Lucky it was the big guy's head and nothing vital. He's not yet regained consciousness, boss, but Wilma says the doctor told her he's showing all the signs that indicate he's mending and though it might be a slow recovery and barring him taking up boxing, he will recover."

McBride turns towards me and continuing to smile adds, "Wilma sends her regards, Tom."

I can hardly speak and I can't explain the emotion I feel. I'm fortunate I'm sitting for I doubt my legs will support me if I try to stand. Without saying anything, Jackson takes hold of the pitcher from the tray and pours a glass of water that he hands to me and with a shaking hand I gulp down, spilling some on my already creased shirt. I try to smile, but fail miserably and I can only imagine how I must look to the others.

"Maybe when you've composed yourself Mister McEwan, you might want to explain your intention to murder Robbie Burns?"

I start at the beginning and hold nothing back, baring my soul as it where. From my first sighting of the man I believe is Robbie Burns to the subterfuge I employed when contacting the Spanish police. I tell of visiting Gordon Roberts at home and asking his advice. I make the mistake of trying to say that Gordon attempted to dissuade me from going any further and suggesting I inform the police, but Jackson interrupts and not unkindly reminds me that is not the Gordon Roberts we both know. "If there's a bad guy to be locked up, I doubt Gordon will hang back and a little thing like protocol and involving us certainly won't stop him," he growls and I realise he must know Gordon at least as well as I do.

I continue and when I get to the part where Gordon and I met with Ina in the Saracen Head pub, Jackson sits forward and listens intently, shaking his head in disapproval at our cowboy tactics.

"You do remember from your days in the Force young man, that there is a procedure for meeting touts these days, Tom?" he asks and as I nod it doesn't escape my attention he has used my forename.

Again I try to claim I persuaded Gordon to accompany me to the meeting, but as far as Jackson and McBride is concerned I can see my explanation is falling on deaf ears.

I tell them of my visit to reconnoitre Joseph Docherty's housed, of sitting in the car park at the health club and my shock on seeing Robbie Burns exit the club and travel to Docherty's home nearby.

My night excursion to Casa El Docherty has Jackson sitting on the edge of his seat. His face turns a ruddy red when I describe the injuries on Ina's face and recognising the barman that I saw in the Saracen Head pub. I can't help myself, but become more animated as I relate seeing Burns arrive back at the house in the dark with Docherty. I catch his glance towards McBride who is feverishly making notes as I talk, while Graeme Fleming seems to be listening intently and Murray, arms crossed, pretends to be bored. I briefly describe my job as an insurance investigator, that earns a guffaw from Murray and glance at McBride, whose face indicates he clearly isn't pleased at the bastards' attitude.

I hesitate slightly when talking about Cathy, but don't dwell on my relationship with her and simply say we enjoyed a friendship that in her case was extra-marital.

"Was she the only one you were shagging then?" sneers Murray. Jackson, his voice low but sharp enough to cause Murray's face to redden, simply says, "Please, Detective Inspector," and it seems obvious to me he isn't happy with the crass interruption.

I decide to answer Murray's question and confirm that Cathy was the only woman I was having any kind of relationship with. Jackson nods and seems satisfied with that. For some reason I choke when describing the finding of Cathy's body and Jackson hands me a refill of water. I sip at the water and remind him, "But you now know about the machete in the boot."

"You said you were being implicated, but by who?" he asks.

I hesitate, not yet wishing to disclose my suspicions and I can see in his eyes he knows I have more to tell him.

"I believe you might have a leak in your Intelligence network, Mister Jackson. When Ina Carroll met with Gordon Roberts and me a couple of nights ago, that's when I learned that Jo-Jo Docherty apparently said something that made me suspicious. She told me that several months ago she overheard Docherty speaking on the phone. Ina thought it might have been someone in England, though she had no way of knowing for certain, but Docherty apparently told the caller that the police, the 'manky mob' he called them, were intent on conducting surveillance on Docherty between Tuesday and Friday of that week."

"What week was that?"

"I have no idea sir," I replied.

"If I might boss," said McBride. "Assuming what Missus Carroll overheard was correct, I've been through the surveillance logs on Docherty for the last six months, checking what days the four teams have been assigned Docherty's file. I've had one of my team research the 'Tuesday to Friday' dates and if what Missus Carroll told Tom about it being several months previously is correct, I assessed a three month parameter period when Docherty was the subject of surveillance on a Tuesday to a Friday. Between the four teams, there were five occasions. You will know this is not definitive, but given the sparse information, it's the best I can come up with."

Jackson sighed and said, "I'm guessing what the answer will be Danny, but how many people had access to the information on those occasions that Docherty will have been the target?"

"You mean aside from police officers and our partner agencies who we inform to avoid cross-purpose surveillance? Civilian Intelligence analysts, cleaners passing through the squad rooms, commissionaires chatting to the guys and opening gates and not forgetting anyone who is vetted and has access to the Intelligence Internet system?"

"Bloody computers," growls Jackson, "So, in essence too many people to account for?"

McBride doesn't reply, but simply nods, his face grim.

"And not forgetting," Jackson turns to me, equally grim faced, "that is if Mister McEwan here is telling us the truth?"

Hearing I'm back to being Mister McEwan again makes me just a little worried.

McBride half raises his hand and says, "There is one more thing if you please, boss. When I had a look through the surveillance logs, there is an entry in the log just over three weeks ago when one of the team reported a strange face in Docherty's BMW jeep and organised a pull for the car from the Traffic to identify the guy. The log says that the guy produced a passport in the name William Arthur McDade. The follow-up check by the surveillance team identified McDade as a known villain, but not currently wanted, so he was merely logged as an associate of Docherty and no further action was taken."

I watch Jackson run a weary hand across his face as he turns to McBride and says, "And the passport he produced as evidence. I'm assuming the Traffic cop checked the photo against the man who produced it?"

"Don't know, boss. That's not recorded in the log and I can only presume so, but DI Murray did say there is a resemblance between Burns and McDade and them being cousins …." he left the sentence unfinished.

"Bloody Traffic cops," snorted Murray, "should be disciplined if you ask me."

But nobody asks Murray and Jackson ignores the self-righteous bastard. Instead, he says to me, "So far you haven't convinced me Mister McEwan that anything you have said is worthy of a witness statement rather than us taking the easier route of treating you as an accused."

"You must realise, Mister Jackson," Martin McCormick breaks his silence and sits forward, "that while I agree my client is of course keen to save himself from arrest, he did voluntarily attend here to make amend for any mistake he might have made and to assist you in the apprehension of the killer of not just Missus Williams and the man you sought, Robbie Burns, but also Missus Carroll, not to mention the assault on Mister Roberts."

"I am aware of this," replied Jackson, "and I'll bring you up to date regarding our suspicions regarding Mister McEwan presently. For the moment, I'd like to hear what your client has to say about his discovery of the body in Weymss Bay."

I admitted that Ina had been tipsy when she mentioned Docherty's caravan and from her vague description of where it was located, I tell them of having taken a chance and driving down there with the intention of finding Burns.

"Of killing him, you mean?" said Murray, the sarcasm evident in his voice.

"Perhaps if we let Mister McEwan finish, eh?" says McBride icily and I know then there is no love lost between these two guys.

"To be honest, I didn't know what I intended doing. There were a lot of things going through my mind. I blamed him for Alice's … DC Foley's death and maybe Cathy's too and every shitty thing that had happened to me since then. I had the machete, yes and when I found out where he was hiding, I took the machete with me because.... well, because," and I hesitate, suddenly uncertain, "I don't know. I don't think I was thinking too straight."

"But you killed him, didn't you," said Murray, standing now, leaning on one hand while pointing an accusing forefinger with the other. A thought crosses my mind that if this is his technique for interviewing suspects, he's shite at it. Such is the fury in his face, his voice raised to a squeaky pitch and for one second I think he is going to vault across and grab at me.

Martin McCormick is also on his feet, an arm protectively across my chest, his voice raised as she shouts, "Mister Jackson! Please control your officer. I have to a good mind to …"

"Silence!" thunders Jackson, now on his feet also. Then he turns to Murray and seemingly controlling his voice, says, "Detective Inspector Murray. Must I remind you again that I am conducting this interview? Please remove yourself from this room and wait for me downstairs in my office. Thank you," then slowly sits down and stares straight ahead.

Murray, stares from me to Jackson, disbelief on his face and without a backward glance, walks out leaving the door ajar. Danny McBride leaves his seat and softly closes the door and as I watch, winks at me as he sits back down.

"Mister McCormick," Jackson addresses him, "please accept my apology for my officer's …." he struggles for the words, then settles for, "…. zealous interview technique."

Martin, his face pale, nods in acknowledgement while Graeme Fleming raises his eyes to stare at the ceiling.

"Now, Mister McEwan, you were about to relate your discovery of the body in the caravan?"

"Yes sir. I knew straight away it was Robbie Burns, but he seemed to have been dead for some time."

"And you know this how?"

"His blood, sir. I'm not an expert, but even I could tell it had congealed and he was cold to touch."

"So you did touch him then?"

"I tried to turn his body while he was lying on the couch and he fell onto the caravan floor. Some blood and matter splashed onto my lower trousers. I cleaned them last night in my hotel room."

"Hotel room?"

I go back a little and tell him about fleeing the caravan, being seen by the young lad and finding the Premier Inn hotel, of cleaning my trousers and this morning, soliciting the help of Martin McCormick to come into police headquarters.

"I regret that DI Murray has had some difficulty coming to terms with certain aspects of the evidence in this inquiry, but you will both be pleased to learn," he cast his eyes down to some notes in front of him, "that once more, the timeline vindicates you Mister McEwan. You seem to be alibi'd for Burns murder. How very fortunate you have been," he sighs, but not without a trace of sarcasm.'

I nod with relief and smile, then in a flash realise that either Murray didn't know about the timeline or has decided to ignore the evidence under his nose. What I can't make my mind up is if Jackson orchestrated the outburst to give him rope to hang himself and I wonder if Martin and I have stumbled into a small, inner plot to set Murray up. I inwardly smile thinking that maybe Murray is more unpopular as a CID officer than I ever suspected. But then again, Murray isn't my problem.

"Did you search the caravan?"

"No not at all," I vigorously shook my head. "Once I realised Poet, Burns I mean, was dead, I figured the best thing I could do was get the hell out of there. No sir, I didn't turn the caravan over at all."

He slowly nods then turns and says to McBride, "Tell him."

McBride stares at me and I read it in his eyes. He's warning me to express surprise, that this is the first time I have heard this, okay?

"You called me, Tom and suggested that Burns might have been involved in Post Office robberies, right?"

"Yes," I reply.

"Well, the inquiry team discovered a bag of money in the caravan and the serial notes of the notes are being checked against the proceeds of at least two Post Office robberies, maybe more. The team also discovered a bag containing a shotgun cartridge and smudges of oil that Forensic tell us is of the type used to lubricate a firearm. Needless to say the gun was gone. Wouldn't know anything about that now, would you Tom?"

"Absolutely not," I reply, but realise that the suspicion a firearm is now in the hands of a killer is just one more problem these guys have to deal with.

"I presume we're relatively up to date?" Jackson breaks into my thoughts.

"Yes sir."

"So, Mister McEwan, we have now arrived at the point where you are going to inform me of your suspicions as to who might be the leak in my Intelligence department, eh?"

"Might I ask first sir, how do you propose to deal with Docherty, given that his association with Burns must lead you to suspect he is implicated in at least harbouring a man wanted for murder and even perhaps the ongoing Post Office robberies?"

Jackson turned to McBride who nods to him, then says, "While we have been here chewing the fat, Mister Docherty's house is the subject of a surveillance operation that was overseen this morning by DI McBride. No other Intelligence personnel are aware of this operation and it has not yet been logged on the Intelligence network. The surveillance team is being supplemented by an armed police response unit from the Support Unit, as well as Forensic personnel, and a Sheriff warrant was earlier this morning granted to permit entry, forcibly if need be, to search for evidence of Burns presence at the house and anything else that might be of interest and with particular emphasis on our missing firearm. The officers at the house await my call to execute the warrant and this will be given when I have satisfactorily concluded our meeting here."

Jackson must have seen something in my face he didn't like, for his eyebrows knitted and he simply said, "What?"

"I can't be certain, Mister Jackson," I slowly reply, "but if my suspicion is correct, I think you should give that order right now. I believe that if Jo-Jo Docherty isn't already dead, he soon will be."

Graeme Fleming has left the room and is accompanying Frankie Jackson to the control room located on the upper floor where Danny McBride tells Martin and me that a police operator has been dedicated to stand-by and monitor the surveillance wavelength for anything that might be of interest to Jackson. "Anything at all," McBride tells Martin and me. They have been gone for about fifteen minutes and for the first time since I set foot in the place this morning, I'm feeling relaxed and fairly confident I won't be arrested.

"What makes you think Docherty might be in danger and that he isn't the killer?" he asks me.

I consider the question and my answer then tell him, "If my suspicion is correct, I think your killer is cleaning house, getting rid of anyone who can connect him with the Intelligence leak."

"But murder?" and I see the doubt in his eyes. "Jesus, Tom. You're talking about three people here and not forgetting the attempt on Gordon's life."

"Four people," I reply and see the surprise in his eyes. "You're forgetting Alice Foley and there might be more when your team hit the house," because God forgive me, but I'm secretly hoping that the bastard Docherty is also dead.

"Alice Foley?" McBride asks, his voice betraying his curiosity and even Martin McCormick sits forward, staring at me like I've finally lost it. I nod and am about to explain when the door bursts open. Jackson enters and I can see he is not bringing good news. Well maybe not for the police because frankly I'm completely indifferent to Docherty's fucking welfare.

"Right, talking's over McEwan," he thunders at me. "What the hell is going on?"

"Boss?" says McBride, then sounding more forceful that he probably means to, says, "Will somebody explain what the fuck's going on here?"

"Your man here," Jackson points a shaking finger at me, "is bang on, if you excuse the pun. There was no reply at the Docherty's house, but his vehicle was parked outside, so the surveillance team leader instructed the response team to put the door in. They found Docherty lying in his bathroom with half his head blown off." They both stare at me and I shrug and tell them why I think, or rather, who I think is the killer.

Chapter 21

Martin McCormick is driving and I know he is eager to ask me questions, but I guess the enormity of my final statement to Jackson and McBride is still reeling through his mind. I suppose he is also surprised that Jackson decided to release me in the meantime, but not without first warning me that he will consult with the Procurator Fiscal to determine if any charges are to be libelled against me. Finally, Martin speaks, but only to ask me where I want dropped off?

"After that bollocking Mister Jackson gave me and now that I know I'm not flavour of the month, I suppose there's no point in hiding any longer, so if you can drop me in Duke Street near to my flat, Martin, I'll be grateful."

He nods and concentrates on his driving which gives me time to gather my thoughts.

Three years have passed since Alice died and there's not a day gone by that I haven't thought of her. Not, as you might think, of a lost opportunity, but more with fondness than tenderness. Like I told you before, I couldn't then and can't now explain my feelings other than try to describe them as sympathetic affection. I suppose time, as they say, is a great healer, but it also causes reflection of what might have been - and what might have been for me was a great life with Lisa and our twin daughters.

At my request, Martin pulls up and finds a bay outside the grocers on Duke Street to permit me to collect some fresh bread and milk.

"I still can't believe it," he says at last, shaking his head. "Of all the people, he is probably the person I suppose the police would least suspect. To be frank, having more or less just come into the whole scene, I didn't quite understand everything that you told DCS Jackson and DI McBride. Look, I know you've been through it all less than an hour ago, but you would you mind going over it again, just for me? Maybe break it down in simple terms? If for any reason I need to construct some kind of defence strategy for you, Tom, I'd like to make a start in my own head as to what you have told Jackson and McBride and why. "

"Okay, just ask if you have any questions," I tell him. "You might recall me telling you that three years ago, when this all kicked off, it began with Alice Foley and I taking part in a surveillance of Robbie Burns?"

"Yeah, that's right. You were in a car together. Somewhere in Lanarkshire, wasn't it?"

"Holytown," I reply, settling back into my seat and the dark memory of that night flashing through my mind. "Just as the bad guys were about to hit the security guy carrying the case with the cash, Alice and I had got out of our car and run to the junction at the Main Street. I was a bit behind her because, frankly," I grin at the memory, "she was faster than me. She got to the corner a step or two before me and she had a quick shufti …. a glance I mean, round the corner and I remember she said something strange. It didn't mean anything to me at the time, but made sense as other things much later fell into place. I can't recall her exact words, but it was something about a car that was parked across the road. The car's headlights were off and the more I think of it, the more I'm convinced she can only have seen the car under the street lighting and in silhouette. The funny thing is," I continue, warming to my story, "Alice said something about it being the same type of car, but she sounded …." I struggled to explain, "Shocked I suppose is the word I would have used then, at seeing the car at all and particularly there. What I now believe is that she recognised the car."

"And you also believe this car she saw was known to her and that's why she sounded surprised?"

I nod and continue, "Anyway, just at that point Burns fired his bloody shotgun in the air and the whole thing got chaotic and to be honest, what she saw completely slipped my mind, but wasn't forgotten. What then happened was that Alice saw the bad guys running off and went hell for leather to cut them off. I tried to follow her, tripped and went arse over tit onto the roadway. By the time I've got myself together, she's gone into the dark and the whole thing becomes totally confused." Even after this time, I find myself chilled just speaking about it. "About ten or fifteen minutes later we found Alice, or more properly, the dog did, lying face down in a pool of water with the back of her head bashed in. The conclusion of the post mortem was murder."

"And this lad you spoke of, your neighbour's son?"

"Young Iqbal," I involuntarily smile. "Car daft he is. Iqbal saw a man leaving my close mouth on the night Cathy Williams was killed, not a resident and someone that Iqbal had not previously seen. I believe Iqbal saw the man who murdered Cathy. As Iqbal watched, the man first moved out of sight and I believe that he was planting the machete that killed Cathy in the boot of my car. Iqbal was about to turn away from the window when he saw the man again and the curious thing is that Iqbal saw him getting into a car that Iqbal couldn't identify; a car of a type and model the lad hadn't seen before. I can't explain it, maybe call it intuition, but it struck a chord with me even then and I had Iqbal look at some cars I found on the Internet. He picked out a picture of the one he had seen the man getting into or rather, the same make and model, with no hesitation."

"This is the car you told Jackson and McBride you suspect Alice Foley had spotted at the scene of the robbery, the same car you also had previously seen and the same type this man you told Jackson and McBride about?"

I nod and turn towards him. "The day after, or more correctly, the morning of Alice's murder, the team were instructed to assemble at Meiklewood Road. Of course, I was in a bit of a state, shock I suppose, but I remembered parking my old jalopy next to a car I hadn't previously seen. A pristine, highly polished black coloured Ford Cortina mark one, a collector's model."

"That belongs or at that time anyway, did belong to your suspect, Alice Foley's husband, this man Sergeant Wallace Foley?"

Again I nod; the bitterness in my mouth too acidic to even reply.

"According to what DI McBride told us," Martin continues, "Foley is the local Intelligence Collator for his division, so I suppose that if McBride can prove he has accessed the Intelligence logs for the operations against this man Docherty, it will at least corroborate your suspicions. However," he sighs, "I have to tell you Tom from an evidential stance, your hypothesis probably isn't strong enough to stand up as evidence in a court. Don't get me wrong though, while I support your theory, I can't believe that Foley would be as stupid to commit so many murders."

"Oh, I can," I bitterly retort, "believe me, I most certainly can. I think he killed Alice because she suspected even then that he was in Docherty or Burns or both their pocket. For money or favours, who knows? I think she was leaving him for more than just his abuse of her, that she was going to turn him in and he couldn't risk that. Her," I hesitate even to use the word, "relationship with me was the ideal opportunity for him. I believe he set up that robbery on the night Alice died, knowing when and where she would be and waited. How he found her in the dark, I don't know, but I'm guessing that he was there in plenty of time ahead of us arriving and was monitoring our frequency. He had access to a police radio, so it couldn't have been that difficult for him. He would have heard where the vehicles were deployed round the area and a local map will have pinpointed where Alice and I were parked up. Then it was simple for him. When Burns discharged his shotgun and the robbery went apeshit, he waits till we get out of the car for the foot pursuit and his luck gets even better. I get separated from Alice when I trip, he follows her into the darkness and … well, you know the rest, Martin."

"And in the confusion you described, he slips away without anyway seeing him." He strokes his chin and asks, "But what about Burns, I mean, surely if he had been arrested, he might have turned Foley in to work some sort of deal with the Prosecution?"

"We have no way of knowing what he told Burns, but if you want my opinion, Foley has probably told Burns the police were already onto him and Foley persuaded him that he was to go ahead with the robbery, but leave himself enough opportunity to get away and sacrifice his accomplices to do so, knowing that in the confused aftermath of the shotgun blast, the police would be too involved arresting the accomplices and this would allow Burns time to slip off into the darkness. Burns probably realised he was identified and if caught, faced a lengthy prison sentence. I believe he wasn't there to commit the robbery, he was there to get rid of the accomplices and I think had planned an escape route, but wouldn't have suspected he was to be implicated for the murder of Alice. No, that was Foley's hidden agenda. He not only set up the police, he set Burns up to. The rest is history. Burns already had his ticket to Spain and that's why we couldn't immediately trace him. The whole episode wasn't about robbery, it was about killing Alice."

"And the man who died in the car accident in Spain, Burns cousin, was he part of the plan, do you think?"

I shake my head. "I've no idea, but again and I'm only guessing, probably not. I think that was simply an accident that Burns took advantage of. It gave him the opportunity to return to the UK with a new identity. It's unlikely the police will discover who authorised the deletion of Burns fingerprints and DNA from the records system, but Foley will undoubtedly know the routine, so he's probably suspect for that too. If as McBride says the Spanish agree to an exhumation of the body, there might be conclusive proof that it's McDade in the grave. But that's not my problem" I grin. "If anything I've told Jackson and McBride is even remotely near the truth, they have a can of worms on their hands."

"Bloody hell," Martin exclaims, "It's like reading a John Grisham novel. So, you believe that having murdered his wife, Foley continued to provide this guy Docherty with information?"

"Yes, I do. I'm also guessing either Foley was too far in with Docherty to get out or maybe even enjoyed the double life he was leading. Only he can tell us. It was a bit of bad luck for him when Robbie Burns returned to the UK and even worse luck that I saw Burns that day. It is likely Docherty has taken advantage of Burns prowess at robbery and set up the Post Office jobs, using Foley's access to the Intelligence system to provide information to Burns, with Docherty getting a silent partner's cut. When Docherty's man told him that Ina Carroll had met two strangers that looked like cops in the Saracen Head pub that night, he beat our names out of poor Ina and I've no doubt told Foley all about out interest in Robbie Burns."

I swallowed hard as the enormity of the story seemed to suddenly hit me.

"Foley knew that if we tracked down Burns, he wouldn't have taken the fall for Alice's murder and given Foley up to work out a deal and the whole house of cards would have came tumbling down about Foley's ears, so that's why Burns had to die. I'm guessing he was worried that either Ina had seen him at Docherty's house at some point or maybe heard his name mentioned. Either way, he couldn't afford to take the chance that she might later recognise him and so she had to die too. It was probably just sheer bad luck that Gordon was with her when Foley struck."

"And the woman in your flat, Missus Williams, I suppose that night you were, as you thought, Foley's real intended victim, but killing her instead he decided to set you for her murder?"

I nod, a lump in my throat and finally say, "Poor Cathy. Likely he's persuaded her to open the door and she's paid for her mistake with her life and if the police had discovered the machete in the car, who would have believed a disgraced, former cop?"

"I suppose there's no guessing who is suspect for killing this man Docherty, then?"

"No, Martin. It has to be Foley cleaning up behind himself. Unless there's someone else who knows of his involvement with Docherty and Burns, then that should be an end to it. If Jackson and McBride accept what I've told them, Foley will be at least detained then subject to arrest. If he has at anytime been in Docherty's house or if there is anything they found in my flat, I'm certain there will be Forensic evidence they can match against him. Nobody can be in attendance at a crime scene and not leave some trace or other. Beside that, they should be able to obtain a warrant for phone records to prove communication between him and Docherty and maybe even computer evidence to further prove Foley's research on the Intelligence network about the times and dates of the surveillance on Docherty."

"What about the Post Office robberies you spoke of? Burns, if indeed he was committing the robberies, presumably had accomplices."

I smile at that and joke, "I'm not a detective any longer, Martin. I need to leave the police something to do."

"Indeed," he thoughtfully replies. "Maybe not a police detective, Tom, but subject to things working out in your favour, we haven't really had the opportunity to discus an opportunity for you, working with my company I mean."

I open the car door to get out and over my shoulder tell him, "Let's screw my current employer into the ground first, Martin, then we'll meet and talk it over, if that's okay with you?"

"I'll be in touch then," he grins, waves and pulls out into the traffic.

I watch him drive off as I turn to enter the grocers.

Carrying the milk and fresh bread in a plastic bag, I hurry from Duke Street into Craigpark Drive and promise myself that after brewing a strong cup of coffee, I intend spending at least ten minutes standing under a hot shower. I feel a sudden chill and I shudder in the winter sunlight. As I slowly walk along the road, the noise of children from the nearby primary school playing at lunchtime echoes through the streets and I find myself smiling. As I approach the flat I think about phoning Lisa and asking how the twins are, knowing I will use the call as an excuse just to hear her voice, but then I reason, she will be at work and probably won't be able to speak. Besides, I then remember, the battery life has expired and it needs recharged anyway. I turn into the entrance towards the close mouth and see Iqbal at the front window, a solemn expression on his face. No, not solemn, more puzzled I think. I give him a smile and a short wave and am surprised he doesn't wave back. I'm inserting the common key into the lock and thinking he might want to speak to me, but when I turn back to his window, he's gone.

I trudge up the stairs and open the door to the flat, then closing it behind me I'm grabbed by my anorak collar and literally hauled off my feet backwards and fall backwards onto the floor and even as I'm falling, I'm thinking the key! The bloody key Cathy took and I realise who is behind me as the plastic bag goes skidding off to the side of me. As I glance upwards in surprise, the first thing that takes my attention is the twin, canon like barrels of a sawn-off shotgun being held inches from my nose.

"We're not going to be difficult about this McEwan, are we?" says a hoarse voice.

"There's nobody with him, Wally," whispers a nervous voice, an Irish accent I hear and I'm guessing that it's Docherty's henchman, Connor McLaughlin. I slowly turn my head and I see his back to me as he peers through the eyehole in the door. McLaughlin then turns and stares wide-eyed at me and I just know he's almost as frightened as I am.

Foley, dressed in a long, black coloured overcoat buttoned to the throat, is wearing blue coloured plastic Forensic gloves and brutally pokes me under the chin with the sawn-off. Small sprays of spit eject from between his lips as he hisses, "Look at me. Right, slowly, get up onto your feet and put your hands in your jacket pockets. Do it, now!"

I turn onto my front and slowly push myself upright. Am I scared? Too fucking right I am for all the time Foley continues to menace me with the shotgun grasped in both large paws and staring into his maddened eyes, I'm not forgetting he's already used it.

So here we are then, the three of us, standing in my hallway; a killer with a sawn-off shotgun, a nervous sounding Irish barman and a terrified former detective, whose bladder is beginning to protest that it needs to pee.

"Thought it might be another one of your floosies," Foley sneers at me. "Maybe give us a little show like the last one did."

I try not to think of the horror Cathy experienced at this madman's hands before he killed her and work at keeping my voice steady. If

I'm going to die, I decide, I'm not giving this bastard the satisfaction of enjoying my fear.

"I suppose that is the difference between me and you, Foley," I taunt him with a lot more bravado that I feel; "I know how to please a woman, but you just know how to brutalise and kill them."

"What the fuck's he talking about, Wally," whines McLaughlin. "What woman?"

I think to myself, he doesn't know. McLaughlin has no idea why he's been dragged here. Foley has concocted some story, but likely it didn't include murdering me.

"Didn't he say …" I begin.

"Shut up!" screams Foley.

"Didn't he tell you," I begin to repeat, "He's already murdered three women as well as Burns and your boss."

Because I'm turned towards McLaughlin, I'm too late to avoid Foley as he lunges across the few feet between us and one-handedly with the barrel of the shot-gun uses it like a club to strike me viciously across the left side of my head. I collapse like the proverbial sack of potatoes to my knees, but I'm still conscious. Admittedly very fucking dazed and sore, but conscious. I feel the blood seeping down the side of my face and with some fascination, watch it drip from my chin onto the floor in front of me.

"What's he talking about Wally? Wally?"

"Shut up, he's talking shite. Just shut up, will you?" he barks in reply to McLaughlin.

I smile, no, not because I'm happy. Far from it because you see, I know if I'm lucky, I might have minutes left to live. No, I'm smiling because I've figured out Foley's plan. You see, I was wrong when I said to Martin McCormick that it was the end of Foley's killing spree; that he had cleaned up behind himself. I not only haven't included myself in the equation, but even more significantly I had forgotten about one more person. The man who was Docherty's contribution to the Post Office robberies, Burns accomplice and who Foley probably suspects was told where the information about the cash deliveries was coming from. And my best guess is that man is Docherty's lackey, Connor McLaughlin.

"He's smiling, Wally, why is he smiling?" says a confused McLaughlin, who then takes two steps over towards me and delivers a boot towards my face, but he's telegraphed his intention and knowing it's coming, I lean into the kick and take it in my left shoulder. It's funny how things cross your mind when you are under pressure, because even though I'm in imminent danger of dying, I see some of my blood splatter onto his lower trouser leg and think to myself 'There's good evidence', only to realise it won't be any use because the bastard will likely be found murdered alongside me, but having seen Foley wearing the Forensic gloves, it will be my prints on the sawn-off shotgun; another set-up.

Having kicked me, McLaughlin turns away and I fall onto my back and though the injury to my head is causing me real pain and I will kill for a couple of aspirin washed down with a Grouse, I can't help myself and aware I'm slurring my words, I goad him. "You Irish prick. Rob a few unarmed postmen and think you're a fucking hard man? Let's see how hard you are when your fat pal here shoves his sawn-off up your arse and he pulls the trigger. You think after doing you boss he's going to let you live. You stupid …"

I don't finish the sentence because quite simply, Foley's boot is pressed down hard onto the right side of my face, forcing me to eat the carpet. Maybe I offended him when I called him fat, I'm thinking.

"I told you once before, pretty boy," Foley hisses again at me, "shut your face."

His boot is still on my head and I'm already resigned to die anyway, so I manage to squeak at him, "Is that why Alice was leaving you? Because you're crap in bed or because you were selling information to your pals?"

The pressure on my head is released and he reaches down with one large hand and grabs the front of my jacket, then half drags, half pulls me across the narrow hallway to a sitting position against the wall beside the front door. Okay, I know my hands are not tied and maybe a movie hero would have lashed out with his fists or feet or some fancy unarmed combat move. But let's not forget I'm in a stupor from a blow to the head and I'm not stupid either, because there are two of them and the biggest one still has hold of a sawn-off shotgun, so give me a break here, okay?

McLaughlin standing to my right still isn't happy and he again whines to Foley, "Fuck's sake, Wally. Tell me what's going on here, man. What's this guy harping on about? You told me …"
"Shut up, Connor, will you just shut up!" then unlike the television, apparently he's made his mind up that a lengthy explanation to the victim isn't necessary and turns and points the shotgun at me, then with an evil smile and an audible click, pulls back the hammer on the first chamber. In desperation, I tell him, "You had better get your story right for your interview, Foley. Mister Jackson and DI McBride won't be that easily fooled."
His eyes narrow and I know I've scored a small victory and I realise he doesn't yet know he is being hunted. Well, guess what? I'm about to take delight in telling him. I feel consciousness slipping from me and make a supreme effort to stay awake.
"I spent this morning with my lawyer at police headquarters telling them about you, how you murdered Alice to shut her up. What you don't know is she saw you that night in your fancy car, the Mark One Cortina and she told me about your deal with Docherty."
I'm lying, but of course I've nothing to lose and every minute is life. "Told me of your association with Jo-Jo, tipping him off when there was surveillance on him." He stood still and I see it in his eyes. I'm right. Alice either did know or suspect he was bent. The shotgun is still cocked and now gripped in both hands, pointing at me. "And you don't know it, but there was a witness who saw you at the caravan park the day you topped Burns."
Okay. I'm lying again, but a few more precious minutes of life are worth it, don't you agree?
"You're bluffing," he says, but can't stop his face from going pale.
"Wally, what the fuck is he on about?" asks an increasingly anxious McLaughlin who now is literally hopping from foot to foot.
I grin at the Irishman, tasting the salty blood that has run from my wound into my mouth and though it takes an effort, I lie again.
"The polis aren't forgetting about you either, Connor. They know about you and the Post Office robberies." He turns Procol Harum, or should I say a whiter shade than pale, puts a hand against the wall to steady himself and for a second I think he is going to collapse. "We need to get out of here Wally. And now," is his response.

I should say, his final response, for Foley turns ever-so slightly and from about six feet, blasts him in the chest with the shotgun. The noise reverberates so loudly in the confined space of the hallway that I think for an instance my eardrums have burst and I watch in horrid fascination as the multitude of small lead pellets spread in an angry scarlet curtain of blood across the surprised Irishman's torso as the shot lifts him off his feet and splatters him across the wall behind him.

"You're bluffing," Foley calmly repeats to me and cocks the second barrel.

So here I am, sitting on the floor with my back to the wall, valiantly trying to stay awake as I stare first at the blood soaked corpse across from me and then at the oversized nutcase who is about to end my life and nothing comes to mind. Not my life flashing in front of me, no thoughts of Lisa and my twin girls, nothing. I simply stare at the two barrels in the hands of the grinning, maniacal bastard and all I can think is, 'Fuck'.

I startle as the door crashes inwards and I watch as something resembling a small black spray can, or that's what it seems like, comes lazily flying through the opening and then the world goes brightly white and my ears loudly pop.

"How do you feel now?" asks the grey haired, middle aged, female paramedic as she fusses at my head and shines a small torch into my eyes.

"What happened?" I try to ask her, but the words sound to me like they've come out like syrup from a syringe. I try to sit up, but I'm gently pushed back down and recognising the brightness and equipment above me I realise I'm lying on a stretcher in an ambulance.

The woman doesn't answer, but simply smiles and half turns to someone behind her and I hear her say, "Two minutes pal, then he's mine and we're out of here. Anything else you can find out when he's at the casualty at the Royal." She moves back deeper into the ambulance and beckons someone forward.

Danny McBride hovers over the top of me and smiles. "Cut that a wee bit fine there I'm afraid, Tom. Stun grenade, but they tell me it's not got any lasting effect. However, you're going to be okay, or so I'm told," he grins and glances up at the paramedic. "I'll not ask you how you feel because you look like shit."

"Foley?" I manage to gasp.

"Arrested and on his way to London Road polis station. I'll not go into details here, but you owe a big thanks to that wee Muslim lad that lives down the stairs, Iqbal is it?"

I nod and feel so weary I just want to sleep.

"Concussion," I think I hear the paramedic say, but I'm not really listening anymore.

Chapter 22

Don't ask me anything about what happened for the rest of that day, for it's a bit of a blur and I know that there was a lot of people hanging about me, but the only face I recall seeing is Lisa. I think she spoke to me and I seem to recall she was crying, but like everything else it made no sense and all I wanted to do was sleep. So, moving on brings me up to now. Four months has passed and things are settled, or as best they can be.

I learned later that Iqbal, my young friend from downstairs was credited for saving my life.

He saw Foley and McLaughlin enter the close mouth and though he didn't recognise Foley, having only seen his back when he exited the close after killing Cathy, his suspicions were sufficiently aroused to have a look outside on the roadway. When he saw the Ford Cortina and recognised it as the same car from the afternoon of the murder, he was so alarmed he run indoors to phone the police and report what he had seen. Though I didn't find out who the operator he spoke to was, they in turn were astute enough to check the registration number and discovered it had been logged just thirty minutes previously by DI McBride as a vehicle of interest. Of course, young Iqbal was unaware of this and when he saw me enter the close, he didn't have a clue about what was about to happen, but figured that rather than try to stop me, he would again phone the police who wisely dispatched their armed response team to deal with a possible threat from Foley. I also later found out Foley was assessed by Danny McBride to be carrying Robbie Burns shotgun.

The team, McBride later told me, had just covertly arrived at my door when they heard the shotgun blast that killed McLaughlin and the rest, as they say, is history.

I was also pleased to learn from McBride that thanks to intervention by Detective Chief Superintendent Frankie Jackson, the Procurator Fiscal decided my value as a witness was much more preferable to that as an accused and all matters relating to my concealment of the Cathy Williams murder weapon was dropped. I know what you're thinking. It seems once again I owe Jackson a debt of gratitude.

As for Iqbal, he didn't just earn my everlasting thanks and friendship for life, but I treated him to a day out at Knockhill Racing Circuit in Fife, where to his delight, he sat with me as my police driving skills returned and I raced a selection of fast cars round the track and to be honest, I had almost as much fun as he did.

Martin McCormick exerted some pressure on the Insurance company and sufficiently worried my now former employer about the threat of litigation that it persuaded them to make me an *ex gratia* payment for what he termed their unacceptable treatment of an innocent man. I can't agree I feel totally innocent about Cathy's death, but equally there is nothing I can now do about it. I wanted to attend her funeral service, but my parents of all people, suggested it might be cause more hurt to her children than the salacious reporting of her lifestyle ever did. I gave the money from the Insurance company to a charity, but don't think of me as a nice guy because frankly, I wasn't being magnanimous; it was my feeling of guilt that prompted the donation that I made in Cathy's name.

Gordon Roberts continues to recover from the trauma of the injury he received and can't recall anything of the assault. Curiously, the neurosurgeon suggested the alcohol he had consumed that evening might have gone some way to anaesthetise him when the blow to the back of his head was struck. He talks of returning to work, but evidently has not taken on board Wilma's comments on the issue. Privately, I believe she will have the final say. On his behalf, I did attend Ina Carroll's funeral service to pay his respects and deliver a wreath, but discreetly remained at the rear of the church. I was humbled by the large turnout and eulogies from her friends and neighbours, all of which I reported back to Gordon, to whom I speak with on the phone every second or third day. I won't make the mistake again of losing touch with him.

Wallace Foley appeared from custody the day after his arrest and pled Not Guilty to a number of charges that included multiple murder, attempted murder, charges related to conspiracy to commit robberies as well as various contraventions of the Police (Scotland), Firearms and Data Protection Act's. Against all legal advice, he continued to plead innocent of all the charges and on a warm spring morning, trial commenced at the High Court in the Saltmarket area of Glasgow. With numerous others, I was cited as a witness and the trial commenced with Forensic and Scene of Crime evidence. The third day of trial was wholly taken by the Prosecuting Counsel taking me step by step through my evidence. The following day, during my cross-examination, I suffered the indignity of Foley's defence Counsel labouring over my supposed sexual relationship with his client's wife, who he suggested to the jury was a cheating and promiscuous tart. As in all such trials, the deceased cannot defend themselves and it falls to the living to protect their good name and character. Unfortunately, I made a right arse of it and I was rebuked by His Lordship after I threatened to come down from the witness box and tear a new one for the smirking Counsel.
Needless to say, the local press had a field day and once again Alice Foley was front page news, but on this occasion for all the wrong reasons.
That night, my evidence concluded, I decided to go back to the flat and murder a bottle of Grouse, but before I got there my phone rang and I was surprised to see on the screen the caller was Lisa.

She had called, she told me, not to gloat but to find out if I was okay, that she had heard on the news about what had happened in court. We spoke for almost an hour and without realising it, I abandoned the idea of getting drunk.

Albeit I was dismissed as a witness from the trial, I attended each day thereafter and listened intently as the witness's evidence, both human and circumstantial, proved his catalogue of crime before the court. His defence was weak and shoddy and in the end, the jury of nine women and six men found him guilty of all the murders bar one; ironically, the murder of Alice Foley was found to be Not Proven, that decision that is unique to the Scottish Criminal Justice system that neither convicts nor proves innocence.

It seemed that while the consensus of public opinion believed him guilty, there was insufficient evidence to prove the charge and I understand the police are not looking for anyone else in connection with her murder. The other related charges, including the attempt to murder Gordon Roberts were mostly guilty, but it was the capital crime charges that settled his account.

His Lordship summed up in less than an hour and describing Foley as without parallel, the most wicked man he had ever the misfortune to sentence awarded him five life sentences with a minimum of fifty years imprisonment before he can apply for parole. The sentence was reported in the media as being so severe that apart from the historical hanging sentence, never before in the annals of Scottish Law had there been such a sentence awarded to a prisoner and given his age, Foley looks forward to dying while imprisoned. I watched as he was led down to the cells. He glanced my way and the malevolence he had demonstrated when pointing the shotgun at me was still pasted to his face.

I felt nothing.

So as I said earlier, we're here now and what does the future hold for me?

Martin McCormick and I met some weeks after I was discharged from the Royal Infirmary to discuss prospective employment with his firm. I commenced work there two weeks ago and partner another former cop, a man called John Logan with whom I have already formed a good working relationship.

The work's varied and sometimes routine, but what job isn't? I had another phone call a couple of weeks ago from Danny McBride, who suggested going for a beer. Curiosity rather than a social need prompted me to meet him and we spent a couple of hours in the Horseshoe Bar. He turned out to be good company and in my new line of work, will prove to be a useful contact and we've had a few beers since that night.

Lisa, according to my small blonde haired spies, is no longer seeing the man they called Uncle Andy and to my reserved delight, informed me she recently moved from her parent's house and into a flat in the west end of Glasgow. I haven't the right to ask, but suspect her father's overbearing and bullying attitude has finally driven her out. We still chat on the phone and on the odd occasion when she delivers the girls to me, she has brought them up to the flat and stopped for a coffee. There's nothing yet between us, but who knows; time will tell I suppose and I keep my fingers crossed. I feel better about myself these days and still occasionally think of Alice Foley, but as I said before, with fondness rather than affection.

One day recently and for some unaccountable reason, I found myself standing in the drizzling rain by her grave at Dalbeth Cemetery on London Road in the east end of Glasgow. The grave took some finding for I had been told her family had the headstone taken away to permit the stonemason to remove the name of 'her beloved husband Wallace Foley', but that said, the grave was neat and tidy and appeared to have been recently tended. As I stood there, uncertain why I had come, an old man was shuffling past, his suit jacket collar turned up and his shoulders bowed against the wet weather, a small black coloured telescopic umbrella carried in one hand and some wilting flowers in the other. With arthritic hands, he took some from the bunch and handed them to me, then peered through rheumy eyes at the temporary white painted, wooden cross that bore just her name as well as both the dates of her birth and of her death.

"Just a wee lassie when she died, eh son? What a shame that the young go before the old codgers like me. You'll miss her, no doubt," he said as he shook his head and moved on.

I smiled at his retreating back, bent down and laid the flowers on the grave, then turned and walked towards the gate.

Needless to say, this story is a work of fiction.
If you have enjoyed the story, you may wish to visit the author's website at:
www.glasgowcrimefiction.co.uk

The author also welcomes feedback and can be contacted at:
george.donald.books@hotmail.co.uk

Printed in Great Britain
by Amazon.co.uk, Ltd.,
Marston Gate.